ALSO BY

THE SOUTHERN GHOST HUNTER SERIES

Southern Spirits

The Skeleton in the Closet

The Haunted Heist

Deader Homes & Gardens

Sweet Tea and Spirits

Murder on the Sugarland Express

THE ACCIDENTAL DEMON SLAYER SERIES

The Accidental Demon Slayer

The Dangerous Book for Demon Slayers

A Tale of Two Demon Slayers

The Last of the Demon Slayers

My Big Fat Demon Slayer Wedding

Beverly Hills Demon Slayer

Night of the Living Demon Slayer

SHORT STORY COLLECTIONS:

A Little Night Magic: A collection of Southern Ghost Hunter and
Accidental Demon Slayer short stories

Murder on the Sugarland Express

The Southern
Ghost Hunter
Mysteries
Book 6

NEW YORK TIMES BESTSELLING AUTHOR

ANGIE FOX

This edition published by arrangement with Moose Island Publishing.

Murder on the Sugarland Express

First Edition

ISBN: 978-1-939661-45-6

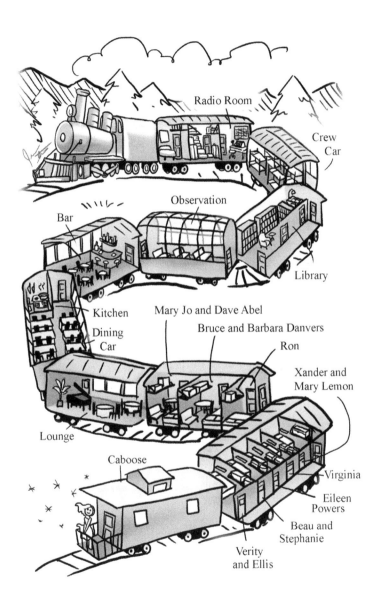

CHAPTER 1

I ran a brush through my hair and fastened a thin gold chain around my neck, keeping one ear peeled for a knock on the door downstairs. Ellis Wydell, my one and only, would be dropping by any minute to personally escort me to the soft opening of his new restaurant.

It was a night for family and friends to see the place, try the menu, and celebrate. Ellis had turned the old Southern Spirits distillery into a fun, modern gathering place with old-world charm. He'd done it to honor his deceased uncle, who had been his original partner on the project, and he'd done it for the town, to restore an old building to its former glory. I was so stinking proud of him. I couldn't wait to see it—even if my ex-fiancé would also be there, along with my almost-and-potentially-still-in-the-future-but-OMG-it's-too-soon-to-go-there mother-in-law.

I took a sip of wine that turned into a gulp. I mean, just because I'd come within a toad's hair of marrying Ellis's brother didn't mean this had to be weird. My relationship with Ellis had nothing to do with the rest of his family. We cared for each other because we were right for each other. Ellis and I were happy together. Ecstatic.

The fact that my wedding to Ellis's brother would have taken place a year ago this very night was just an awkward, strange coincidence.

It wasn't like I hadn't seen the rest of the family since knocking Beau into the cake and storming out of the reception.

He'd had it coming.

Beau had cornered my sister the night before the wedding and tried to kiss her. She'd fended him off and told me everything.

Like any girl with a lick of sense, I went to Beau that night and told him I wouldn't marry him. But he showed up at the church the next morning anyway. Beau wouldn't rest until he'd humiliated me in front of everyone we knew. Then Virginia Wydell sued me for the cost of the lavish ceremony and reception, forcing me to sell almost everything I owned to pay her back.

By the time the dust cleared, I realized I'd dodged a bullet. But Beau and his mother didn't see it that way. As far as they were concerned, Beau was a catch and I should have been proud to march down that aisle and call myself Mrs. Beau Wydell.

The ruined wedding had led to a frenzy in the Sugarland rumor mill that only got worse when I decided to become the local ghost hunter. It hadn't helped that I'd taken on Ellis's Southern Spirits property as my very first case—or that I'd started dating Beau's black-sheep brother. But that was finally settling down. Now I just needed to blend in for the grand opening. The focus should be on Ellis and the restaurant. He certainly deserved it.

I took a deep breath and applied pale pink lipstick with a bit of gloss on top. This was just one more speed bump on the road to happiness. I truly cared for Ellis and couldn't be more excited to see his new place. Why, this very afternoon, he'd called to say that he'd made one final touch to the restaurant that would surprise even me.

I fingered the tiny gold skunk pendant on my chain, a gift from Ellis. Time to go. I slipped out of the bathroom and bounded down the wide wooden staircase of my lovely ancestral home. Six generations of my family had lived and died here, and I would as well. I belonged here. I loved everything about the place.

Except for the ghost of a 1930s gangster who waited for me just past the bottom stair. Frankie "The German" didn't appear happy to see me, either. He planted a hand on the antique newel post and glared at me like I'd just stolen his last barrel of hooch.

Well, I didn't have time for his antics tonight.

"Evening, killer," I said, sidestepping around him.

"Hold it right there." The ghost formed again in the hallway directly in front of me, blocking my path to the kitchen.

Frankie appeared in black and white, but I could see through him. Mostly. He wore a 1920s-style pin-striped suit coat with matching cuffed trousers and a fat tie. Oh, and he had a bullet hole in his forehead, courtesy of the last person he annoyed while alive.

Sometimes, it wasn't so hard to understand why it had happened.

"My house, my hallway," I said, pretending not to notice the way he loomed over me. He could take the angry specter act somewhere else. I'd been afraid of him at one time, but we'd pulled each other through enough harrowing and downright jaw-dropping adventures that I no longer startled at the appearance of the gangster hovering above my original red oak floors. "I have to make sure Lucy is settled in before I leave."

My pet skunk never minded when I had the occasional evening out. She liked to catch up on her sleep. But she did enjoy being cuddled before I left. And with Frankie floating around downstairs, she probably needed an extra snuggle or two. She might not have even eaten her dinner.

Lucy wasn't particularly fond of my resident ghost.

Frankie allowed me to pass, but he wasn't done. "Make it

quick," he said, straightening his tie. "I got a hot piece of business going."

"Please, not again." The last time he'd seized a wild hair, I'd walked outside to find an entire ghostly racetrack in my backyard, complete with a bookie booth. "I don't think I can take it."

"It ain't for you," he said, as if the idea were preposterous. "It's a romantic gesture for Molly, and you're about to blow it."

"Aww..." The frustration drained out of me. "How sweet." Frankie had opened his heart a bit since he'd met his girl. Molly was a cute, Victorian-era ghost he'd fallen for during our last adventure. Sure, it had only been a few short weeks since they'd gotten together, but their budding romance appeared promising all the same. "Is she here? I'd love to say hi." Only I couldn't without his help.

Frankie had to lend me his power if I wanted to see any other ghosts besides him. He wasn't particularly fond of doing it since the drain on his energy made parts of him disappear. In fact, I had found myself bribing him on more than one occasion when I needed to get in touch with our town's spiritual side.

The ghost stopped in front of the hallway mirror, and I couldn't help but notice how he cast no reflection. He checked his watch while I took the opportunity to fluff my hair. "Molly will be here any minute and, no, you can't see her." He ran a finger under his collar and yanked, as if it were too tight all of a sudden. "You'll start telling her stories again."

I dropped my hands to my sides. "Oh, come on. The one about you and the urn is a classic."

Frankie and I had met after I'd done a bit of housecleaning. The ugly old vase I'd found in the attic had needed more than the quick and dirty cleaning I'd given it with my garden hose, but I'd done my best. While I was at it, I'd dumped out the loose dirt inside and rinsed it into the roots of my favorite rosebush, thinking I'd replace it with some fresh water and a nice, fat rose.

Only it wasn't a vase; it was an urn, and by rinsing Frankie's earthly remains so completely into my garden dirt, I'd bound him to my property.

I'd been as unnerved as he was.

Our only saving grace was that I hadn't done a bang-up cleaning job. A smidge of Frankie's ashes remained inside the urn. That meant I could take him places with me, as long as I didn't mind being the girl with an urn in her purse.

And I did take him places. Just this morning, we'd gone to the library.

It was the least I could do considering the circumstances.

He rolled his eyes, and I took advantage of his distraction to scoot past him.

"I should tell her about the time you got spooked in a haunted house," I told him.

"Hey, I told you Rock Fall mansion wasn't your typical haunted house," he protested, and I swore I saw his cheeks flush. Poor gangster. "I don't deal in Egyptian curses," he insisted.

That case had actually turned out well, although I didn't think Frankie would appreciate the reminder.

"I'll be out of your way in a sec," I promised, finding my pet skunk next to the kitchen island. She'd emptied her food bowl and had somehow decided that it would make a good bed. She snuggled with her back legs and furry little rear inside, the rest of her hanging out, which didn't seem to bother her in the slightest. She lifted her head and curled her tail out when she saw me.

"Did you get enough dinner?" I asked, reaching down to scratch her between the ears.

Only she spotted Frankie first and took off like a shot for the parlor.

"Darn it," I said, watching her go.

"Good. She was sitting on a clue."

"Frankie." I turned to find him behind me, holding a small white basket with a handle. I couldn't have been more shocked if he'd been holding a kitten. "Classy," I managed.

He let the basket disintegrate into thin air and pointed a finger at me. "This is none of your business. You're supposed to be gone."

"It's my house," I told him. "I didn't know you'd be playing Romeo tonight." I'd have made kissy noises if I didn't think it would make him bolt.

He smacked a hand against his forehead. "I should have just stuck to my place. But Molly said she wanted to go somewhere new."

Ellis had installed a utility shed out by the pond that was all Frankie's. His private retreat, if you like. I could understand the appeal of going out.

"You should definitely put forth the effort," I agreed. "Even small romantic gestures can mean a lot to a girl." Then it hit me. "You should make her a mixed CD." Did people do that anymore? "Maybe a mixed digital playlist."

His jaw slacked. "I have no idea what you're talking about, and I most definitely don't need your help romancing a girl."

The kicker was, he might. Before Molly, I was willing to bet Frankie hadn't had a serious date in almost a century. That basket certainly didn't look like him. And even though I was no expert in the ways of love, I was a girl and I knew what girls liked. "Show me what you're doing for her tonight," I pressed. "Just one peek and, after that, I'll wait outside," I promised. "I'll even take Lucy."

She'd be happier out on her patio pillow, anyway.

The ghost groaned and then hit me with his power.

I gasped. Not because it hurt, but because I hadn't expected him to do it. Perhaps some part of Frankie really did want my help.

His energy settled over me with a heavy, prickling feeling that reached down to my bones. In a million years, I didn't think I'd ever get used to it. Moments later, my senses opened and I could see the other side.

My dated kitchen appeared much the same as it always did, with pale yellow walls and an oak-topped island. Frankie's urn sat

6

next to a cookbook I'd borrowed from the library. The avocado green wall phone stood waiting by the laundry room, its perpetually tangled cord trailing down to the floor. I had no kitchen table, no real appliances. I was still recovering from my brush with financial doom, courtesy of my once-soon-to-be mother-in-law.

I had to find an easier way to say that.

Ghostly rose petals shimmered into focus, leading from my back door through my kitchen. They branched off at Lucy's bowl, and a folded note rested underneath it.

"Is this one of your clues?" I asked, taking a closer look. I accidentally brushed the edge of the ghostly note. It felt cold, with a wetness that seeped into my skin.

"Stop right there!" Frankie made a motion to block me, but he knew as well as I did that any touch between a ghost and a living person gave both parties quite a shock.

"It's private," he insisted, "a scavenger hunt. She likes games. And I'm not finished. I still have to dim the lights, write a poem, and light twelve dozen mini votive candles around your tub."

Lordy. "You're borrowing my grandmother's antique claw-foot tub?" I asked. "The one I bathe in every day?"

He shot me a cat-ate-the-canary grin that faded as soon as a knock sounded at the back door. "Oh no. She's early."

Perhaps that was a good thing. That way, he didn't have time to unleash a swarm of monarch butterflies or hire a classical music quartet. And I still wasn't keen on having him in my tub— ghost or not.

I opened the door, and instead of Molly, I found my handsome boyfriend, Ellis. He wore a white button-down shirt with jeans, along with a smile that showed off the dimple in his chin.

"How did I get so lucky?" I wondered aloud, much to his delight.

Molly hovered right behind him, her dark hair done in a pretty updo, her black dress hugging her corseted curves.

"I'm not ready yet," Frankie protested, like Romeo's caustic country cousin.

I slipped outside and closed the door. "You look gorgeous," whispered my broad-shouldered date as he leaned down to kiss me on the cheek.

Behind him, Molly gave a heartfelt sigh.

I took Ellis's hands in mine. "Molly's right behind you."

"Well, hello," he said, turning, as if he could see her. He'd never have that power, at least I didn't think he would. But it didn't stop him from acknowledging her.

She batted her lashes. "Always a pleasure," she said, with a lilting twang. Molly hadn't gotten out much before she'd met Frankie, and even the simplest social gestures seemed to delight her.

"We're going to Ellis's new restaurant," I explained. "I'm so proud of him," I added, squeezing his hand. "Southern Spirits is amazing."

He grinned, and I could still see the slight scar under his eye from when he'd saved me from a killer. If anything, it made him even sexier. "Molly and Frankie are invited too, of course," he said.

A crash sounded from my kitchen.

"Truly?" Molly clapped her hands together. "That's where Frankie's gang hides out. I've been wanting to go."

"It's a little dark where they are," I hedged. Not to mention frightening. Dozens of the South Town Boys had been gunned down in an illegal speakeasy built into the caves underneath the property. They'd tried to shoot me the last time I'd ventured into the ruins of the club hidden below Southern Spirits. It had been six kinds of scary because when I was tuned in to the ghostly side, their bullets could actually kill me.

It was definitely no place for a lady.

Much better for her to stay behind and enjoy the surprise her gangster boyfriend was cooking up for her. I cracked the door. "Frankie…"

"I want to go see Southern Spirits," Molly finished for me.

The ghost appeared at my door, his tie askew and a box of matches in his hand. "No," he said to his girlfriend. Then he turned to me. "Go get Suds," he hissed. "The doves escaped, there's chocolate sauce all over the floor, and I'm out of matches!"

"Er, Verity," Ellis hedged, checking his watch. "Are you ready? At this rate, I'm going to be late to my own party."

"One second," I told him.

We couldn't leave Molly standing out on the porch while her out-of-his-mind boyfriend chased down chocolate-covered birds and tried to set fire to however many candles he had scattered all over my house.

He was lucky I liked his girlfriend. And that the mess was his to clean up on the ghostly plane. Otherwise I would have been a lot more upset about what he was doing to my ancestral home.

I pasted on a smile. "Let her inside the house," I said through gritted teeth. "Ellis and I have to go."

"Why don't you want me to meet your friends?" she countered. "Suds likes me."

Frankie dug a finger under his collar. "Suds ain't like the rest of my friends."

That was true. Suds hadn't even known he was dead until Frankie and I unearthed him in the tunnel underneath the First Bank of Sugarland. Once Suds had gotten over the shock, he'd been as good an ally as I'd get on the other side.

Molly's face fell. "Are you ashamed of me?" she asked Frankie.

"Don't be crazy," he said, flinging a hand out, chilling my arm when it whooshed past. "I'm ashamed of them."

"We really have to go," I said, taking Ellis's arm.

"We do," Molly agreed, holding her ground.

I heard a chorus of squawks from inside my house and a bone-rattling crash.

Frankie shot a wide-eyed look at me. "Do doves and swans get along?"

"I'm getting your urn," I said, ducking past him. "You're coming with us."

"I've got it under control," he insisted, watching me pluck his final resting place from my kitchen island.

"We'll leave your troubles behind," I promised. He'd see. I deposited the small brass urn into my shoulder bag.

"That's not how it works." He followed me out onto the porch as I locked the door behind us. "It never works out that way."

$\sim$

MINUTES LATER, Ellis had his radio tuned to classic jazz as his truck rumbled down the tree-lined road toward Southern Spirits. Frankie and Molly sat in the back, she with both arms wrapped around his bicep. He looking like he'd swallowed a bug.

"Cheer up," she said, giving him a shake. "I'm sure your friends are just as deliciously exciting and unpredictable as you."

"That's what I'm afraid of," he muttered.

Whitewashed fencing gave way to an old limestone wall. Moss clung to the top. The rock wall rose higher on both sides of an open iron gate.

We turned into the elegant drive flanked with decorative greenery. A large brick building stood at the end, with wide wooden carriage doors at the front. Tall windows with green trim lined the first and second floors, sheltered under red brick arches, with a wood turret off the back. White, hand-painted letters on the red brick read "Southern Spirits since 1908."

A crowd of at least fifty waited outside. For us? I hoped not.

"What's going on?" Ellis murmured, slowing his truck. "I told them to relax at the bar. Have some drinks, enjoy the new place." His mouth tightened when we saw Virginia Wydell out front in a white suit and heels, directing the crowd. "My mother, on the other hand, wanted me to make a big entrance."

But that wasn't him. Neither were the spotlights shooting up into the night, nor the pole lights casting their glare over the crowd, obliterating the soft ambiance of the outdoor bulbs Ellis had strung at the entrance to his new place.

Leave it to Virginia Wydell to turn everything into a spectacle.

I spotted Ellis's father among the crowd. He was a silver-haired, Armani-suited, older image of Ellis. The man was perpetually at work or out of town. People said he was unstoppable, but I always wondered if he was just avoiding his wife. He hovered on the edge of the crowd, his cell phone to his ear, per usual. Most likely on a business call.

Ovis Dupree, guest reporter for the *Sugarland Gazette*, pointed his camera at us as we pulled up. Ellis's mother leaned over the wiry, eagle-eyed Dupree, her sleek blond bob brushing his ear, as she no doubt delivered last-minute instructions.

As if Ovis listened to anyone.

Near the edge of the crowd stood my ex, Beau Wydell. Sugarland's golden boy, he was tall, with Chris Pine good looks and a cocky smile he currently directed at me. Heaven knew what he was up to.

I was well on my way to ignoring him when Crazy Louie, the gangster ghost who had once vowed to end me, emerged from the crowd right behind Beau.

I sat up straighter and gasped. "No."

"Don't worry," Ellis said, parking the truck. "He won't bother you."

I stiffened as Beau hurried to open my door. A lock of blond hair fell boyishly over one eye, making him appear as playful as he was handsome. It was a calculated move.

"I'm not worried about your brother," I said.

I mean, normally, playing nice with the man who'd made a pass at my sister then let his mother try to ruin me would be enough to make me want to run.

But this time, it was the gangsters who emerged from the crowd behind Louie that made my muscles seize up and my mouth go dry. Two dozen of them, dressed in suits and packing heat. Crazy Louie had promised to make me pay after I'd knocked his skeletal head off what was left of his body down in the speakeasy. It had been an accident—I was trying to pick his pocket at the time—but try explaining that to Lou.

The gangster didn't "do" apologies.

Lou glared at me with murder in his eyes, and I stared down the gaping barrel of his gun.

"Frankie!" I pleaded. "Unhook me. Now!"

Beau opened my door. "Good to see you, sweetheart." His expression was warm, his voice mocking.

Lou grinned and took aim.

I lurched out of the truck with nowhere to run, nowhere to hide.

Frankie ripped back his power at the same moment Lou opened fire.

The shock of the ghostly energy rushing from my body sent me stumbling sideways. Needles of pain whipped down my body. Beau caught me before I hit the ground, and I swore I felt the icy sting of ghostly bullets an instant before they became harmless phantoms of the lethal slugs that would have killed me.

I gasped and stared up at Beau. I wasn't hurt. At least I didn't think so.

A laugh bubbled out of me as I gripped hard onto Beau's arms.

I was alive!

Beau smiled back at me with bright-eyed delight, and the *pop-pop-pop* of the reporter's camera guaranteed that a picture of me swooning in the arms of my former fiancé, on the anniversary of the biggest wedding scandal in Sugarland history, would be all over the front page tomorrow morning.

My only hope was that the Sugarland rumor mill was finally tired of me.

CHAPTER 2

"*How* bad is it?" I asked the next morning.

My little skunk snuggled in the covers next to me while Ellis grabbed the newspaper from my front porch and walked it back in. At least he didn't have to go far; we still slept on my futon in the parlor because I'd been forced to sell most of my furniture to pay for the botched wedding.

"Let's see," Ellis said in that carefully neutral tone he'd no doubt perfected on the police force, the one that usually meant trouble.

Lucy toddled toward Ellis as he slid the plastic wrapper off the newspaper. She liked crinkly things.

"It could be worse," Ellis said, the futon cushion dipping as he sat next to me and scanned the front page. "You didn't get shot by a gangster."

"If that's the bright side, we're in trouble," I said, scooting over to see.

He tossed the rest of the paper down next to him, and Lucy snurfled between us, shoving her nose into the plastic wrapper and whipping her tail back and forth.

Sure enough, the front page of the *Sugarland Gazette* featured a large black-and-white picture of me in Beau's arms, holding on for dear life, gazing up at him. The headline read "The Past is Alive and Well at the New Southern Spirits."

How awful. It was one thing for Beau to publicly humiliate me. He'd made a sport of it. But to pull his brother into it was a new low.

"At least they mentioned your new restaurant," I said, unfurling the page all the way. "And look. There's a picture of it here on the bottom." It was small, but it was there.

"Look at him," Ellis ground out, glaring at the image of his brother, who wore the hungry expression of a hero on the cover of a romance novel. "He's way too happy to be swooping in to rescue you."

For Ellis's good and the good of everyone, I'd tried to get along. I'd tried to be friendly, but one hard stumble and Beau had taken advantage.

My ex liked to think everything that happened with the wedding was all a big misunderstanding and that I was really secretly still pining for him. Never mind the fact I avoided him whenever I could.

Ellis's baby brother could turn a blind eye to almost anything as easily as he could turn on the charm. His brash, fun-loving attitude was what had snagged me in the first place. Still, I'd learned what he was really like, and there was no danger of me ever getting close to Beau Wydell again. Ellis knew that. But I suppose even the most confident man needed to be reminded now and again.

"Okay, so your brother is a jerk." I climbed over the paper and into Ellis's lap, crushing any and all mention of yesterday. "It's you I want," I said, wrapping my arms around his neck. I captured him in a kiss. "You realize that, don't you?" I asked against his lips.

"I do," he said, his arms snaking around me. But he was still tense. I could feel it in the way he held me.

"Talk to me," I said, brushing a lock of hair from his forehead.

He sat rigid, staring at a spot past my shoulder. "I'm not angry that you tripped into his arms. I'm not angry at Ovis for taking a picture, or the paper for publishing it." His gaze found mine. "I'm angry that my baby brother thinks he can take you back."

I shifted on his lap. "It makes me mad too," I admitted. But Ellis needed to get along with his brother even more than I did. Family was important. I didn't want to see his broken. "Tell him how far out of line he is," I suggested. "Lay it out there and give him a chance to see his mistake."

Ellis sighed, letting some of the tension unwind. "I'd explain how well that usually works with him, but you already know."

All too well. "At least I ended up in a pretty good spot," I said, nipping at his ear.

"That you did," he murmured, flipping me over onto my back, smiling as the laughter bubbled out of me.

Whenever we were alone—just the two of us—our relationship worked. It was wonderful.

Then the temperature of the air dropped ten degrees, and Frankie shimmered into existence right next to the bed.

"Well, that was an unmitigated disaster," the wiseguy groused, cigarette in one hand and his Panama hat in the other.

"Do you mind?" I asked, shooting the ghost the stink-eye.

Ellis plopped his face against my shoulder. "I thought you said he promised to stay out of the bedroom."

"This is the parlor," Frankie countered, taking a drag, as if he were the one who should be offended. "I got an afterlife, you know. You two have been holed up all night."

Ellis sat up reluctantly and I did the same.

"It's called sleeping," I said, adjusting the straps on my nightie.

"Then you're doing it wrong," the gangster countered, blowing a smoke circle.

"What do you want, Frankie?" I asked, giving up any pretense of civility as Lucy flattened herself against Ellis. He sheltered her against his chest and grabbed for the wrinkled paper with his other hand.

"I need to go by Molly's place." The gangster stepped closer and rubbed his jaw. "She said she was fine after last night, but I don't think she liked it when I tackled Crazy Louie."

I'd have liked to have seen that. "Did you explain to her that you were only trying to protect me?" Surely she'd understand.

"Who said anything about *you*?" he scoffed. "Lou had my gun! I was this close to getting it back. But then the band started up, and once your head was off the platter, the guys just started fighting for the fun of it."

"Sounds lovely." I was familiar with his gang's shoot-'em-up parties. Gun battles were a sport for them—it wasn't as if any of them could die again. According to Frankie, gunshots stung *"like a mother,"* and fatal shots would only knock a ghost out for a couple of hours. Then a terrible thought occurred to me. "Molly wasn't hurt, was she?"

"I lost sight of her until Sticky Pete clocked me over the head and I fell down at her feet. She wasn't too happy. Said fighting wasn't romantic."

"I'd have to agree with her there."

"I was winning, too." He flicked the end of his cigarette with his thumb, and the half-inch of ash at the end fell off and disappeared into nothingness. "She ran back to her place, said she wanted time to think. I need to go by there and make a grand romantic gesture before she decides I'm some hooligan."

He was a hooligan.

"Frankie," I began, weighing his request. This didn't exactly mesh with my plans for kissing my boyfriend until we forgot all about this morning's headline.

I glanced at Ellis, who was reading the article in the paper. His shoulders stiffened as he studiously ignored his phone rattling on the hardwood by the bed, buzzing with incoming texts.

We couldn't catch a break.

Frankie cleared his throat, and I returned my attention to the squeaky wheel. "So your urn is in my purse, and you need me to drive you to Molly's so you can attempt some outlandish declaration of love."

"He's not leaving until you do," Ellis said, eyes on the paper.

True. But in all honesty, I didn't think another dozen doves was the answer.

I also knew he wouldn't let up until we'd tried. I slipped out of bed and attempted to locate my shoes. "Frankie, you've got to stop it with the grand romantic gestures. Go to Molly this morning, but talk to her. Take her on a walk. Just be yourself."

He barked out a laugh. "You and lover boy might get your kicks lying around in bed all day, but I got Molly to like me by taking her on that picnic in the cemetery, by drawing her picture, by doing stuff."

I retrieved a clean sundress from the laundry room off the kitchen. "I get that, but none of those gestures matter if you can't be yourself."

He furrowed his brow. "Like I was last night?"

"No." Maybe he didn't need to show her *all* sides of himself. At least, not right away.

"Then I need a gesture," he concluded.

The newspaper crinkled as Ellis held it up. "Hey, I found the real article about my restaurant. Buried on page 18A."

Seeing as the town newspaper had only one section, that didn't bode well. "Some people start reading from the back," I pointed out. Or maybe that was just magazines.

"At least the story is positive," he said, folding the paper back. "The food critic liked the bacon macaroni and cheese."

"What about the shrimp and grits?" I asked.

"Also a hit." He smiled. It was his grandmother's recipe. "They did a nice paragraph on my uncle, and Ovis even included a few pictures of the ghost bar."

Ellis had surprised me by decorating the large antique wooden bar with photographs and memorabilia dedicated to the lives of some of the ghosts we'd met in Sugarland. He'd framed pictures and letters from Colonel Clinton Maker, the Rough Rider who kept an eye on the place. He'd put a replica of Frankie's second favorite gun in a glass case, surrounded by vintage pictures of my wiseguy and his gang. He'd also included tintype photographs of Molly and some of the "forgotten" girls we'd met on our last adventure.

It was so personal. So thoughtful. So *him*.

I slung my dress over my shoulder and went to wrap an arm around him. "Now we need to do something for you."

He deserved it. Ellis worked so hard.

"I want to get away." He plopped his head back against me. "Just you and me and no one else," he added, directing a look about five feet from where Frankie actually stood.

"We need it," I agreed.

The ghost rolled his eyes.

Ellis adjusted the paper and showed me the quarter-page advertisement on the back of the paper, near the story about Southern Spirits. "Take a look at this."

NEED AN ESCAPE?
BOARD THE NEWLY RESTORED SUGARLAND EXPRESS VINTAGE TRAIN FOR A LUXURY RAIL JOURNEY YOU'LL NEVER FORGET. EXPLORE THE WILDS OF THE TENNESSEE MOUNTAINS FROM THE COMFORT OF YOUR OWN LOVINGLY RESTORED RAILCAR.

"I could stand to escape for a few days," I told him, now more than ever. I took another look at the ad. "'Be a part of our once-in-a-lifetime maiden voyage from Kingstree, South Carolina, to our hometown of Sugarland.' It sounds expensive."

He leaned over and kissed me on the cheek. "It'd be my treat. I have some vacation time coming at the police station. The restaurant is finished. I have all my permits. We don't open until next month." He drew me down onto the bed. "Just think of it: no work, no responsibilities. No Ovis."

"No Beau," I said, watching his phone buzz with a text from his brother.

"My mother will be too horrified about this morning's headline to even bother with being scandalized about this," he added cheerfully.

"I could ask Lauralee to take Lucy," I said, warming to the idea. Lauralee was my oldest and dearest friend. Recently, she'd bounced the idea of taking my little skunk for a weekend, just to see if her boys were responsible enough to commit to a pet of their own. It would certainly be a good test.

"I'm going, too," Frankie said, snuffing out his cigarette on the wall. "A trip out of town will make Molly forget all about the gang fight. Plus, I owe her for the incident with the band."

"No offense, but you're one of the people we're getting away from," I told the ghost. "And what happened with the band?"

"Never tick off a tuba player," Frankie said, shaking his head. "They're tougher than they look. Anyway, unless you want me to be alone and lonely for the rest of eternity, I'm going on that train ride."

A knock sounded at the front door. "Yoo-hoo! Verity," a woman called over the creaking of the hinges as she let herself in. "My girls and I made you a 'congratulations' casserole to celebrate your reconciliation with Beau Wydell. We really couldn't be happier for you. He's the hottest bachelor in the county, you know."

I smelled sausage and eggs before Cordelia Masters turned the corner into the parlor and watched me leap out of the bed I'd shared with Ellis.

Her smile fell, and I could almost see the flower in her hat droop along with it. "For you and…Beau," she said, awkwardly holding the covered dish between us.

She stared from me to Ellis, as if we'd been caught doing something we shouldn't.

"Sorry to disappoint," Ellis said, standing, not bothering with a shirt.

I pasted on a gracious smile and realized I still had my sundress draped over my shoulder. "Thank you, but as you can see, I'm not back with Beau," I said, allowing her to keep the still-steaming casserole. "That's over. It's been over for a year now. No matter what the papers say."

She blinked a few times. "I'll have to call Louisa May, then, and tell her to cancel the cake."

Ellis drew up behind me. "I think that would be best," he grated out.

Cordelia had left the front door open, and I heard another car pull up the gravel drive. "Have a nice day," Cordelia said, backing out, practically running as she called out to the next visitor, "Sadie, park the car. I have news—" The screen door flapped in her wake.

I turned toward a frowning Ellis. "You're right. We need to get out of town."

CHAPTER 3

*B*y noon the next day, I was in the parlor, packed and ready to go. And not a minute too soon. The Sugarland grapevine had sprouted a dozen new tendrils even I hadn't seen coming.

Lauralee had gladly taken Lucy while I'd avoided two more casserole pushers and fielded a phone call from my mom in Florida, assuring her that, no, I did not lose my mind and rekindle a romance with Beau.

Ellis had bought us last-minute tickets on the Sugarland Express and was coming to pick me up.

Now all I had to do was escape a tortured ghost.

"Stop being difficult," Frankie said as I closed the suitcase I'd borrowed from my sister, Melody. "You and I both know it's a mistake to leave me here alone."

"What's the difference? You do whatever you want, even with me around," I said, sitting on the case in order to zip it shut. My sister had lent me far too many shoes. "Besides…" I tried to think of a polite way to say it as the zipper snicked closed, but settled on pure honesty. "I don't want to see ghosts on this trip."

"That is insulting," he said, "but I will take the high road."

He couldn't find the high road with a map.

Ellis's truck rumbled to a stop out back. "That's my ride." I smiled.

Frankie stiffened. "You're just going to leave Molly standing on your porch."

"No," I said, dragging my suitcase through the kitchen toward the back door. "I'm going to leave her with you."

Frankie trailed behind. "Can I be honest?"

I paused. "Do you really want me to answer that?" This was Frankie we were talking about.

"I don't want to hang out with *you*. I've got to do this for Molly." He yanked off his hat and ran a hand through his hair. "I mean, what if she decides I'm boring and breaks up with me? I can't take her anywhere new or exciting, not without you. I'm trapped here."

True, I had grounded him. Quite by accident. But still, it put him at a disadvantage.

He pointed his hat at me. "If Molly ditches me, it'll be on you," he warned.

"You can't blame me." But he would. If there was trouble in paradise when I came back, I didn't relish defending myself over and over again. Once Frankie got an idea in his head, it was hard to shake it loose.

And I was rather fond of Molly.

"Fine," I said, hoping I didn't regret it. "You can go—on one condition." I'd find a way to explain to Ellis why I felt the need to bring two ghosts on our romantic escape. "I want to forget you're even there. No snarky comments, no sharing our room, no popping in on us in the morning."

"Hot diggety dog!" He slapped his hands together as he passed through the back wall on his way to tell Molly. "You won't regret it."

I hoped not. But there wasn't too much time to ponder. I'd

barely stuffed Frankie's urn in my shoulder bag before Ellis opened the door and we were off.

~

W<small>E</small> <small>ARRIVED</small> <small>IN</small> K<small>INGSTREE</small>, South Carolina, that night with enough time to grab a quick bite before it was time to board the train. Formal dinner on the Sugarland Express wasn't until nine o'clock, which was later than we were used to eating.

I still hadn't figured out a way to tell Ellis that Frankie and Molly were canoodling in the flatbed of the pickup truck.

Never didn't seem like an option.

I mean, I could keep it a secret. It wasn't as if Ellis could see Frankie and Molly. Still, that kind of dishonesty made me uncomfortable.

"Relax," Ellis said as he pulled up in front of a gorgeous old railroad station that had been converted into the Last Stop Grill. The two-story brick building boasted arched windows with red awnings and a wide outside platform with tables overlooking the old tracks. "This was one of the busiest stations in this part of the country for decades. Frankie should find a lot to occupy him here."

"Wait. You know he's here?" I gaped as Ellis killed the engine. "How?"

"You keep sneaking looks at the flatbed behind us," Ellis said, pocketing his keys. "It doesn't take an expert to know Frankie talked you into coming."

"That ghost is stickier than a possum in pine tar," I agreed, reaching for my purse, feeling a bit guilty. Ellis had treated me to this trip so we could be alone together, and I'd allowed my ghosts to intrude.

"Can't say I'm happy about him tagging along," Ellis said, popping open the door. "I assume he'll stick to his own business."

"That he will," I promised. And while we were discussing it... "Molly's here, too."

He shook his head and tried to hide the hint of a smile. "I figured."

"Thank you," I said, growing a bit misty-eyed. Ellis had every reason to be annoyed with me, yet he'd given me the benefit of the doubt.

He was one of the good ones. We just needed to catch a break.

My eye caught several couples dining outside, smiling and laughing without a care in the world, or so it seemed. I wanted to be one of them.

Ellis opened my door. "You think any harder and you're going to break something," he teased, offering a hand to help me down out of the truck.

"I just don't want anything to go wrong on this trip," I said, walking with him toward the wide front doors. It seemed like wherever we went, trouble followed.

"The trip will be great." Ellis wrapped an arm around my shoulders. "We're leaving our worries behind." He drew me tighter. "Trust me."

"Of course." I wished I had his confidence. I let out a long breath and tried to relax. "It'll be fine."

I glanced back at the truck and caught the eye of the gangster, who gave me the thumbs-up.

I ignored him.

"Let's eat," Ellis said, in the tradition of guys everywhere.

We entered the old station, and I was captivated. Built in 1906, the warm wood trim and antique maps on the walls carried the kind of nostalgic charm that made my spirit warm and my heart go pitter-patter.

Three long wooden benches in the waiting area—most likely original—stretched out, as if waiting for the next train to roll in. The gilt bronze and crystal tiered chandelier above reminded me of the one from my home that I'd been forced to sell.

It had graced the parlor for as long as the house had stood. There was no telling where it was now, or what would become of it. I fought back a twinge of pain for my family heirlooms scattered and gone. I couldn't recover everything I'd lost, but I could hold onto the hope that someday my home would be this warm and full again.

We visited the hostess stand and were escorted to a lovely table on the patio overlooking the tracks. In fact, most of the restaurant seating was under the large awning outside. The station itself wasn't that big.

"You like?" Ellis asked, admiring the vintage-inspired Southern Railway place settings.

"I love," I said, sinking back into the cushioned chair.

This was our chance to be a blessedly normal couple. Well, as normal as we could get with an urn in my purse and two ghosts in the back of the truck.

An age-stained clock face hung from the hand of a brass, art deco angel. The doors stood open, and the smell of old brick and wood drifted from inside, mingling with the fresh summer air.

The waitress had barely poured two glasses of sweet tea for us when my phone pinged.

"It's Lauralee," I told him. "I hope she hasn't run into trouble already."

"Go call her back," he said, relaxing with his drink. "I'm fine here."

The waitress directed me to a small brick patio at the rear of the building, where two other women chatted with their babysitters.

I smiled as I dialed my friend's number. For the first time in a long time, I could honestly tell her that I was taking care of myself. Ellis and I would prove that we could do this. We could be normal. Savor the simple things. Enjoy three whole days without the threat of scandal, tragedy, or murder.

The phone rang, and for a moment, I let myself imagine a life like this, with Ellis.

"Sweetie," she exclaimed the moment I answered. "I'm so glad you called back. We have an issue," she said, her voice lowering. "I'm sorry to bug you on vacation, but I figured I should get your take."

"Oh my," I said, dismayed that crisis mode felt distressingly normal as well. I braced my back against the wall. "Is everything all right?" When I'd dropped Lucy off last night, Lauralee had assured me that my little skunk would be in for the vacation of her life. And while I had no doubt about Lauralee's ability to control chaos—my friend had four boys under the age of eight, and her house was still standing—Lucy wasn't used to following anybody else's rules.

Even after I'd specifically talked to her about being a good houseguest.

"Everything's great," Lauralee said, to the sound of kids laughing in the background. "The kids love having an animal around. But..." She paused. "Is it okay if Lucy sleeps in bed with my oldest? Because she already did last night."

"That's no problem at all," I said, pushing off the wall, both relieved and glad that Lucy had warmed up to her temporary home so quickly.

"Oh, and I know you said she loves yogurt, so the two youngest made her a parfait."

"They take after their mother." Lauralee was one of the finest cooks in town.

"Someone has to use the crystal from my wedding," my friend said. "Of course, Hiram didn't want to be outdone, so he's going to teach Lucy to give him a high five."

"You realize she's only staying with you for three more days," I said, heading for an arched door that appeared to offer a shortcut back into the restaurant.

"Once you sleep under our roof, you're one of us." Lauralee

laughed, her humor cut short when we heard a crash behind her. "Gotta go!" she said, with a smile still in her voice.

There was no one like Lauralee, and I was grateful to count her as a friend, but for once I was glad she was in Sugarland and I was here.

I passed into a lovely travel-inspired bar area. Leather club chairs, brass lamps and side tables, and artfully displayed vintage luggage reminded me of the days when traveling was an experience to be savored.

A reclaimed wood table served up a variety of books on classic cocktails, scenic railways, and good cigars, topped by a quirky iron sculpture of an old locomotive.

The space stood empty. It was early yet. I'd have to show Ellis this room after dinner.

A few details like this could really dress up his Spartan bachelor pad. Slowly but surely, he'd been stashing the candles, the tall jar filled with decorative balls, and all of the knickknacks I'd bought him, claiming they blocked the TV or they got in the way when he ate his microwave meals on the coffee table.

I slipped my phone into my bag and was about to get back to my date when Frankie shimmered into view in front of me.

He held up his hands. "I know you don't want to see me, but I have news."

"You're right. I don't want to see you," I said, moving past him.

He reappeared directly in front of me. "This is the station where the Pokipse Gang robbed the nine o'clock special," Frankie gushed.

My bag slipped off my shoulder. "I'm not even sure what that means," I said, adjusting the strap. "And what happened to not talking to me?"

"This is important," he insisted. "I just met Joe Pokipse out back. He and the gang made off with more than three hundred dollars in gold, and it's buried right outside." He was like a kid on Christmas. "Half that's mine if you dig it up."

Did he hear himself? "We are not digging up gold. We're not teaming up with Joe Pokipse. I am on vacation, and you are on a date."

He sighed, as if I were the difficult one, and hit me with a wave of power that made me catch my breath.

"Frank—" I began, reeling from the shock of it, forcing myself to breathe deep as the prickling energy raced down my arms and soaked into me.

"Relax and enjoy it. I have lots of spare juice now," Frankie said, as if that were the issue.

Molly had made him a more powerful ghost. I wasn't sure if it was the "joining" of their energy (in ways I'd rather not think about) or if it was merely the fact that he was happier and more in touch with his feelings than he'd ever been, at least since I'd met him.

Either way, he wasn't as stingy about sharing his ghostly power, which was certainly different. Not to mention inconvenient because, for once, I didn't want it.

The ghostly side filtered into view around me. In stark gray, I saw three rows of benches, like the ones in the lobby, plus a petite Molly standing next to Frankie.

She gave a small wave. "Hi, Verity. He shouldn't have done that."

"Exactly. He should be focused on you while I'm on vacation," I said, directing my ire at the gangster.

Frankie looked from his girlfriend to me. "I am focused on Molly. This is how I'm gonna get the cash to show her a good time," he said, as if that were the solution to everything. He leaned close to me. "Now, the gold is under a big oak tree. You cut it down, and then you get a shovel—"

"No," I said. "I'm going back to dinner with my boyfriend." I strolled past him, out toward the lobby area and the doors to the patio.

I was not going to get wrapped up in his ghostly shenanigans. I wasn't even tempted.

"Wait. Hold up," Frankie said, keeping pace with me. "I'm just trying to give Molly a taste of what we do for a living. You know, impress her. Flash some gold around."

He was trying to take advantage. "I don't see you," I singsonged under my breath. "I don't see any of this."

The ghost of a woman in a ragged traveling cloak blocked the door to the patio where Ellis sat. She turned to me and lowered her hood. Her skin clung to her cheekbones, giving her a skeletal appearance.

"Excuse me," she drawled slowly, her Southern accent thick. "Do you have the time?"

Not in her dimension. But darn it, I didn't want to be rude. I checked my watch. "Ten after seven," I said, attempting to edge around her toward the door.

The skin around her eyes was so thin I swore I could see her eye sockets as she gazed up at me. "Do you know when the next train will arrive?"

Possibly never.

I'd heard stories of ghost trains, but I'd never seen one. And it appeared as if she'd been waiting for a long, long time.

The shimmering woman watched me expectantly, and I cringed at the thought of her waiting endlessly, stranding herself for eternity. She needed to start living her afterlife in a way that made her happy.

I drew closer to her and spoke to her as if she were someone's great-grandmother, which, for all I knew, she might have been. "The next train may be a long time coming," I said gently. "I think it's best that you move on."

She nodded, and I wasn't sure my words had any impact. Then I watched her slowly fade until she disappeared entirely. I hoped she'd gone into the light.

That was the last ghost sighting I'll have while on this vacation, I promised myself as I stepped out into the light of the patio.

Ellis had ordered a potato-skins appetizer for us and was talking with an older couple at the table next to him.

I dropped a kiss on his cheek and joined him.

"It's just never been done before," said the woman at the next table. Her husband had his nose buried in a book on vintage locomotives. He looked familiar, with his pale eyebrows and gold-rimmed spectacles. A half-eaten slice of carrot cake sat between them, with two forks.

"Mary Jo was just telling me about the new Sugarland Express," Ellis said.

"There's nothing new about it," she said, her colorful glass earrings swinging as she spoke. "It's been completely restored using cars and parts from several original-model turn-of-the-century trains. They did a spectacular job. We drove from Foley for the maiden voyage. Everyone in Dave's classic train club wanted to go, but the trip came up rather suddenly and sold out just as fast."

"I heard they finished early and wanted to get moving," Ellis said, nudging the platter of skins my way.

I slid two onto my plate.

"Six more sleeper cars are in the works. They'll be adding each of them as they finish restorations, but it's a small train to start," Dave said. "They're smart to be conservative. I think they want to get their feet under them."

"I think it's perfect," Mary Jo said, digging her fork into the slice of cake. "And a wonderful way to meet people." She nudged her husband.

He put down his book and held out a hand. "Dave Abel."

"As in Abel Windows and Doors?" I thought he looked familiar. Now that he'd pulled his nose out of the book, I recognized that Jay Leno chin and ready smile from his regional commercials.

Foley was only about an hour northeast of Sugarland. Abel did big business, especially in historic home renovations.

"That's me," he said. "Are you in the market?"

"Not everyone needs a door, hon," his wife said as we shook his hand. His grip was strong. In fact, Abel was built like he'd worked a lot of restoration jobs himself. "Mary Jo," she said, giving a little wave. "Ellis has already told us all about Sugarland and showed us pictures of your pet skunk." She winked. "Such a cutie."

I didn't know how to respond for a moment. Was Ellis the cutie, or was my skunk? I wasn't sure. And I certainly wasn't used to people going out of their way to approve of our relationship. "Thanks," I managed.

If Mary Jo noticed my hesitation, she didn't make an issue of it. "It's a small train, so we'll probably be seeing a lot of you," she added pleasantly. "We're in compartment number 1. Number 2 as well," she added, slightly embarrassed. "They made the two compartments into a double with a separate bedroom."

Hey, I didn't blame her a bit if she could afford it. This was obviously a passion trip for them.

"We're in compartment 9, near the back," Ellis said, pulling out our tickets. They were exact reproductions of the originals, down to the crisp linen paper, flowing script, and the ornate engraving of a vintage steam engine rushing down the tracks.

"The care taken with this restoration is amazing," Dave said, leaning over to show Ellis a spread from his book. "This is the part I was trying to find. Now this is the original engine block…"

A cold hand rested on my shoulder, and I felt the wet, ghostly chill straight down my arm.

"I need to speak with you. Most urgently," a voice rasped, causing goose bumps to erupt over my ear.

Darn it. Frankie hadn't turned my power off.

I turned and saw a ghost with a white moustache that curled at the ends. A watch chain stretched from the side pocket of his vest.

It ended in a bulge between two round shiny buttons at the front. He wore white shirtsleeves and a dark hat with a brim, and I didn't mean to stare, but it had the words *Sugarland Express* embroidered across the front.

His pale eyes bored into me. "I know you can see me," he insisted. "I watched you earlier, talking to those two troublemakers."

That about summed up Frankie. I still had hope for Molly.

"Excuse me," I said to Ellis and the nice couple as I slid out of my chair. "I need to take care of something before we go."

The ghost standing at our table seemed to be a former train conductor. I had no idea what he could possibly want with me, but seeing as I planned to get on the Sugarland Express in less than an hour, it seemed like a good idea to find out.

A flicker of warning touched the back of my mind. I didn't like going off with strange ghosts. Still, I was curious about what he had to say.

"This way," I murmured, leading him back to the waiting room turned bar.

We passed underneath the archway, and out of the corner of my eye, I saw him pull out a flask and sneak a hearty swig.

I was glad he wasn't driving our train today.

"We have a problem," he said, reaching for me.

I pivoted out of his way and wondered if he had control of his faculties. Ghosts never voluntarily touched the living. It was jarring for everyone involved. "What's wrong?" I asked. Perhaps I could help him, although we were set to board at eight o'clock. That wouldn't leave much time.

"I can't take that train out again," he said, looming over me. "Ever."

"All right," I said. Whatever had happened to him, it was over now. "You don't have to ride the Sugarland Express tonight," I assured him. "A living conductor has taken charge. Your journey is complete."

"It is not," he bit out. "You brought me back."

Come now. I braved a step closer. "I hardly think it's my fault."

"You and everyone getting on that train," he said, waving his flask.

"Listen—" I began, trying to think of a way to talk him down.

The ghost's eyes hollowed and his voice drew low. "The Sugarland Express was a fine train. The best. Or so we thought. But she was heavy. On her maiden voyage in '29, a bridge collapsed under her, and she plunged into the river below, killing everyone on board."

Stars. "That's terrible." That part of Sugarland history had definitely gotten swept under the rug.

The ghost drew closer. "The wreck is still at the bottom of that river today. I stayed with it until every one of my passengers ascended to the light or moved on to haunt a better place. Finally they left me at peace. But now you've called me back." His cold breath iced my cheek and shoulder.

"I think you're taking this too much to heart." He should be free. "This is a different train." The first one was at the bottom of a river.

"The new owner salvaged the original bell," he said ominously, "and they placed it on the locomotive of your train."

"Well, that's just one part," I said, trying to ease his anxiety.

"It's the soul of the train," he snapped. "And the name: the Sugarland Express. They named it after my train. They made it look like my train. They've resurrected the spirit of the Sugarland Express." He scrubbed his forehead with his hand. "That's not all. We had a...distressed soul on board. If the Sugarland Express pulls out of the station this evening, I may not be the only one returning."

That didn't sound good. "Okay, well, help me, then. Tell me what to do about it." There was no sense tempting fate.

"Destroy the new Sugarland Express," he ordered, with the fervor of an old preacher. "Melt down the bell."

"Um…" I didn't see how I could pull that off.

I mean, I'd just gotten ahead financially after my last adventure. Destroying a multimillion-dollar train would definitely put me back in the red.

"Do it," the ghost insisted. "Otherwise, it might be you at the bottom of that river."

I studied the desperate warning in his eyes, the sheer terror written over his features. He'd suffered greatly. He was still dealing with the aftermath of the wreck.

Still, I didn't see how a tragedy from 1929 could possibly affect a state-of-the-art train today. Yes, the new Sugarland Express had the name and the bell of the old one, but it also had all the latest equipment and conveniences. The bridge today would be inspected and maintained.

And as far as souls coming back, there was nothing I could do if another ghost from the past chose to haunt the new train. With any luck, I wouldn't even see him…or her. I meant it when I said I'd decided to take a vacation from Frankie and his power. As soon as he unhooked me, I was done seeing ghosts on this trip.

Still, it hurt me to see this ghost suffer.

"Maybe it's time to let it go," I said as gently as I could. He needed to stop torturing himself. The wreck was tragic, but it was over and done.

His face fell, as if the battle were already lost, which I supposed it was. We couldn't change the past.

"That last journey was tragedy from the beginning." He closed his eyes briefly, all the fight draining out of him. "I should have turned back after the murder."

Hold on. "Murder?" I asked.

He gave a small nod, his focus drifting to the window. "We never caught the killer, and it was a heinous crime." He cleared his throat. "Less than a day into the journey, the train got stuck in the mountains in a freak snowstorm." He gazed at me with a haunted look in his eye. "While the train was stopped, a killer struck. A woman was found stabbed to death in her locked compartment. She looked a lot like you."

This was getting worse and worse. "Now you're just trying to scare me."

"I wish I was." The conductor removed his hat. "But it's true. The killer was never found."

"Well, at least we won't be having any snowstorms on this trip." In fact, I hoped the train had a good air conditioner.

The ghost eyed me warily. "The woman was killed while everyone on board was in the dining room. Everyone had an alibi."

"It's over now." The killer was long dead.

Only I knew firsthand that death didn't necessarily stop a person bent on justice...or vengeance.

"We never found any prints in the snow or evidence anyone had come inside." He folded his hands behind his back. "We couldn't get a signal out. The police department never got to investigate. I tried," he added, his expression pained. "But there was nothing. No one. I'm responsible for the safety of the passengers under my care. I let them down," he added quietly.

"There was nothing you could do." It had been a tragedy, no doubt. But it was over now. The old Sugarland Express didn't exist anymore. It was part of history, a forgotten one at that.

"You can still keep the train from going out again," he said, getting agitated. "You can keep the passengers from boarding."

I couldn't stop a train. "You're giving me too much credit." I couldn't tell people to avoid a vacation because of a murder and a wreck that had happened to a different train in a different age. Most of the hauntings I'd investigated had to do with ghosts clinging to real places and objects from their pasts. The original Sugarland Express lay rotting at the bottom of a river. "This isn't even your train, not really."

He drew so near I could feel the chill of him in the air. "Then why was I called back?"

The corner of his mouth tipped up as I drew a harsh breath.

His eyes narrowed. "There's no getting around it. Set foot on the Sugarland Express and you'll be boarding the ghost train as well. Don't say I didn't warn you."

I drew my shoulders tight and forced myself to calm. "It will be all right."

"Tonight the cursed bell will ring again…"

I'd make Frankie turn his energy off. "We'll get through this." If anything happened, they needed Ellis and me on board.

Not that there was anything to investigate.

I'd lose my mind if I opened myself up to every past tragedy and every sad ghost.

He ignored my distress. "If you insist on going out, if you're determined to begin the journey again, then know this." He closed in. "It began with the killing. If you can stop that, maybe you can change the rest. Help me protect the passengers in the murder car," he ordered. "We cannot allow tragedy to strike again in compartment 9."

I stared at him.

"Promise," he insisted.

I wanted to. I desperately wished I could make that vow and stick to it. Ellis and I were in compartment 9.

$\mathscr{I}$ stood rigid by the vintage suitcases I'd found so charming only a short time ago. No wonder the compartment had been available. The owners had probably booked all the other ones first. Even people who didn't have ghosts interrupting their appetizers could sense the paranormal. It was that prickling feeling on the back of your neck when you knew you were not alone, or the odd sense to avoid a darkened set of stairs. Most people learned to trust their instincts, and mine were telling me to stay far, far away from compartment 9.

I hurried back to the table and whispered the whole story to Ellis. And him being the man he was, he took immediate action. His call to the tour company was short and direct. When he hung up, he turned to me.

"They're trying to switch us to a different sleeping compartment. We'll know before the train leaves in a half hour." He checked his watch. "Speaking of such, we'd better get going." The Abels had already vacated the table next to us.

"Sounds good," I said, winding my hand in his.

Not every guy would be so sweet about his girlfriend changing vacation plans based on a ghost sighting.

He touched my shoulder. "You okay?"

He really was handsome with his brow knit like that. I appreciated his care and the effort. Still, I couldn't hide a wince. "We bought the last tickets available. It's a full train." He walked me through the open doors and into the main lobby. "I don't know if there's anywhere else they can put us."

He gave a sharp nod. "We've done all we can. Let's try not to worry about it."

"I'll do my best," I said, letting him walk me past the long waiting benches. This was his treat, our chance to get away from it all. I'd already brought ghosts along. I hoped he realized how grateful and touched I was that he'd planned this getaway for us. We'd figure out a way to handle the issue with our sleeping arrangements.

I mean, the murdered ghost hadn't come back to haunt the train. Well, as far as we knew.

Ellis opened the door for me, and we left the Last Stop Grill.

The new, modern train station stood just down the street. Ellis ferried us down and left me with the luggage while he returned the truck he'd rented for our one-way drive. Ironically, he'd rented the same type of Chevy pickup he drove at home. That was Ellis. He knew what he liked.

I took a seat on the metal bench out front and resisted the urge to call my sister, Melody. When she wasn't at the diner, she worked part-time at the Sugarland library. Melody had all sorts of half-finished college degrees and was a whiz at research. If anybody could tell me the history of the doomed train, she could.

But I wasn't going to get involved.

Still, I hadn't met a ghost yet who'd appeared to me without a good reason. The old conductor had seemed genuinely worried, and I couldn't shake the feeling that we might be headed for trouble.

It wouldn't hurt to know what had happened.

I pulled the phone from my purse and dialed my sister's number. She answered on the first ring, because that was Melody.

"Why are you calling *me*?" she asked by way of greeting. "You should be way too busy wining and dining."

We weren't on the train yet. "I want to run something by you…" I told her about my encounter with the ghost.

"Excuse me," she said to whatever library patron she'd been helping. I heard a bump and a rattle, then the click of her heels as she walked. "Listen to me, Verity, and listen good. It doesn't matter what happened on some train a hundred years ago. You are going to have fun. You are going to have romance. You will have the freaking time of your life, and that's an order."

"We are. I mean, we've already started." Except for the issue with the ghost.

"You don't need to get involved. You're on vacation. Tell Frankie not to show you any more spirits."

"I'm trying to avoid it," I assured her, "but it won't hurt to know what we're up against." I waited for her response and got none. "So can you look into the murder on that train? I'd also like to know more about the accident that killed all those people."

"Oh, all right." She sighed. "As soon as I finish helping Mrs. Porter with her genealogy project," she added, the lilt returning to her voice. "It seems her great-grandfather, the pastor, had a secret family."

"It's always something." History was rarely as neat as most people made it out to be.

We said our goodbyes, and I was about to tuck my phone back into my purse when I heard voices coming from the cobblestone alley between the train station and the diner next door.

"Don't you walk away from me," a man threatened.

"I have my needs," a woman snapped. "You have to let it go."

I kept hold of my phone, ready to dial 911 for the woman as I peeked around the corner.

A blonde in a blue dress and sky-high black heels faced off

against a guy who had the body of a quarterback and the snarl of a gangster.

Believe me, I knew. I'd seen plenty.

He loomed over her and curled a hand over her bare shoulder, a little too close to her neck. "You and I both know it's not over. He can't give you what you want."

She looked at him for a long moment, refusing to back down or even flinch. "Are you saying you can do better, Ron?"

A vein bulged on his neck. "I'll fix it." He jerked back his hand and walked away, toward the street on the other side.

The woman exhaled and shook her hair from her shoulders. She was cooler under pressure than anyone I'd ever seen.

She'd stood up to a man twice her size. She'd come back at him while he'd had her cornered. And she wore heels on cobblestone. Talk about a force of nature.

I drew back before she saw me, and stood beside my luggage as she strode out of the alley and toward the Last Stop Grill. I kept an eye on her until she made it safely inside.

"Hey," a voice said right next to me. I jumped. "It's just me," Ellis said, with a steadying touch on my arm. "Did you just see a ghost?"

It was a reasonable assumption, but, "No."

"I got a call back from the tour organizers. We've been switched to compartment 10," Ellis announced, pressing a tip into the hand of a young, skinny porter who began gathering our luggage.

"Fantastic," I said. Ellis had come through again. I shouldn't be surprised. Relieved was more like it.

"Compartment 10 is smaller," he conceded, "and the bathroom a bit tighter. I'm sure the other couple will be pleased with their upgrade."

I stiffened. "Other couple?" They were putting someone else in the hazardous compartment? Of course they were.

"It's a full train," he explained. "I'm sure it will be fine," Ellis said, taking my arm and escorting me away. "Any other couple wouldn't even know if the conductor was in bed with them," he murmured into my ear.

"True," I said. It made sense.

Yet I couldn't escape the notion that I'd put an innocent couple in grave danger.

CHAPTER 5

*M*inutes later, we stood in front of the new Sugarland Express. The shiny black metal sides gleamed, and an elegant gold stripe raced just under the windows. On each car, flowing gold script framed by magnolia branches proclaimed the Augusta Belle Rail Lines to be the height of luxury and sophistication.

Steam billowed from the engine.

I spotted Dave and Mary Jo Abel farther up the platform. She waved at us while he directed the two porters loading a rather large trunk into the front of the train.

"Ready to go?" Ellis asked.

I tried to steady my heart when the old engine bell rang three times, like a summons. Or a warning.

Clang.

Clang.

Clang.

Just because that bell had been resurrected from the wreck of the Sugarland Express didn't make it a bad omen. At least that was what I tried to tell myself.

Frankie waved at me from inside the dining car, a drink in

hand. He and Molly didn't have to worry about pesky things like boarding times and lines. Once I'd carried his urn onto the station property, he had free rein.

Knowing Frankie, he'd taken full advantage.

While the train had a ghostly conductor, it seemed many of the porters and ticket takers had gone to the light.

That had to be a good sign, at least.

Now that I knew where the gangster was, I motioned for him to cut off his power. If this was going to be a real vacation, I needed to leave the spirit world behind before I even set foot on that train.

At first, Frankie squinted at the slashing motion I made with my hand over my neck. Then he got it. I saw him grin and felt his power lift.

Thank heaven and hallelujah. Ellis and I would at last know what it was like to be a normal couple.

I'd barely breathed a sigh of relief when an unseen force jerked Frankie from the window.

Goodness. I hoped he was all right. We knew of at least one active ghost on the train. There could be more.

He couldn't have offended anyone so quickly, could he?

A gray-haired porter leaned out of the train about six cars up. "All aboard the Sugarland Express!"

He put down a shiny silver step, and we all lined up to be among the first passengers to board the newly restored train.

"Thank you!" I said. "You know, I may just check out the dining car," I said, pivoting to the right. Not that I wanted to spend my trip chasing after Frankie, but the ghost drew trouble like a duck on a june bug.

A second porter blocked my way. I recognized him as the one who had carried our bags inside. "I'm sorry. You can explore the train after we secure your compartment." He couldn't have been more than twenty-five, and so near to skin and bones I swore he'd have to run around in the shower to get wet. I could easily slip past him and be on my way.

Ellis was the one who stopped me. "I'm sure Frankie is fine," he said, guessing the source of my agitation as he handed our tickets to the lead porter. "Let him go."

"I'm not used to doing that," I admitted. I'd allowed Frankie to come along on the condition that he keep to himself, and I had to abide by that as well. It wasn't like I could solve every problem for him, in this world or the next.

The ghostly realm had become too much of a distraction, and part of that was my fault. But today, we could start fresh. I could relax more and worry less. I could ignore the way a sudden gust of cold air whisked past my shoulder.

Clang.

Clang.

Clang.

They really needed to stop ringing that bell.

The older porter nodded to Ellis. "Number 10. A lovely choice. Come this way," he said, his back stooped as he led us down a narrow hall.

The new Sugarland Express boasted two long sleeper cars at the back. Windows lined the left side as we made our way toward our compartment. Sleek cabin doors punctuated the polished wood to the right, their gold-leaf numbers guiding us. I glanced over my shoulder and saw the second porter following with our luggage.

"There are five compartments per sleeper car," the older porter said, leading us past compartments 1 to 5. He pushed open a polished wood door with an oval window and led us through a small transition area and into the next car. "All rather elegant."

We followed him past compartments 6, 7, and 8. I hesitated at compartment 9 before moving along to the door at the very end.

Compartment 10 opened on a compact, luxurious room with a plush red velvet couch on the right, next to a table with a lamp and a silver bowl filled with oranges. My thoughts trailed back to my little skunk, Lucy. She loved oranges—all fruit, really. And from what it sounded like, she was getting plenty at Lauralee's house.

The young porter stowed our luggage in a discreet cabinet next to the couch while his superior showed us how the little table under the double windows pulled out into a place to stash books and magazines, or to enjoy a drink.

I admired the rich paneling on the walls and the white spa slippers with the Sugarland Express logo lined up in front of a small door. "Is that the bathroom?"

"It's really quite remarkable," the porter said, as if he were experiencing it for the first time as well. "This section holds your entire vanity area." He slid open the door to a sink and a shaving mirror as well as shelves for our toiletries. "And a small shower back here," he said, showing us a compact, but gorgeous shower area. "A luxury they didn't have in 1929."

"I'll take it," I told him.

"The beds unfold from above the couch," the porter continued. "I'll be back tonight to turn the room." He gave a nod and left, sliding the door closed quietly behind him. The other porter had already gone.

I turned to Ellis, smiling. This was it. "You did it."

"We did it," he said, taking me into his arms. I was just about to kiss him when we heard muffled voices next door.

"The people in compartment 9," I said, trying to make out what they were saying.

It sounded like a woman and a man.

"Try to let it go," Ellis said, glancing in that direction. "They should be safe if they can't see ghosts."

I hoped that was true. Yet the conductor had seemed so frightened. "I've just seen so much tragedy in the last year. If I can prevent something more from happening, I will."

"And?" Ellis prompted. He knew me too well.

"We can at least talk to them about trading back," I said in a rush.

His eyes twinkled as he drew me close. "I understand the need to make a difference," he said, resting his forehead on mine. "It's one of the reasons I joined the police force." He laced his hands behind my back, holding me securely. "Still, I can tell you now that those people aren't going to want to switch back. They were upgraded to our luxury car for free."

He was right. They'd probably think we were making it up. Most people didn't want to hear about ghostly conductors or murders or trains that went bump in the night.

So I put my mind to enjoying my time with Ellis, to unpacking, to the little things I enjoyed so much, like organizing my toiletries just so on the vanity area behind the sink.

But as we dressed for the formal welcome dinner and I heard the woman's giggle, I couldn't keep those people off my mind. I would take the opportunity to meet them tonight, perhaps gain the woman's confidence so that she'd feel comfortable turning to me for help if she needed it.

We might not encounter them at dinner. Our table had already been assigned. But there was a champagne toast in the lounge car to celebrate our departure, and a social hour in the bar car after.

I adjusted the straps on Melody's yellow silk cocktail dress. It would be more than suitable for both occasions. And while it was a bit tight in the hips and the bust, I didn't think Ellis would mind. From the look he gave me while I lifted my hair for him to fasten my necklace, I'd say the dress was a hit.

"You don't have to wear your skunk necklace all the time," he said, brushing a kiss along my ear.

"I like it," I said, lowering my hair. It reminded me of Lucy and of him. So what if it wasn't cocktail-party chic? It was mine and I loved it.

Somehow, Ellis's dress shirt had wrinkled in the time it had taken for me to dress, but that was all right. He slid on a dinner jacket that mostly covered it. Put him in a parka and he'd still be the most handsome man on the train.

"We have five minutes before the champagne toast," Ellis said, opening the door for me.

From the window, I could see well-wishers on the platform, waving to the passengers already at the farewell gathering in the lounge. And as Ellis closed our door and straightened his tie, I couldn't help but pause in front of the closed door to compartment 9.

Yes, I could seek them out in the bar later, but we were neighbors. There was no harm in introducing myself.

Perhaps I could slip a warning in with a hello, or at least mention that Ellis was an officer of the law, just in case they needed assistance sooner rather than later.

Okay, it sounded strange even in my head. But I had to do this, even if it might be a little awkward.

Nothing could have prepared me for what happened next.

At the sound of my knock, the door to compartment 9 opened and I stood face-to-face with Beau Wydell.

CHAPTER 6

I stared.

Ellis cursed.

Beau simply smiled. "Hi, Verity."

"How did *you* get here?" I choked out, my throat tight, my head buzzing. The train was booked full. We'd bought the last tickets. We'd barely even gotten tickets, but Ellis knew a guy.

My date stood fuming behind me. "Beau is an investor in the train," he said tightly.

And there was the guy.

"When I found out you were coming on our maiden voyage, I decided I couldn't miss it," Beau added. His tone was light, but when I turned, his eyes were on me, his expression fierce. "It was my pleasure to book the last two cabins. One for you and one for me."

Nothing like a power struggle between two brothers, with me in the middle.

"When were you going to tell me Beau was involved?" I asked Ellis. No wonder he'd been cagey about how he'd gotten us last-minute tickets. Silly me, I figured he'd had some innocent contact in town and was enjoying the surprise.

A muscle in his jaw twitched. "It shouldn't have mattered. I thought my brother was doing me a favor," Ellis gritted out. "I had no idea Beau would have the bad taste to tag along."

Beau planted an arm on the doorjamb. "It's my train," my ex said simply.

"You did this on purpose." Ellis glared at him, drawing me away from his brother. I was glad to go. "This is out of line, even for you."

"Oh, relax," Beau said, as if we were the ones causing the problem. "Mom always says a good businessman manages the details of his ventures personally, so here I am. I have to make sure everything runs smoothly this first time out. And I'm going to be busy enough with my own date." He turned to me. "She's hot. And smart. I think she might be the one."

I fought the urge to roll my eyes. I hadn't heard of him dating anyone in town. And I'd know since the Sugarland grapevine had us as an item again.

"Don't get all jealous and possessive," Beau warned me. *Me!* "You had your chance."

"And I ran," I said, a little more forcefully than I should.

That was the problem with Beau. He could be charming when he wanted. He could even be kind. But then he'd turn around and pull a stunt like this and act like it was normal. Well, it wasn't. This was wrong on about a hundred different levels.

Unfortunately, there was nothing we could do about it now. We were stuck with Beau, on a train. For the next seventy-two hours at least.

"Goodbye, little brother," Ellis said, placing a hand on my shoulder to escort me to the lounge car.

I'd never been one to crave a stiff drink, but at the moment, I certainly wouldn't turn one down.

Beau walked along behind us. "Stephanie is already at the launch celebration. I think you'll like her."

Perhaps. But I didn't exactly plan on getting to know her.

I glanced behind me and caught Beau's wolfish grin. He was having fun, the jerk. As if I cared one way or another whom he was dating. I just didn't want him along on my romantic getaway.

I opened my mouth to tell him as much when the door to the lounge car slid open and Ellis came to an abrupt halt.

A piano played "I've Got You Under My Skin" for the dozen or so patrons that I could see talking and laughing in the long, perfectly appointed car. White velvet curtains framed the windows above plush couches set into the walls on both sides. A woman in a pink dress leaned over to speak to a fellow passenger, and I couldn't help but recognize the rigid set of her back and the elegant lines of her shoulders.

Please, no. It couldn't be.

She straightened in the cold, regal manner that could only belong to Virginia Wydell.

"Surprise," Beau said with relish.

"Mother?" Ellis choked out.

Virginia froze for a second, a gasp escaping her thin lips.

"Meet my investment partner," Beau said, an unmistakable twinkle in his eye.

Virginia appeared blindsided as well.

"I had to get the money from somewhere," Beau said, a touch defensive, but nowhere near as ashamed as he should be.

Virginia's stunned gaze darted from Beau to Ellis to me. "How?" she stammered.

"It's...good to see you, Mother." Ellis stepped stiffly into the bar car. "Let's talk." I let the door slide closed after him.

That left me trapped between cars with the rat. I turned to my ex. "I don't know what kind of game you're playing," I said under my breath, "but it's not going to get us back together, and it's certainly not going to make this an easy trip for any of us."

Beau lost the grin. "That's the kicker, Verity. As soon as you decided to date my brother, you made this harder than it ever had to be."

I ground my jaw, but didn't deny it. Of all the men in Sugarland, I'd chosen to date the brother of my ex. That was one of the reasons I was having trouble moving forward with Ellis. It was never going to be an easy road. "I didn't fall for your brother on purpose," I said, as if that made it better.

Beau gave a mocking chuckle. "Well, sweetheart, I didn't do this on purpose, either. I saw an opportunity and I took it. Just like you." He glanced through the round window at his mother and brother deep in talk, then back to me. "You could have walked away and left Ellis alone, but you didn't. Now you're sharing a bed with my brother. You're taking a vacation with him. Hell, you might pop up at family Christmas this year. I'm just showing you the mess you've created."

The door slid open, and Ellis and Virginia stood on the other side. "Come and join us, Verity," Ellis said, holding a hand out to me as he glared at his brother. "Beau will find a way to get along without you."

I stepped into the bar car. "Hello, Virginia," I said as politely as I could. She hadn't chosen this any more than I had.

"Verity." She tried for warmth and failed as we both selected a glass of champagne from a waiter with a tray. Virginia took a hasty drink.

Ellis dragged Beau farther into the car for a tense brotherly chat, and I left them to it.

"Imagine," Virginia said, steeling herself with a second, even bigger swig of her champagne. "First Beau shows up with a gold digger clinging to his arm when he should be focused on the launch of the train, and now…you." She gestured vaguely at me. "I'm going to have to spend the whole trip making sure my sons don't do anything ridiculous."

"I think that already happened," I said, downing a rather large sip of bubbly.

Virginia barked out a laugh, to my surprise and hers as well.

"I don't know what I did to deserve this," she said, holding up her glass with mocking familiarity.

"Want to brainstorm?" I asked, only half-joking. I had no answers.

At least we weren't even pretending this was anything but a giant mistake.

Ellis and I couldn't get away even when we were getting away.

The crowd had filled out in the few minutes since I'd arrived. A handsome man with a dark beard and an air of command stood at the head of the car and clinked a fork against a glass. He wore a uniform exactly like the old conductor's, right down to the Sugarland Express emblazoned across his cap. "Let us all make a toast," he announced. The train whistle sounded, and well-wishers began waving from the platform outside. "To the Sugarland Express."

"To the Sugarland Express," we repeated, holding up our glasses.

Clang.

Clang.

Clang.

Went the cursed engine bell.

The train lurched and pulled away from the station.

"Lord save us," Virginia murmured.

He just might have to.

CHAPTER 7

I'd like to say things improved over dinner, but I'd be lying.

As the train sped into the wilds of South Carolina, we made our way one section up to the dining car. True to his plan to humiliate me, Beau had placed Ellis and me at his table. All of the other tables were full. I knew because I checked.

"We can eat in our room," Ellis suggested against my ear.

We could. But I wasn't going to give Beau the satisfaction of knowing he'd gotten under my skin. Again.

"It's fine," I said, locating the name card at my place. I'd have to face his family sooner or later. I kept my expression pleasant and serene as Ellis assisted me with my chair.

My dear, deceased grandmother would be proud of my grace and poise, especially since I was seated directly across from Beau.

Ellis took the chair next to me, glowering at his brother the whole time, while Virginia retreated to the exit near the kitchen, conversing with the busboys, the waiters, pretty much anybody she could order around, while sending our table death stares every so often.

I got it. She was in survival mode. For once, I knew how she felt. We were both stuck in this ridiculous revenge plot of Beau's.

Even then, I wasn't quite prepared to contain my surprise when a tall blonde slipped into the seat next to my ex.

"Hi, hot stuff," she said, planting a sweet kiss on Beau's cheek.

It was the woman I'd seen arguing in the alleyway back in Kingstree.

She'd drawn her long hair into a polished twist and wore dangling pearl earrings with a lavender silk dress that hugged every curve yet still managed to appear both classy and expensive. It also exposed her sleek back and pooled at her sides, making it clear she wasn't wearing a bra.

She was as strong as I remembered her, with a rigid bearing and a steely gaze. You'd think Virginia would have liked that a little bit. Unless she was competition.

Beau gave a self-effacing chuckle, clearly taken with the attention from his new flame. "Stephanie, meet my blue-collar brother, Ellis," he said, with a wry twist to his mouth, as if it were funny that Ellis had chosen a career in law enforcement over a guaranteed job in the family legal practice.

"It's a wonder they allow me at the table," Ellis lightly quipped, shaking her hand.

"It's a wonder she doesn't fall out of that dress," Virginia drawled, commanding a seat at the head of the table. She shook out her napkin. "Although Beau does have a point, dear Ellis. An old distillery is nice, but you could be investing in more upscale enterprises like this one."

Even his success would never be enough for her.

"I'm happy with my life and Southern Spirits," Ellis said, as if her dig hadn't bothered him in the slightest. But I knew him, and I saw she'd hit pay dirt.

I had to give it to my boyfriend that he could be cordial at a moment like that. Ellis didn't fight the flood. He just stood strong while the muddy water rushed past him.

He'd been knee-deep in this battle ever since he'd decided to follow his gut rather than be told how to live his life. I admired him for it, but it was sad that his own flesh and blood never would.

"Not everyone can be a titan of industry," Stephanie concluded, running a hand along Beau's arm.

"Not everyone has it in them to fight for what truly matters," I mused, looking her dead in the eye. "I like a man who is willing to stand up for the little guy."

Ellis gave a small smile. "Stephanie, this is Verity."

They'd obviously met before. Without me. That was all right. I knew I wasn't exactly invited to Sunday dinner.

The blonde across the table flashed a quick, shallow grin. "I know exactly who she is," she said, with a bit too much relish, as if she'd sized up the competition and found me lacking. Well, if she saw me as competition, at least I had more material on my dress, and all of my underwear, too.

Just then, the man from the alleyway passed by our table. I'd recognize him anywhere. For one thing, he was built like a college quarterback. For another, I'd paid special attention to his sturdy jaw and wiseguy features because I'd fully expected to have to describe them to the police.

What was he doing on the train?

He caught eyes with Stephanie, and I wasn't the only one who noticed. "Do you know that guy?" Beau asked. "I saw him watching you on the platform, too."

"I've never seen him before in my life," Stephanie remarked, so smooth and innocent that it sounded like the truth.

"He spoke to you ten minutes ago at the bar," Virginia corrected Stephanie. I had to give her credit. She didn't miss a thing. And she never hesitated to act. "You seemed quite agitated by him."

Stephanie blinked, wide-eyed. "He was hitting on me. I told him to stop."

Virginia gave her a long look. "You don't have to give us the whole story, dear," she remarked, shooting a warning glance at her youngest son. "Every woman has her secrets."

Beau tried to smile and failed as an awkward silence settled over the table.

Stephanie smoothed her hair. "It honestly isn't my fault if men are attracted to me," she said, looking to me of all people for support.

It wasn't that I was in favor of awkward silences, or conniving girlfriends, or whatever Stephanie was trying to pull. But all I could think about at that moment was that this could very easily be my life.

Here I sat, watching Virginia snipe at Beau and Stephanie, trying to hold my tongue, and failing, as she and Beau tore Ellis down for the terrible crime of being a good, solid person. Then there was Stephanie, who waged a battle for supremacy that she'd have to fight all by herself, because I wasn't about to join in. And if she truly was "the one" for Beau, she'd be with us for some years to come.

I was frankly done with all of it and we hadn't even gotten the bread yet.

It wasn't as if Ellis would alter the direction of his life due to continued criticism. It wasn't like Stephanie would suddenly confess and tell us all about that guy from the alley. We weren't going to change the world here. We just needed to get through dinner.

So I counted on the trick that my grandma had taught me, one that her mother had taught her. I changed the subject. "This is a great train."

Stephanie shot me an indulgent smile. "Don't you just love what Beau has done with the Sugarland Express? He's so creative."

Virginia pursed her lips, and I had a feeling I knew who was behind the success of the enterprise, but I wasn't going to be the one to say it.

Beau wasn't either. "What can I say? I'm a perfectionist."

Ellis laughed despite himself, which seemed to annoy Beau and placate his mother.

To my great relief, the bread arrived.

One course down. Maybe I could skip dessert.

"The Sugarland Express is wonderful, from what I've seen," I said, reaching for the breadbasket. "And it was fun to have appetizers at a historic train station before boarding."

"You ate at the Last Stop Grill?" Stephanie asked, as if I'd told her we'd picnicked in the truck bed—which we had from time to time. "I hear that place is a run-down allergy trap. I'd never set foot in it," she said, eschewing Beau's offer of bread and Ellis's choice of dining.

I'd tried to be reasonable. I'd tried to change the subject. But I was not going to sit here and take that. "You didn't seem put off by any of that when I saw you walk into the Last Stop this evening," I said, buttering my slice. I couldn't help it. She'd gotten my goat.

Her eyes widened. "I did not," she said quickly, but I could tell I'd hit my mark.

"Verity is terrible at keeping secrets," Virginia said conversationally, with an edge of steel, "but she's almost always right." She glanced back at the man from the alleyway, as if sensing there was more to the story. "Your friend from the bar is traveling alone, which is strange for a man his age. I wonder what he's even doing on this train," she said, eyeing Stephanie.

Beau's girlfriend sipped her wine.

"I'm just glad I decided to come," Beau said, lifting a glass. "The train is magnificent. It'll bring tourism dollars to Sugarland and put us on the map again."

I'd toast to the last half of that. But as I lifted my glass, I felt a distinct chill in the air.

Not two seconds later, Frankie rose straight out of the table in front of me, his hat askew so that I was looking straight at the bullet hole in his forehead.

"We need to talk," he stated, as if I didn't have other things to do at the moment.

I reached around him to clink my glass with Beau's.

"Real nice," the mobster said, as if I were ignoring him instead of merely working around him. "Look, I don't know if it's a chick thing or what, but Molly met a ghost that looks a lot like you, and now she's worried about her."

I pasted on a smile as Ellis made his own toast to our town's rich history. I was in the middle of dinner. Surely Frankie could see that.

"Wait, sweetie," the gangster said to the empty space by the breadbasket. "Don't talk yet. I gotta give Verity a dose of energy."

He wouldn't dare. I didn't ask for it. I didn't need it. In fact, I'd expressly asked him to take it back shortly before boarding.

I braced for it anyway.

A blaze of power hit me square between the eyes, and I stifled a gasp as it raced with hot, needlelike fury over my skin. *Jerk!* I ground my teeth and tried to keep my serene dinner smile in place as the otherworldly energy settled deep down into my very core.

"I'm sorry," Molly said, surveying the table as she shimmered into view over the breadbasket. "I really wish it could wait." She tucked a lock of hair behind her ear. "But there's a cute blonde ghost who reminds me a lot of you. Sweet, Southern. She even has a pet squirrel."

I could not talk about this now. I tried to say it with my eyes as I raised a glass and pretended I'd heard Ellis's toast.

"Anyhow," Molly continued, as if I were somehow free to have this conversation, "she was at peace, haunting her ancestral home, when she was drawn back here—right to her death spot!"

I kept my face carefully neutral and gave up trying to clink glasses.

The conductor had warned me about more ghosts returning. I'd hoped he would be wrong.

"So this girl came back," Frankie said, the unlikely voice of reason. "Maybe she wanted to haunt someplace new."

"She never wanted to see this train again," Molly said. "She was murdered in compartment 9."

I gulped my wine.

Stephanie gave me an odd look. Beau chuckled. I put the glass down.

Molly leveled her gaze at me. "On the first night of the journey, the original train was stopped due to snow on the tracks. It was like an avalanche. In the confusion, her killer struck. What if he's on the train now? What if he does it again tonight? It's a bad idea to take the same route as the original train. She'll have to go through it all again."

My word. That would be awful.

I remembered Ellis saying we'd travel on historic tracks, but certainly not on the exact same itinerary.

"Excuse me," I said, clearing my throat, directing my question to Virginia. "Are we traveling the same route as the original Sugarland Express, the one that went off the bridge?"

Molly cringed at the mention of the crash.

Virginia merely nodded and let the waiter place a salad plate in front of her. "Why yes. We felt historical accuracy was critical for the success of this project. In fact, our dinner tonight follows the same menu. Same selection of wines." She smiled. "We're traveling the historic route, down to the whistle-stop." She seemed pleased for the first time that night as she nodded to the man refilling her wineglass. "Of course, we're grateful to be traveling over a modern bridge."

She said it to be humorous, but it didn't lighten my mood a bit.

"See?" Ellis nudged me. "Maybe you're having an effect on my mom."

He'd meant it as a compliment. Virginia hadn't exactly been a stickler for historical accuracy before. And now, the one time she tried, it was looking like a very bad idea.

It made me cringe inwardly to realize the ghost conductor might have been right. We were certainly inviting trouble.

"Well?" Molly pressed, obviously expecting me to do something about the fate of my ghostly doppelganger.

Beau said something into Stephanie's ear that made her snicker at me. Those two really needed to grow up. And I had to face facts. The girl in compartment 9 was long dead.

"You can't change the past," Frankie warned.

"We need to help. Or at least try," Molly insisted. "How hard is that to understand?"

Dang it. It wasn't hard at all.

"She's been watching you, Verity," Frankie murmured into my ear. "She wants to be like you," he accused, "which stinks because I don't even like you."

I fought to keep my smile pasted firmly in place.

Ellis leaned close to me. "Ghost trouble?"

"Frankie," I murmured.

It was all he needed to know.

"Tell her she's not an amateur sleuth," Frankie pleaded. "This is our romantic trip, not a ghost-hunting, mystery-solving debacle like you always fall into."

Didn't I know it.

But it didn't even seem like they needed me for the argument. "How can you not care?" Molly demanded. "Where's your heart?"

The gangster glared at me, and if looks could kill, I'd be floating in the middle of the table with Frankie and his girlfriend.

Seconds later, the brakes screeched on our train.

"Hold on." Ellis took my arm to steady me.

The Sugarland Express slowed too quickly. The train rocked back and forth, rattling our plates and glasses.

Stephanie grasped for her toppling wineglass, reaching directly through Molly, who winced and disappeared. Frankie followed.

Virginia stood, bracing a hand on the table.

Mountains rose up on either side of us.

"Nothing to worry about," the man in the white jacket announced as the lights flickered. "Remain calm," he ordered, before the lights failed and the train plunged into darkness.

CHAPTER 8

a woman screamed.

I grabbed Ellis's arm.

"I'm right here," he said, holding me tight.

Brakes squealed. A glass shattered on the floor, the spray wetting my ankle.

The locomotive swayed dangerously to the side, and panicked voices surrounded us.

What is it?

Are we crashing?

Oh, my God. Oh, my God. Oh, my God.

A chair at our table toppled to the floor. Virginia's voice sounded over the chaos. "Remain calm!"

Dim emergency lights flickered on. The train lurched, and Virginia's hip slammed hard against the table. I held on, wincing as my glass of red wine toppled over my hand and onto the front of Melody's dress.

Beau remained rooted to the spot, breathing heavily across from me.

Virginia pushed off the table and left us.

"Where does she think she's going?" I exclaimed, holding Ellis tighter.

"I don't know," Ellis said, slipping out of my grasp as he staggered to his feet. He was going after her. Dang him and his need to be noble all the time.

"Stay here," he ordered, pushing away.

Fat chance.

He was heading for the front of the train.

I stood and started to follow him, hoping I was making the right call. I couldn't let him disappear into the darkness without me.

If we got out of this, I'd appreciate my life more. I'd be more thankful for the little things. I'd be nicer to Frankie.

The train jumped and shuddered.

I'd never leave my house again.

I braced myself as the steel walls surrounding us gave one final shiver before the train ground to a dead stop.

A woman sobbed. Others gasped for breath.

"Call for help," a woman's voice urged.

"I can't get a signal," her partner shot back, surprised.

Well, we were in the mountains, so that made sense. At least we were still in one piece. For now.

The original train had also made an unscheduled stop in the mountains, and one of its passengers had died that night. The similarity made my skin crawl. And I couldn't just wait for Ellis to save the day. I might technically be on vacation, but I had a sinking feeling that I was going to have to get to the bottom of the tragedy on the Sugarland Express before this trip was over.

As if I wasn't dealing with enough, the ghostly conductor flickered into existence by my side. "Miss Verity," he began.

"I—" Couldn't I have a normal dinner? Just once, a real date, a getaway without Ellis's crazy family, or Frankie's interruptions, or long-dead people and their problems that became my problems and—

"Come with me," the dead conductor urged, "quickly."

In the gray glow of the ghost, I saw Dave Abel wrap his arm around his wife, Mary Jo, who was rubbing her wrist.

"What's going on?" It didn't look good.

"Someone has broken into the radio room," the ghost conductor said, beckoning me toward the front of the train. "One of the living. He's tearing it apart."

That didn't make any sense. "Who would do that?" I asked, following the ghost.

I sidestepped chairs and broken dishes as my fellow passengers pulled themselves back together.

"Faster," the conductor pressed as my heel sent a fallen tray skittering sideways.

I doubled back and grabbed it to use as a weapon. If there was already a man in the radio room, there was a good shot he'd planned the train stoppage.

Or he knew who had.

I reached a shadowy hallway at the front of the dining car and found myself running upstream against two waiters and a cook heading toward the frightened passengers.

"This way," the cook said as his beefy arm brushed my shoulder.

I let them pass and soon found myself alone in the hall outside the small galley. They'd left the door open. Knives littered the floor. Nobody would even know if one was missing.

The emergency lights flickered and died.

I pressed on. I couldn't be that far behind Ellis and Virginia. At least I hoped that was the case as I entered the deserted bar car.

"Ellis?" I asked, trying to spot him in the faint silver glow from the ghost.

Shadows swathed the bar at the front.

Ghostly gray light illuminated leather club chairs clustered near the windows, and the faint scent of cigar smoke hung in the air. Each chair, each smoking table, each art deco wall sconce glowed gray. The restoration was so perfect, the merging of the ghostly plane with reality so complete, that it took my breath away.

Virginia had reproduced the doomed train down to the last cup, glass, table, chair, and cursed bell. Even the bottles behind the bar lined up.

What should have been a triumph made my stomach sink.

This was where the passengers of the ill-fated train had laughed and drank and toasted their journey to death.

The ghostly conductor hovered at the far end of the car. "Hurry," he pressed.

"Of course," I said, but as I pressed forward, the hollow thunk of a bottle hitting the floor stopped me in my tracks.

My gaze shot to the bar, where all of the bottles appeared to be in place.

Then I heard the rhythmic thunk-thunk-thunk of a bottle rolling and saw it advancing down the center aisle, directly toward me. I held my breath as it stopped cold at my feet.

At least it was real.

I blew out a breath and picked it up. It felt icy against my hand. Perhaps it was merely a chilled bottle of white wine that had become dislodged in the commotion.

I could set it right and be on my way.

"Miss Verity," the conductor urged.

I forced myself to remain calm. "Coming," I said.

With shaky hands, I placed the bottle on the bar. Then, with a nod to the ghost, I pretended it was perfectly normal when the door between the cars slid open on its own.

I followed the glow of the conductor as he guided me through the dark space between the cars.

The emptiness of the train pressed at me, and even though I knew there were people stranded in the dining car and that Ellis and others must be up ahead, I felt very much alone.

The ghost jolted, as if he'd seen something or heard something.

"Hurry," he pressed. He doubled his speed, and I struggled to keep up, following the light of the ghost as he sped through a domed observation car. Where modern trains simply had seats, this car featured plush couches in rows, with wide windows that curved up over the seats to form a clear glass roof. The night sky glinted above us.

He was moving too fast.

I slammed out of a passenger car and into the void between. A shadow rose up out of the blackness and grabbed me.

"Help!" I screamed as an iron grip drew me closer.

I knew better than to run headlong through the dark after a ghost, especially with a potential saboteur on board.

"What are you doing?" the stranger demanded. It took me a second to recognize it was Virginia.

I was almost happy to see her.

"Someone broke into the radio room," I said, grabbing hold of her arms. "They're tearing it apart. Where's Ellis?"

"With the conductor. There's a problem on the tracks." She pulled away from me and bent down, coming back up with her cell phone light on full glare. "You made me drop this. We're lucky it didn't break." She shone it on me. I held my hand up and blinked against the sudden brightness. "How do you know there's trouble in the radio room?" she asked, as if I were under interrogation.

"A ghost told me," I snapped, ready for her to dismiss me.

"Let's go," she said, thrusting the door open behind her. "Three cars up. It's a communications station now. I have the key."

"Let's hope we need it," I said, pushing ahead of her.

I had to give her this: Virginia was pragmatic. I, on the other hand, seemed to have learned nothing from my vast experience running headlong through haunted places.

We passed through the library car, Virginia's light bouncing off hardwood bookshelves as well as a large picture window. A pair of plush reading chairs flanked a table topped with a bust of Edgar Allan Poe. I had to come back here.

From there, I hesitated before a narrow hallway with no windows on either side. "Crew compartments," Virginia said, her voice hushed. "We're almost there."

We pressed on.

We had our saboteur directly ahead of us. Trapped.

Unless he'd already gotten off the train.

"Here," Virginia hissed, pushing open a small door to our left. I held up my tray, ready to defend us. Virginia shone her light inside and gasped.

A laptop computer lay crushed on the floor. Next to it, several smashed black boxes bled green processing boards and tangled wiring. An antique hardwood desk, built into the wall, bore scratch marks from the destruction.

Virginia uttered a curse I'd never heard her use before. "That was our state-of-the-art communications system." Her hand shook as she shone her light over the destruction. "I can't believe this."

I bent down to inspect the damage closer, careful not to disturb it. "Do you have any idea who could have done this?"

"No," she shot back.

The room was so small I could have spread my arms and touched both sides. There was nowhere for the perpetrator to hide.

He had escaped. Or perhaps he hadn't been flesh and blood to begin with.

The overhead lights snapped back on, startling us both.

I blinked, my eyes adjusting to the brightness.

Virginia drew a hand to her chest. "It's impossible to count on cell phones or other wireless technology this far into the mountains, so we installed our own hotspot, along with a backup radio," she said, locating it with her toe among the rubble. "We had our entire comms system in this old radio room."

And now it lay smashed on the floor.

"Is there any other way to contact the outside world?"

She gave a shaky nod. "Of course. The conductor keeps a radio in the control room." She stiffened and then dashed from the doorway of the radio room. I was right on her heels.

We ran past the conductor's sleeping quarters and into the control room of the locomotive.

The ghost conductor stood next to the main panel at the front. "You're too late," he said, as if it were my fault, as if I could have prevented any of this.

I saw what I assumed had been the radio receiver torn from the panel.

"Now we *are* in trouble," Virginia said, her voice stark.

All right. I blew out a breath. *Think.*

The headlamps on the locomotive shone out ahead of us, where Ellis and two other men worked together to push a small boulder off the tracks.

"Is that what stopped us?" I asked.

"Rocks fall onto the tracks. It's rare, but it happens," Virginia said, without relish. "The driver saw it and was able to stop."

"We stopped too." The ghostly conductor looked out the window to the men on the tracks. "It didn't keep us safe for long."

That was enough. At least for me. I didn't know what was unfolding here, but it wasn't worth risking our lives. "We need to head back," I said, "put this engine in reverse and get out of here." We were less than a day into the trip. Kingstree was a lovely town. I wanted to get back there as soon as possible.

Virginia glared at me. "You're out of your mind."

No, I was scared. Virginia had cursed our journey with her obsessive historical preservation, although I didn't think she'd want to hear that, especially from me. "Our comms system is down. I'm sure the passengers would understand."

"That we quit our maiden voyage?" Virginia snapped. "I think not." She leaned close. "You need to learn the value of tenacity, my

68

dear. It does apply to more than your shameless pursuit of my son."

I wasn't going to dignify that with a debate.

Instead, I forced a brittle smile. "Ask Ellis if he minds," I said, slipping out of the cab and down onto the tracks.

"Get back here," she hollered. "We need to guard the radio room."

I'd leave that in her very capable hands. Besides, there was nothing left to smash. I needed to see what we were up against.

It didn't take the men long to notice me hobbling along the rock-strewn rail bed in heels.

"She's injured," Ellis's stout companion declared, his eyes catching my stained dress.

"It's just red wine," I called out.

The air was hot and filled with swarms of tiny insects drawn by the lights.

Ellis reached me first. "You should get back on board. This isn't safe."

"Well, it's not so safe on board, either," I said, not as long as someone was desperate enough to sabotage our trip. Ellis gave me a quizzical look as a second man reached us. He was in his mid-forties, fit, with a short brown beard shot through with gray. "Verity Long," I said, holding out a hand.

He took it. "I'm your conductor, Eric Manning."

Yes. I'd seen him earlier when he made his lovely toast to our trip. "There's something you need to know." The third man, whom Ellis introduced as the engineer, joined us, and I told them about the willful destruction of the communications system, leaving out any mention of the ghost. I'd tell Ellis that part later.

"Whoever did it must still be on board the train," Conductor Manning said. "There isn't a road or town around for miles."

"They could be hiding anywhere out here," Ellis said, eyeing the woods near the tracks. "I hate to say it, but this might not have been an accidental rockfall. You said yourself the boulders could have been placed there. For all we know, our vandal had transportation out of here."

"I didn't hear any motors," Manning said.

Ellis sighed. "I didn't, either."

The driver scratched his chin. "If a vandal wanted to do damage, he'd have placed the rocks on that bend up there. With the boulders on the straightaway like they were, I was able to see them and stop."

"Besides, why would someone sabotage a passenger train?" Manning added, looking from Ellis to me.

That was the million-dollar question.

"We should head back to Kingstree," I told them. "I said the same thing to Virginia." I didn't mention she'd disagreed. She would make her position clear enough. I had a feeling she'd only stayed back to keep an eye on her locomotive, but it wasn't like I could keep her out of the discussion for long.

"I'll make that decision," Conductor Manning said.

Yes, well, I hoped he made the right one.

The engineer nodded, deferring to Manning. "I'll get underneath and double-check the brakes," he said, "and make sure we didn't damage them on the stop."

"Good." Manning looked back at the cleared tracks. "Care to walk ahead with me?" he asked Ellis. "Make sure everything looks good? Maybe check out some of the areas around the track."

Ellis nodded, his hand absently going to the gun he kept tucked in a back holster. "Climb on board," he urged me, giving my arm a reassuring squeeze. "I'll be back in a minute."

"Sure," I said. I'd just join his mother again. No doubt she'd be thrilled to see me.

I retreated toward the train, realizing I'd also ruined Melody's heels in the rocks. Thank goodness I had an understanding sister, although I would replace both the dress and the shoes, even if my bank account wouldn't appreciate it.

Dull light shone from under the bottom of the locomotive as

the engineer began his safety check. I glanced over my shoulder and saw Ellis's and Manning's flashlights drawing farther down the tracks. The line of vision was good here. We had been lucky. I turned and walked backward, watching them.

"Verity," said a voice behind me, causing me to trip for a moment over my own feet.

The heels didn't help, either.

I turned and saw Molly just off my right shoulder.

"You scared me." She should know better than to sneak up on me like that. That was her boyfriend's job.

She'd arranged her hair into a stylish twist, with a few stray wisps floating in an unseen breeze. "Frankie's going to kill me for telling you this, but I was heading back from the powder room when I saw something suspicious." She led me back toward the train. The lights of the locomotive caught her silvery form, almost obliterating her from sight.

"Was it a live person damaging the train?" I asked, leaping over the side of the tracks, following her.

"Worse," she said grimly. "I saw a dark, menacing shadow," she warned, "entering compartment 9."

CHAPTER 9

*T*made my way back through the train, glad for the lights this time. There was no one in the library car or the observation car or anywhere else up front at the moment.

The place felt strangely empty, but at least I wasn't jumping at every shadow.

"This is not the same train as before," I reminded myself.

Only I could see the eerie ghostly overlay of the doomed train, so similar to the new one. It glowed stark and clear in the dark. Which was probably why I liked the lights so much.

Keep it together.

There was no tragedy attached to this trip, no murder on board, nothing to suggest tonight's incident was anything other than a close call triggered by someone who might not have Virginia Wydell's best interests at heart.

The list would be long on that one.

I mean, if we were going to suspect anyone with a grudge against the queen bee of Sugarland social projects, we'd have to add about ten more cars to the train to fit them all on board.

I entered the bar and found it occupied. A balding bartender in a smart navy jacket poured a Manhattan through a cocktail strainer while a waiter loaded a glass of red wine onto his tray.

The two appeared startled to see me. I was rather a mess.

"Goodness. Have you been up there all alone?" the bartender asked, placing a skewer with three dark cherries on top of the drink.

"You look like you've been through the wringer." The waiter handed me a towel from the bar. As if that would scrub red wine out of silk.

"Thanks," I said, appreciating the effort. I made a few dabs for show. "Virginia Wydell needed me," I added, not going into details. But I did have a question. "Have you seen anyone else come through here since the lights came back on?"

"Just you," the waiter said.

"As soon as we had power back, Beau Wydell sent us up here," the bartender added, accepting the towel back from me. "He figured the passengers could use some liquid courage," he added, holding up a glass to me.

I liked that offer better than the towel, but I had work to do.

"Thanks, but no thanks," I said, on my way again. "I have to go."

I passed into the darkened area between the cars and nearly jumped out of my skin when Molly's head popped out of the door leading to the dining car.

Her skin glowed white. Her eyes burned with excitement. "We need to hurry if we're going to save the girl in compartment 9!"

"All right," I told her. "No need to jump out at me like that." Frankie made a habit of it, and I'd had enough heart palpitations. "We need to keep our wits about us. That shady-looking ghost you saw might be an official occupant of compartment 9." It wasn't like the dead woman could claim sole ownership. There could be plenty of spirits on board, and it never paid to assume anything about a ghost you didn't know. I'd learned that the hard way. If Frankie were here, he'd tell her the same thing. "Where is Frankie, anyway?"

Molly waved off my concern as she glided ahead of me down the hallway. "He thinks he can distract me with some big romantic surprise in our room." She skimmed a hand along the nape of her neck and sent her dark hair flying. "I'm not allowed in right now."

No wonder she'd been wandering.

"Where are you two staying?" I asked, passing the galley. They'd closed the door and hopefully cleaned up the knives.

"He's turned the caboose into quite a love nest," she said, with a wriggle to her hips.

It had to be better than Frankie's last attempt. "We'll call him if we need him," I said, giving pause at a flurry of agitated voices from the dining room.

The discourse rose in pitch and volume as I stepped out into the chaos.

The floors had been cleared of dishes and debris, but the tables were still a mess of half-eaten plates and toppled stemware. Passengers huddled around tables and in groups, talking and clutching stiff drinks.

"There you are!" Beau said, standing up from a chair near the front. "What happened? Where is my mother? And Ellis?" he asked, looking past me. "You left me to deal with this alone."

"It's not my train," I said, navigating through the tense seating area. I could feel everyone's eyes on me.

"What happened up there?" Beau pressed, sticking close to me.

"There was a rockfall on the tracks," I said, raising my voice so the other passengers could hear. "We stopped just in time. The train is fine. In fact, the brakes worked perfectly," I added, watching my fellow passengers relax at the news.

They didn't need to know we had no communications system anymore.

"Thank God," Beau said as I located Molly at the back of the car and headed for her. He sidestepped a chair to keep pace with me. "Will you look at me for a second?"

"I have to keep moving," I said. "I'm following a ghost."

He wrinkled his nose. "At a time like this?"

"Tell me about it," I said. As if I could explain about the trouble in compartment 9 to him of all people. Then again, this was as good a time as any to tell him the truth. I drew him to a private spot near our ruined table and kept my voice low. "A woman was murdered in your room back in 1929, shortly before the original Sugarland Express crashed."

He held up a hand. "It's a different—"

"The bell is the same. The spirit is the same. The ghosts are in a tizzy," I told him. "You gotta trust me on this one."

Beau broke out into a grin. "Is this the kind of crazy stuff you tell my brother?"

He wasn't listening. "I'm trying to warn you. It's why Ellis and I switched cars."

His smile faded. "I shouldn't have let you on the train. I hated seeing you with him at dinner tonight."

"Beau, focus." He had a group of frightened passengers on his hands, not to mention a saboteur on board. "Listen. What just happened is worse than a near miss with a rock. While we were stopped, someone snuck up front and messed with the train's communications system. They could have been using the power outage as a distraction. Was there anyone missing from the dining room before the train stopped?"

He shook his head. "I was too busy with dinner to notice."

"What about after the power outage?" I asked. "When the lights were out or, heck, after they came back on—was anyone unaccounted for?"

Beau went a little pale. "Let me think," he said, his expression going blank. "Dave and Mary Jo Abel helped me calm everyone down." He glanced to where the couple I'd met at the Last Stop Grill stood talking with a very young woman and her husband.

"They bonded with the honeymooners. The girl was freaking out." Beau took a sip of his drink, whiskey from what I could smell. "The communications system? Damn."

"Who else?" I pressed as Molly waved at me frantically from the back of the train.

"Coming," I mouthed to her.

But this was real life. This came first. I wanted to get Beau's take on what had happened right after the blackout while his memory was fresh.

"There was Eileen, the journalist," he continued. "I don't see her now, but she was here when the lights came back on."

"Could she have gone to the front of the train during the blackout?" I pressed.

"I don't know," he scoffed. "Did you see her there?"

A terrible thought occurred to me. "I might have seen someone." In the bar car, when that bottle rolled out, I'd assumed it had been supernatural or just a result of the train's jarring stop.

But what if there had been someone hiding behind the bar?

Someone who had torn apart the radio room and made their escape…

They also could have slipped back into the dining car without anyone noticing. The galley had been empty and the train dark.

Still, I couldn't think of a reason why a journalist would stoop to sabotaging a passenger train. "What is Eileen reporting on?"

Beau shot me a look of scorn. "The unforgettable maiden voyage of the Sugarland Express," he said, with mock joy, before downing his drink in one gulp. "She's an Arts and Leisure reporter for the *Memphis Herald*," he said, chewing on the ice.

Hmm…yes. She would be one he'd want to impress. "At least she can't go anywhere yet," I said, looking at the bright side. "You still have time to impress her."

It had to be all uphill from here.

I scanned the train car and noticed another significant absence. "Where's Stephanie?"

Beau shook his head. "I don't know. Bathroom or something." He leaned against the wall between two windows and waved off the question. "She was talking to that couple sitting at the back table, celebrating their fiftieth. They reminded her of her grandparents."

Or they were by the door and that made it convenient to slip out.

But if that was the case, she'd have gone toward the back of the train and not the front.

"Has he been here the whole time?" I asked, pointing at the man who had confronted Stephanie in the alley back in Kingstree. She'd called him Ron, if I remembered correctly—the Ron she'd claimed she didn't know.

"He's been here." Beau shot him a glare. "He's been riling up the passengers, telling them we're running an unsafe train. I'd like to drop a few rocks on him."

I placed a hand on his shoulder. "Hang in there." Beau might not have taken charge of the train like Virginia or Ellis did, but he'd held down the fort with the passengers. And he cared. It was more than I could say for the mysterious Ron, who tipped back the last of his drink and shot a dirty look back at Beau. "Keep an eye on him," I added.

Beau pushed off the wall. "I'll get him another scotch," he said, as if he'd rather pour one over his head.

Hopefully that would keep Ron in the dining car with the rest of the passengers. Most of them. As of now, we were missing Stephanie and the journalist. Plus we had a ghost issue in compartment 9.

I might as well see what I could learn about all three of them.

I followed Stephanie's presumed route toward the back of the train.

But as I pushed my way into the first passenger car, I halted. The door at the opposite end of the car slowly glided to a close. I'd just missed...someone.

Well, that was interesting, considering Stephanie should have been gone for a while. The journalist, too.

I picked up the pace, jogging through the car, trying to ignore the glow of the ghostly train all around me. I reached the next car and caught a glimpse of lavender silk disappearing through the door at the other end.

Stephanie.

She'd been running as fast as I had.

I wondered how much Beau knew about his new girlfriend.

"One more car," Molly said. She hovered slightly behind me. I'd forgotten she was even there.

She was right, though. It appeared Stephanie was headed for her compartment, number 9, which, according to Molly, happened to contain a shady-looking spirit.

Perhaps Beau's girlfriend would let me inside to investigate. If anything, it would give her a good story about her man's crazy ghost-hunting ex.

"Let's go," I said, jogging down the hall, eager to catch up with her, maybe even intercept her as she entered her room.

But when I was about ready to open the door between the cars, I saw her through the window. She stood looking down the hall toward the caboose at the end.

I ducked away from the window as Stephanie's head turned in my direction.

I wasn't even sure why I did it. I had a right to be there.

Yet I wanted to see what she would do if she didn't know she was being watched.

Beau's girlfriend didn't disappoint.

Instead of entering her own compartment, I heard her knock on a door. I peered through the edge of the window as she murmured a greeting, then slipped into compartment 8.

Well, now that was interesting.

The door clicked closed behind her.

"Who's in 8?" I whispered to Molly. It seemed Stephanie knew more than a few people on the train.

"Whoever it is, she's probably not trapped with a murderer," Molly hissed, stopping at compartment 9.

"Poke your head in," I whispered, keeping a lookout. "I can't go into Stephanie and Beau's room."

"Yes, you can," Molly said as the lock clicked.

Of all the... "How did you do that?" I reached for the handle, turning it easily. She definitely had more skills than Frankie.

"It's hard. It takes a lot of energy to push the little tumblers." She brought a hand to her forehead and glided back a few steps. "I feel a little faint," she confessed.

Not only that, her image had faded. Frankie was going to kill me if I made his girlfriend disappear.

Her eyes widened. "Let's go," she implored.

I turned back to the door.

It was a horrible invasion of privacy.

"Please," Molly begged, joining me.

I couldn't prevent a murder that had happened almost a century ago, but I could try to give the ghosts peace. We'd only stay a minute.

"Here goes nothing," I said.

Frankie's girlfriend peered over my shoulder as I opened the door.

Molly screamed.

We were too late. The ghost of a young woman lay facedown in a pool of blood on the floor, her long party dress tangled around her legs. Her arms were splayed outward, and a fox fur stole lay crumpled next to her, complete with the animal's front paws and head. Its dead eyes stared up at me.

"Poor girl," I whispered. One cheek rested on the stained carpet. I bent to see the rest of her face. She'd been about my age. My size, even. I wasn't sure if it was a warning or a macabre coincidence.

"I should have followed that scary-looking ghost instead of getting you," Molly sobbed. "I should have told Frankie. Or confronted it myself. I should have been braver."

I wished I could give her a hug. "Bad things happen. It's not your fault."

But in the back of my mind, I also wished we'd gotten here even five minutes sooner.

We'd just missed the killer. "See if she's still breathing," I said, bending over the body.

Cripes. What was I thinking? This young woman had been dead for a hundred years, and she was a ghost. I couldn't stop a murder on the ghostly plane. There was no way to change what had already happened. Otherwise Frankie would have found a way to erase that bullet hole in his head.

The girl's glassy eyes stared without seeing.

I scanned the room for other ghosts or for any sign of who might have done this.

Molly knelt next to me and felt the girl's neck. "She's dead," she said, her voice small.

I studied the ugly wound on her back. "They stabbed her," I said, staying clear of the blood.

Molly gently closed the woman's eyes.

"She won't be like this for long," I assured Molly. I'd watched Frankie get into gun battles with the gangsters on the other side. A mortal wound would usually knock them out for a few hours, but nothing more. "Can you tell me what her killer looked like?"

Molly's hair fell like a curtain over her cheek. She brushed it back behind her ear. "It was a dark energy with ill intent, no more than a jagged shadow, but it was as real as I am."

I didn't like the sound of that.

"She could be your sister," Molly said, giving voice to the elephant in the room.

"I can see where one might think that," I admitted, not at all sure I liked where this was going.

I'd escaped compartment 9.

Too bad this woman hadn't.

"Verity, we've had a rockfall. And now this killing. What if the rest comes true? What if our Sugarland Express goes over into the river?"

"It won't," I said. Surely we were headed for a modern bridge, one that had been inspected according to the latest safety standards. Besides, we might be on some sort of strange ghostly loop, but I had to believe the conductor would decide to reverse the train back to Kingstree and end this cursed trip.

The compartment door opened and Beau walked in.

"Verity," he said, clearly surprised.

"Oh, my word." I stood quickly. "I came to check on your ghost," I said by way of explanation. "I'm so sorry to intrude."

"I get it," he said, closing the door behind him. "It's kind of cute," he added, loosening his tie, drawing near enough for me to smell his spicy cologne.

"She died," I said, turning back to the ghost that he couldn't see.

Beau knit his brow. "Isn't that what ghosts do?" he asked, trying to understand. But it was so much more than that.

The poor girl had begun to fade from his floor. I wished I could have spent more time with her.

"Maybe the ghost wants you to have a seat on the couch with me," he said, winding an arm around my waist.

I jumped like he was on fire. "Hands off," I said, twisting out of his reach.

I couldn't believe he'd actually touched me. Half his shirt was unbuttoned, revealing a tan, gym-hardened chest. How had he gotten it undone so fast?

"Hey, whoa," he said, holding his palms up. "I'm not the one sneaking into your room. Although maybe you'd like that."

"This isn't about you," I insisted. I didn't know how to make it clearer. "You have a murdered ghost *on your floor—*"

Not for long, though.

Molly let out a sigh as the woman disappeared completely.

"You can stop pretending." Beau shot me a grin, running a hand through his hair, rumpling it. "I know we had a moment there at the opening of Southern Spirits. I just didn't think you'd have the guts to act on it."

We were getting nowhere. And…yuck.

"I can't believe you'd be willing to betray your own brother like that."

"You could say the same thing to Ellis," Beau shot back.

"My boyfriend is the most honorable man I've ever known," I said, heading for the door.

"Then why are you in my room?" Beau asked.

"Exactly," I said, shoving out the door and straight into Ellis's arms.

"Hey there," he said, catching me. "We found her." He glanced over his shoulder to Virginia, who stood right behind him.

"This isn't what it looks like," I said as he took in Beau's rumpled hair and half-done shirt.

"It never is," Ellis grumbled.

The younger Wydell had the nerve to shoot Ellis a satisfied grin.

"Grow up, Beau," Ellis added, releasing me and taking my hand instead.

Virginia rolled her eyes. "God bless my family before I kill them."

"I was investigating a ghost murder," I told Ellis.

Beau braced an elbow on the doorjamb. "I hear that's what they're calling it these days."

His mother shot him a withering look. "Stop causing trouble. We have enough." Before I could enjoy her response too much, her accusing glare settled on me.

CHAPTER 10

"*I*'m just trying to help," I said, holding my hands up. "You told my conductor to turn the train around," Virginia declared.

Oh, that.

I glanced away and noticed Stephanie for the first time. She was leaning against a window in the hall like a catalog model. And she made no bones about sizing me up.

Ellis placed himself between his mother and me. "I told Conductor Manning the same thing. We have no comms system, no backup navigation. It's not smart to keep going."

"We're moving ahead as scheduled," Beau said over them both, and I could tell from the smug twist of his lips he said it just to spite his brother. Beau hadn't even bothered with the issue until now. "I am the boss," he reminded us.

Virginia opened her mouth, presumably to tell him just where he could put his #1 Boss mug, when the door at the front of the train car slid open.

A fifty-something redhead with short layered hair and solid, sun-freckled arms stepped into our car. She carried a glass of wine and appeared startled to see our party of five crowding the hallway.

Virginia's expression tightened into a benign, if somewhat fractured hostess smile. "Good evening."

"Sure." The woman slid a key card into the door to compartment 8, keeping an eye on us.

Ah, the journalist.

She'd evidently made it up to the bar, or at least to the dining room, after Stephanie's visit to her compartment earlier.

The two shared a fleeting look.

"I'm ready for bed, too," Stephanie announced, slipping past the lot of us. She wrapped both her arms around one of Beau's and leaned up, exposing her swan-like neck, her ruby lips hovering beside his ear. "As long as I have some handsome company," she purred.

Who did she think she was? Jessica Rabbit?

Beau broke out into a wide, wolfish grin. "At last. A girl who knows what she wants."

Oh, ick. I would praise the day when Beau found a good woman to move on with, even if he didn't deserve one. But Stephanie wasn't it.

She had another agenda. I could feel it in my bones.

I watched, speechless, as she drew him into the room. The door slid closed behind them.

Beau's girlfriend hadn't even blinked a false eyelash at the fact that I'd been alone with him in his room and then come bursting out faster than a greased thunderbolt.

Ellis handled it fine because he trusted me. He knew I could manage his brother's antics. But Stephanie should have at least questioned my business with her man.

I eyed Virginia. She had to have noticed.

"Bless your heart, Verity," she said, crossing her arms over her chest. "You're trouble, but she's worse."

"Goodnight, Mother," Ellis said, touching a hand to the small of my back as we retreated to our room next door.

"I'm not even offended," I told him once we were out of earshot. I was glad Virginia would be keeping an eye on both of us. I had nothing to hide, but I wasn't so sure about Stephanie.

Ellis merely grunted and headed for the minibar next to the table by the window.

"How long has Beau been seeing her?" I asked, skirting around him on my way to the closet attached to the vanity.

"A couple of weeks." Ellis appeared ready to say more, but he stopped himself and instead focused on unscrewing the cap on a bottle of water. He took a drink and stared out into the darkness and the shadows of the mountains rising up on all sides of us.

I got it. I'd rather dance the polka with a porcupine than discuss Beau's love life, but I couldn't get around it. "Stephanie is up to something."

Her girlish giggle floated through the wall.

"What gave it away?" he asked, taking a long swig of water.

He wasn't going to make this easy.

"You know what I mean. Just now, the way she propositioned him in front of all of us, that's not normal."

He paused to swallow, still not looking at me. "I try not to think too much about my brother's love life."

I sighed and turned to the miniscule closet. If I could accomplish one thing, perhaps it would simply be to change out of my itchy, wine-stained dress.

I reached past Frankie's urn to grab my robe off the top shelf when Stephanie shrieked and giggled. That did it. I grabbed the hanger below and a simple green shift instead. No way was I staying in here to listen to...whatever they were doing.

Ellis remained at the window.

He was usually so observant, so ready to discuss a mystery as it unfolded. His brother had really gotten to him.

Still, we were stuck and in trouble. After she had lied about knowing Ron and then snuck out of the dining room, I couldn't help but think Stephanie had something to do with it.

I tried again. "It's just that—"

"Verity," he snapped, his back to me, "let it go."

His words stung.

Stricken, I ducked into the small bathroom to change. Ellis had never shut down on me like that. I didn't know what to make of it.

I understood that while Beau mostly annoyed me, this entire situation had a real ability to hurt Ellis. I just wasn't sure what to do about it.

I smoothed the green dress over my hips.

Truth be told, I wasn't too keen to head out with him anymore.

He stood waiting for me when I stepped out of the bathroom.

"I'm sorry," he said, "I shouldn't have barked at you like that." He hung his head. "My brother can be a sore spot."

"I get it." I let out a sigh. "It's all right. Really."

But Ellis didn't look relieved. Not one little bit.

He lifted his gaze to mine, his jaw so hard a muscle in his neck jumped. "I'm just so sick of the way Beau looks at you. It's not your fault."

I nodded. "I didn't encourage him." He had to realize that.

"I know." He walked toward the window. "You avoid him whenever you can, but that doesn't even matter to him." He stared out at the darkness. "My baby brother expects to get whatever he wants, just because he wants it. Like it's his due. It's always been that way." He gave a sharp laugh. "Hell, everyone back home expects him to get it too. With casseroles."

I wound my arms around his back. "Don't pay any attention to the biddies back home." I'd learned firsthand how fickle they could be. Beau might be the flashy younger son, but middle child Ellis was smart, loyal, and always there when anyone in Sugarland needed him. He'd chosen public service not for the attention or the praise, but because he believed it was the right thing to do. Ellis was worth ten Beau Wydells.

He turned and drew me close, resting his chin on my head. "Everybody expects me to roll over on this one and give my brother what he wants, but I'm not going to do it."

"You'd better not." I gave him a squeeze. "I'm certainly not going to give up so easily."

He gave a small chuckle, a real one this time. "You're what's keeping me sane."

I leaned up and gave him a kiss on the chin. "We'll make it."

He smiled. "I know we will."

I was glad to hear him say it, and happy to see him smile as well. Ellis was a keeper. Not only was he a good man, but we also had the same ideas about life, love, and mystery solving.

"This will cheer you up," I said, stepping back, snagging his water bottle from the table by the window. "When you were up front, I saw Stephanie sneak off to meet with that journalist in compartment 8." That got his attention. I took a swig of his water. "Stephanie also knows the man we saw in the dining car, Ron. I saw them talking in Kingstree."

"Nice work," he said, genuinely impressed. I loved it when he took pride in my observations. "I'll start keeping tabs on her too," he promised, wincing when her amorous gasp rang out from the next compartment. "Except for now," he added, offering me his hand. "Let's—"

"Go," I finished for him, leaving my evening wrap behind as we escaped.

~

"To the bar," Ellis said, already tugging me toward the front of the train.

"A stiff drink sounds great," I promised, "but I want to check on Molly first."

And, yes, I realized I was the one who'd vowed to let the ghosts enjoy their trip while we focused on ours, but that was before the trouble we'd encountered tonight.

So I told him about Molly and Frankie's appearance in the middle of the dinner table and the adventure after. "Molly discovered the ghostly body with me," I explained, leading him toward the back of the train. "It really shook her up. I'd like to see how she's doing."

"You're just now mentioning that?" Ellis asked.

"It's been a busy night."

He didn't argue.

The first time I'd stumbled across a murder victim, I had nightmares for weeks. The second time, as well. Now, it was becoming too much of a habit, but it was still shocking and disturbing every time to witness a life snuffed out. Even if this one was a tragedy from the past, poor Molly had witnessed it up close and personal.

Ellis and I shared a compartment in the very rear of the last passenger car. The two ghosts had holed up in the caboose, which should be right behind us.

"It may be locked," Ellis warned, pushing open the door at the back. We stepped out onto a small balcony. A metal walkway, fenced by two flimsy-looking railings, led to the caboose.

"Didn't your mom renovate this part?" I asked as the walkway swayed under our weight.

He shot me a dubious look. "I doubt passengers are allowed back here, so this part might just be painted to look good to the casual observer."

"Great." I tried not to think about what it would be like to walk here once the train started moving again.

"It had to have passed inspection," Ellis said, evidently trying to look on the bright side. "Whatever my mom might have done, I'm sure it's standard practice."

The place still didn't inspire much confidence.

The warmth of the night seeped into my bones as I knocked on the door to an old-fashioned black caboose.

"Molly?" I asked. "Sorry to interrupt," I added, pushing the door open.

What I saw made me stop short.

It appeared as if Frankie had hitched a mountain cabin onto the back of our train. That was the only way I could think to describe it. My buddy was obviously the dominant ghost, which meant he could make the space appear the way he envisioned it.

Typically, spirits used this ability to make their surroundings look the same as they did when they were alive. Frankie had used it to create a love nest.

The interior of the caboose appeared four times larger than it actually was, with a roaring stone fireplace, an old-fashioned stargazing scope, and a ginormous king-sized bed in the corner.

Only, Frankie was nowhere to be found.

Molly sat by herself on a bearskin rug next to a bucket of champagne on ice, crying.

"Sweetie," I said, hurrying toward her.

"He's not here," she said, scrambling to her feet. "I don't know where he could have gone."

I resisted the urge to fold her into my arms. It wouldn't be comforting for either of us. "Did you two have a fight?"

"No," she said, wiping her eyes. "I haven't even seen him since the train stopped." She sniffed, her eyes swollen and her cheeks flushed. "He said to stay out of our room until he came to get me. After we discovered that poor girl, I needed him. I figured he'd be here, or *somewhere* on the train, but he was nowhere to be found!"

"That is strange," I admitted. He couldn't leave, not with his urn in my compartment. And while Frankie had a tendency to disappear on me, he'd never do that to his girl.

"He was working on a surprise for me. I've been teasing him about wanting to play 'hideout' with a gangster."

That was too much information. "Okay, look. Frankie is way

too into planning these kinds of dates for you," I said, in the understatement of the year. "I'm sure he just lost track of time." He was probably out gathering heart-shaped rocks or finding fake pistols that shot chocolate sauce.

"No." She shook her head vehemently. "He's always on time."

"Frankie?" I asked. He'd come an hour late to my birthday party and he couldn't even leave the property.

Her eyes shone with tears. "I'm afraid something dreadful has happened." She gulped. "I mean, first we find that dead girl and then Frankie goes missing."

"Let's not jump to conclusions," I insisted, even though I was starting to get a bad feeling about it. If that young woman we'd found had been forced to reenact her own murder, then we had a very demented, dark spirit to contend with if it was still on board.

"Do you think I should search the train again?" she asked.

"Ellis and I will do it." Molly could move faster, but we didn't know what we were up against, and she was in no state to be careful or discreet. "You stay put in case Frankie comes back."

She gave a weak nod and a smile. "I hope I didn't start all of this when I met that girl."

"It's not your fault," I assured her. She was just a sweet Southern girl who liked to be friendly. "It'll be all right," I added, taking my leave.

Ellis had watched the entire thing from the doorway, although he could only see and hear my side. "Frankie trouble?" He didn't even bother to act surprised.

"We need to find him," I said. "She's really worried."

He gave a quick nod. This was his territory. "Where did she see him last?" He allowed me ahead of him, no doubt keeping an eye on me as we returned to the main body of the train.

"The dining car, I think," I said, entering the familiar comfort of our passenger car. "That's where they were right before the train stopped."

Ellis brushed a spiderweb out of my hair. "It's amazing what you can get out of a hollowed-out, spider-infested caboose."

I smiled back at him. "Not to mention ghosts at the dinner table. Let's go."

We made our way up, fully prepared to investigate the dining car, when an unexpected sight greeted us in the lounge.

While it seemed as if most passengers had retreated to the bar or retired to bed, a lone couple in a pair of plush chairs at the far end leaned close in hushed conversation.

A large piano stood behind them, and I stopped short when a potted palm between the piano and the wall rustled. I could swear I saw the shadow of a person hiding behind it, listening.

"Ellis, Verity." The woman's head turned, and I saw it was Mary Jo Abel. She beckoned us over while her husband stood and met us halfway, shaking Ellis's hand.

"You look like you need to sit," he said, gesturing to a pair of identical lounge chairs across from them.

"In a minute." I smiled, stepping behind the seating area and toward the sleek baby grand. Was someone spying on the Abels?

That would be beyond strange, but it certainly wasn't out of the question.

"This is a lovely piano," I mused, cautious as I approached the potted palm.

"Ah, yes." Ellis joined me. "I'll bet it looks just like the original," he added, with a nod to Dave.

"Very high maintenance," I accused as, lo and behold, I saw a familiar pair of ghostly wing-tipped shoes peeking out from behind a blue and white Asian pot.

"Frankie's in the plant," I hissed into Ellis's ear before beaming brightly at the couple we'd met on the restaurant patio.

"Of course he is," Ellis said, glancing up as the vent above us kicked on and sent a wave of cold air down onto the potted palm. The draft had caused the rustle, but I was looking at the real problem.

"Get away," Frankie hissed. "I've got this figured out!"

"Obviously," I drawled. I was about to say more when Dave Abel joined us.

He adjusted his gold spectacles and grinned like he did in his Abel Windows and Doors commercials. "Gorgeous night, isn't it?" He stood next to Ellis, taking in the view.

Sometimes, I wished I could simply talk to my ghost in peace. Instead, I smiled brightly and went to join Mary Jo.

I could not fathom, and probably didn't want to know, exactly what Frankie had done in the past two hours that had him reduced to skulking behind the foliage, but there was nothing I could do about it right now.

Except bide my time and hope he stayed there.

I took the chair across from Mary Jo, the one by the window with a nice view of the piano and the potted palm.

"Isn't it terrible?" Mary Jo asked before I'd even smoothed my dress over my knees. "We thought this would be the trip of a life-time, and instead we're stranded on a desolate route in the middle of the night. I'll bet Dave's train club buddies wouldn't be so jealous now."

"It's not even eleven o'clock," I said, checking my watch. "I'm sure we'll be on our way soon."

"Dave might love his classic trains, but I've about had it." Mary Jo leaned forward in her chair. "First night of the trip and we've had a near wreck on an unsafe track. Not to mention a botched dinner. I'm getting hungry."

"I brought granola bars," Dave said, as if he'd been saying it for the past hour. He glanced behind him as the waiter slipped into the car with a bottle of wine and a tray full of glasses. "I'll just be happy when my cell phone works again."

"Complimentary refill?" the waiter asked as he filled their glasses. That brought Dave and Ellis back into the circle. The waiter placed two more glasses on the small round table in front of us.

"Wine for you as well?" He lowered the tip of the bottle toward

Ellis and me.

"I'll pass," I told him. The way tonight was stacking up, I needed my wits about me.

"Fill it halfway, thanks," Ellis said, joining me, his gaze on the potted palm, as if he could flush Frankie out by sheer force of will.

Dave took the seat opposite Ellis and tried his phone again. "I should have checked in with my office hours ago. We're working overtime to wrap up a music hall restoration job in Memphis, and it kills me to be out of touch, but there's no signal out here." He glanced at the retreating waiter. "They had a hotspot on board, but word is that it was wiped out, along with the entire communications system. It's unbelievable."

"You know trains," Ellis said, "how hard would it be to sabotage a system like that?" he asked, leaning back in his chair, as if he were merely curious.

"Not bad. You'd just have to beat the hell out of it," Dave said, "which is why this is so disturbing. Haven't these people heard of a door lock?"

"Did you see the damage?" Ellis asked.

"They wouldn't let me look," he huffed, "as if I'm the problem." He ran a hand under his chin. "I couldn't fix it anyway. Word has it they were running the XPL system on overdrive. It's housed in steel casing with a backup system with built-in wiring, but that doesn't do you any good against a punk with a baseball bat."

"I'm sure the room was locked." Ellis's mother never left anything to chance. "Someone either picked the lock or had a key."

"Whatever security they had, it wasn't enough," Mary Jo said, as if the rockfall and sabotage were Virginia's fault.

"I realize you're frustrated," I said. We all were. "But I wouldn't blame the people who renovated the train. You might not know Virginia Wydell, but I do, and she doesn't do anything halfway."

Ellis shot me a curious glance.

What? I raised my brows. I was telling the truth.

93

I might not want Virginia planning my life or judging my romantic prospects with her son, but she was an excellent businesswoman. I had to give her that.

Besides, despite my perfect justification in disliking her, I was starting to feel sorry for her. She worked too hard to be criticized for events she couldn't control. Especially when Beau would no doubt steal the limelight when things went right.

Maybe I did need a stiff drink.

Dave patted his wife on the hand. "We should be fine if the train's navigation systems are still working. And even if they're not, we're the only ones on these remote tracks. There's nothing to do but press forward." She shot him a worried glance. "We can't call for help and we're already in the mountains."

"We could go backwards," I suggested, hoping for an ally.

"Too risky," Dave said. "There's no driving cab at the rear of this train. Just a decorative, hollowed-out caboose."

"Mrs. Wydell gave him a private tour this afternoon," Mary Jo said with an affectionate eye roll.

"She did." Dave nodded. "From the spiderwebs, I'd say she wasn't expecting me to ask. Still, there's no way to navigate the train on that end. If the engineer tried to drive backwards, he wouldn't be able to see where he was going."

"Darn." I winced. I hadn't thought of that.

"At least we'll be traveling slower now," Dave said, trying to reassure me.

It had the opposite effect. I shot a worried glance to Ellis. "It would be nice to be out of these mountains as soon as possible."

"The scenery is supposed to be the main attraction," Mary Jo said, shaking her head.

"I'll talk to the conductor," Ellis said.

"Won't do any good." Dave took a sip of his wine. "Now that we're in the mountains, a restored train like this can't travel more than thirty-five miles per hour. Any faster is too dangerous on these tracks."

"Lovely." I didn't relish being isolated in the backwoods, even if we were moving.

Just then, I spotted a ghostly figure out the window. He wore a conservative black 1920s-style suit and a fedora. He glanced over his shoulder as if to assure himself he was alone. Then he shone a light on the ground near the tracks.

I looked to Frankie, who had moved to the other side of the palm, away from the other ghost. The gangster held a sheet of music over his face, reading it like a newspaper. Frankie was obviously avoiding the stranger.

This might be the dangerous spirit Molly had seen.

"Would you like to go for a moonlight walk with me?" I asked Ellis. At his questioning glance, I added, "It's a lovely evening, and the train is stopped."

Mary Jo followed my gaze. "Out there? At this hour? Oh, honey. That's not safe."

"The train could start without you on it," Dave added.

The man on the tracks raised his chin and looked directly at me.

"Stay away from him," Frankie's voice sounded in my ear, sending chills down my neck.

Maybe I should, but that ghost might have seen what had happened out on the tracks tonight. He might have witnessed a spirit fleeing the train after the murder of the young woman in compartment 9.

As I stood, the lounge car rattled on the tracks. My stomach dropped as the train began to inch forward.

"There. See?" Dave coaxed, attempting to comfort me.

It didn't work.

I pressed a hand against the glass, watching the ghost as he watched me. He grew smaller as the train gained speed.

"Too late," I murmured. And I could have sworn I saw the mysterious man nod in grim agreement.

CHAPTER 11

Out of the corner of my eye, I saw Frankie glide toward the back of the train and through the wall.

Not so fast.

He kept his face hidden behind the ghostly sheet music and probably thought I wouldn't make a scene following him.

He'd be wrong.

If I wanted to figure out what was going on around here, I had to get on his tail right quick.

"Excuse me," I said, standing so fast that I rattled the wineglasses on the table in front of us. "I need to fetch my...wrap." Good thing I'd left it in the room. "I'll be right back," I said to Ellis, who had already begun to rise.

I could certainly handle Frankie, and given the opportunity, Ellis might learn something more from the Abels. Both Dave and Mary Jo had remained in the dining car during the sabotage, but Dave seemed to have a better idea than anyone how this train worked. I'd also seen them trading stories with several of the passengers after the incident in the dining room. Their knowledge on both counts could prove valuable.

Ellis caught my drift. "I'll be right here," he said, sinking back into his chair. "Maybe we can figure out what's going on."

God bless my man and his mad detective skills.

Meanwhile, I hurried out of the lounge car in pursuit of the mobster.

Frankie was moving fast, but thanks to luck and a pair of low heels, I caught up with him halfway through the first passenger car.

His opaque gray body fuzzed at the edges, from stress, no doubt. And he'd gone transparent to the point where the warm light from the hallway sconces shone down through his head and chest.

"Frankie," I hissed, mindful of the passengers who had retired for the night.

He whipped around, eyes wide. "Will you stop badgering me? I'm in crisis mode."

Yes, well, it wasn't all about him. "Molly is worried sick." He hesitated, and I caught up with him. "She's sitting in that lodge room you made, crying her eyes out."

He dropped the bravado. "Holy smokes." He ran a hand through his hair and checked his watch.

"Does that thing even tell time anymore?" I asked.

He dropped his arm. "Works just as well as it did the day I died," he said, getting defensive, "if I remember to check it." Ghosts didn't usually worry so much about minutes, or even years passing. "I care about time for Molly."

Oh brother. I supposed that was sweet.

"I gotta go see her," he said, backing up. "If it's safe."

"What do you mean, 'if it's safe'? What's happening with you?"

"I'll explain it to Molly." He turned and hurried toward the back of the train.

I followed hot on his heels. "Does it have something to do with that ghost I saw outside? The one in the suit? I saw how you hid from him."

Frankie passed through the door between cars and I shoved it open after him.

He whirled on me, forcing me to dodge him in the small space, his desperation a living, breathing thing. "That suit is a federal officer tasked with tracking the mob." He sneered at my surprise. "We call him the Trap because you never see him coming." He jabbed a finger at his chest. "Only I did. I spotted him and I ain't about to let him collar me."

"Okay, stop," I said, trying to take it all in. "How do we know he's even after you?"

"He didn't get on this train looking for me, but he'll recognize me. I'm sure he's seen my mug shot. I made the top fifty wanted list right before I died."

He said it as if it were an accomplishment.

"I don't think he's chasing you," I insisted. There'd be no way for him to know we'd be on this train, or that Frankie would be out of Sugarland, where he'd been haunting the past eighty plus years.

"Doesn't matter." Frankie pulled out his gun and checked the bullets, as if the man would pop up from the tracks below us. "When he sees me, he'll nab me." He slammed the chamber of his gun closed. "The guy never forgets a face."

Well, maybe he wouldn't know Frankie if his mug shot hadn't been plastered up in every police station from here to Chicago.

Guns weren't the solution. "You can't shoot him," I said.

"Yeah," Frankie said, thinking, "he'd just come back mad."

Not my point.

My temples were starting to ache. I brought a hand up to massage them. I understood this was hard for him. I shouldn't lecture. I shouldn't judge.

I shouldn't have brought a dead gangster on my vacation.

Still, I had to say it. "It would have been so much easier if you'd lived a better life."

"What fun would that have been?" he asked, with no trace of guilt.

Okay. We'd think about this logically. We still stood between cars. The train rocked hard to the side, and I placed a hand onto the soft rubber bumper to steady myself. "What's this guy even doing on board?"

"He went over a bridge on some bad rail trip," Frankie ground out. "We considered it a stroke of luck at the time." He slammed open the ghostly door behind him, as if it were the train's fault. "He was onto us."

"How so?" I asked, keeping up with him.

"The fellas and I had a big deal going right before I bit it," Frankie said, passing through the door and into the next car, walking and talking.

"I remember," I said, following. He hadn't given me details on their supposedly big score. He never gave details. But he'd told me a little.

"Yeah, well, the Chicago boys were sloppy. The Trap had an entire task force after us." He glanced over his shoulder. "If he catches me, he'll lock me up."

I stopped him. "Maybe in 1929, but not now. There has to be a statute of limitations on...whatever you did." Frankly, I didn't want a list.

Frankie rolled his eyes. "You act like time matters."

"Think about it another way," I challenged. "If this Trap guy did find you and lock you up, I could just take your urn back to my house. Problem solved."

Frankie was grounded to my property. He'd be forced to return with me...and then I'd be sheltering a fugitive.

Oh boy. I wasn't sure if that was a good idea, considering I was dating the law.

"He'd find me," Frankie insisted. "He'd probably put me under house arrest at your place." He shuddered. "I'd be there for the rest of your life at least. Then who knows who I'd have to live with after that." He stopped and turned to me. "Worse, once they have the guards assigned and they see what a sweet place you have, they could decide to turn your entire property into a prison for ghosts. I'd be sharing my shed with convicts!"

My ancestral home would be the Alcatraz of the spirit world.

Frankie drew close. "I'm telling you, this could be the end of life as we know it. This guy is relentless. And smart. He thinks funny, always one step ahead," he added as the officer himself opened the door at the back of the car.

"Holy smokes," I whispered under my breath.

Frankie hung his head. "I'm dead," he muttered.

It was the man I'd seen outside on the tracks. Same dark black suit. Same short, fat moustache, curled at the ends. His attention veered to Frankie.

He knew.

The Trap gave no reaction when he saw us, other than a slight upward tug at the right corner of his mouth. At the same time, he made no attempt to hide his study of the gangster, his hooded eyes under dark brows assessing, evaluating.

I might as well break the ice.

"Oh, hello," I said as if I'd just seen him, as if we were running into each other after church instead of in the hallway on a haunted train, where I was the only one living.

My grandmother had always taught me, when in doubt, manners count.

The investigator's moustache twitched. "Miss," he responded, touching the brim of his hat.

He spoke with an accent.

"Are you French?" I asked, ignoring the elephant in the room. Or in this case, the Frankie.

"Belgian," he answered, his words crisp. "I am Special Investigator Julien De Clercq." He walked toward us slowly, in no hurry as he tightened the noose. "I died on this train." His attention returned to Frankie. "You did not."

Frankie remained frozen in place. He kept his profile turned to the officer and then slowly lowered the brim of his hat over the bullet hole in his forehead.

The gangster was well and truly trapped. He couldn't cut and run without me and his urn, and I couldn't escape the moving train.

Besides, even if we wanted to flee the scene, we still had Ellis up front and Molly waiting in the caboose.

I tried for a carefree laugh that sounded a little too high-pitched, even to my ears.

"He's with me," I said of the suddenly mute Frankie. "We're on vacation. We had no idea about what happened all those years ago. I'm so sorry for your...situation." I halted before I stepped in it, but De Clercq had already focused his attention back on my mobster.

"I've only just returned to this train," he said, distracted, drawing closer to Frankie. "You look familiar."

That was it. We were done.

Frankie nodded, his jaw working. "I hope so. I worked in the St. Louis office."

Oh no he didn't.

"Bootlegging Division," Frankie added, warming to his role. "Racketeering. Illegal weapons," he added with relish, as if he'd enjoyed his job, which I supposed he had. He leveled his gaze at the lawman. "I'm betting we've been on some raids together."

Not on the same side.

"Badge number 118. Frankie Lawson," Frankie said, holding out a hand.

My throat went dry. Impersonating an officer? It would never work. The only thing Frankie knew about lawful, decent, virtuous types was that he wasn't one of them.

De Clercq left him hanging. "I've seen that name on reports," he said slowly. I could see the wheels turning. He didn't believe it. He couldn't believe it. Frankie had said it himself. This guy was a brilliant lawman. No gangster in his right mind would try to get closer to him.

Which, come to think of it, explained our problem in a nutshell.

De Clercq raised a finger and pointed it to Frankie's forehead. So much for covering it up. "You get that on a raid?" he asked, referring to the bullet hole.

Frankie shook his head. "Jealous girlfriend," he quipped, and they both shared a laugh. "Right after Carter Dugan and I busted the guys who shot up 'Jelly Roll' Hogan's house."

"I remember that," De Clercq said, warming. "Old Jelly Roll ended up a state senator."

"You can't get 'em all," Frankie said, shaking his head as De Clercq nodded.

Wait. No. This could not be working for him.

It was as if he was used to lying and cheating and getting away with it, which I supposed he always had, but this was a bad idea on about fifty different levels. And of course, I couldn't say a word or I'd get him arrested—which he deserved, by the way.

"Glad to have a lawman of your caliber on board, Lawson," De Clercq said, holding out his own hand this time. Frankie shook it. "Can I have a word?" The officer glanced at me. "In private?"

Because I was the problem.

"She follows me everywhere," Frankie groused. "Ignore her."

"Oh, yeah. Sure," I said to the guy who had insisted on joining me for this trip.

De Clercq looked me up and down and then withdrew his attention as if I didn't exist anymore.

"I'd like your opinion on a case," he said to Frankie, who didn't care about any cases I'd ever worked to solve. "We've had a murder in compartment 9."

Oh, my goodness. "Yes. I walked in on the scene," I said, stepping forward, eager to learn more. Maybe I could help. Yes, I'd promised myself I'd stay out of ghostly business this trip, but I couldn't just ignore what had happened to that poor dead girl.

De Clercq held up a hand. "Miss, please. Leave this to the professionals. Otherwise, I'm going to have to ask you to leave." He turned to the mobster. "After you," he said, leading Frankie inside compartment 9. Frankie!

The gangster treated me to a jaunty wink. Then he walked straight through the closed door behind De Clercq, leaving me behind in the hallway.

Frankie was in and I was out.

I rested my hands on my hips, trying to absorb that turn of events.

I shouldn't care. I wasn't supposed to be looking at the ghostly side anyway. But it still burned my rear.

Frankie didn't earn it. He didn't deserve it. He wouldn't even know what to do with the opportunity. I was the one who should be helping the ghost investigator.

I blew out a breath. If I thought about it logically, it was just as well, seeing as my ex-fiancé and his girlfriend were probably dead asleep after that exhausting bout of *enthusiasm* I'd heard through the wall earlier. I certainly didn't want to knock on the door and tempt Beau to answer in his boxers, or worse. I should just leave the ghosts to it. But for someone to pick Frankie—Frankie—over me to solve a murder mystery!

He'd better be taking good notes.

As if.

I paced the hall.

He'd better be sorry.

Who am I kidding? Frankie is never sorry.

He'd better be loud, at least.

I tried to listen through the door, plastering my ear up against the slick, cold wood.

Silence.

At this rate, the only person who would get an earful would be me if Virginia happened to wander down the hall, or if Beau opened the door.

No such luck. Instead, De Clercq himself caught me as he glided through the wall next to me.

"A nosy one, you are," he said, pausing in the hallway.

"I've been known to use that to my advantage," I said, a bit haughty as I faced him. "I've solved several tough cases."

Despite the protests of a certain gangster.

De Clercq turned to my buddy instead. "Well, Frankie, that's all we know," he said, keeping an eye on me. "One dead girl, one crumpled note, and my investigation outside revealed no footprints, no evidence of outside entry or escape. The killer is still on this train, just as I suspected nine decades ago."

"Very interesting," Frankie said in the detached tone he got when he wasn't listening. "However, we must consider this," he added, holding up a finger. "I am on vacation."

"You are here for a reason!" De Clercq snapped. "I don't know why you boarded the mortal train and I don't care. You're with us now and you will help me solve this case."

"I'll partner with you on the investigation," I said to the detective.

He ignored me.

"The murdered girl is back," he said to Frankie. "I'm back. And so far, I've encountered three other passengers, all of whom I suspected as potential killers before our fatal crash. Each of them was connected to the dead girl in some way. Each of them has been drawn back as well, and I'm convinced one of them is the killer. We have two days to solve this murder and free the ghosts of the original Sugarland Express before our train goes over the bridge again and wrecks. You realize it has nowhere else to go," he added ominously. "I failed in 1929. I need to solve it now. If I can't, I fear we'll be doomed to play out this murder over and over until justice is served."

How horrible.

"I need you," the detective continued. "The clues usually come together so easily for me. In this case, I am blocked. I need your unique point of view, Officer Lawson," he said to Frankie. "After all, you are the man who busted Egan's Rats in St. Louis."

Frankie waved him off. "Their liquor was lousy anyway." Then he quickly corrected, "They would have gone down without us."

"Help me solve this case," he pressed, "and you'll be saving us all."

Frankie considered it for a moment. "Well, when you put it that way," he said, holding out his hands. "Sure. Why not?" He took a step toward the rear of the car, then another. "All for one and one for all, right?" He pointed a finger at the detective. "If it's all the same to you, I think I'll start in the caboose. Work my way up."

De Clercq gave a short nod. "If you think it wise. In the meantime, I'll question the conductor about the scrap of paper I found on the body," he said, dissolving away, as if they had a plan.

Frankie saluted him and did a little dance through the back door toward his girlfriend and his fake lodge.

"Now you just wait right there," I ordered, stopping him short. I think I surprised him. "It's bad enough to lie to the police."

"Investigator," he corrected. "And it's called hiding in plain sight."

I caught up with him. "He cares about that girl and the other trapped ghosts." I couldn't imagine reliving a deadly wreck over and over, every time the new Sugarland Express went out. "We need to save those people from a terrible afterlife." De Clercq seemed smart. If he could bring the killer to justice, he could put the ghosts to rest. "He needs help solving the case."

Frankie raised his brows. "Which you said you'd stay out of because you're on vacation."

Come now. "It's not like I can enjoy my vacation when it means five people will die over and over again."

Frankie started heading for the caboose again. "You made it quite clear that you didn't want to see ghosts."

Seriously? I kept pace with him, holding onto my temper by a thread. "If you wouldn't keep blasting me with your power, I wouldn't have seen any of this. I never would have met the original conductor. I wouldn't have walked in on a body. Ellis and I would be happy in compartment 9, and my biggest worry would be about my jerky ex and his mother."

"Excuse me for having extra power and a girlfriend," Frankie shot back.

"You said you'd leave me alone," I ground out.

Frankie threw his arms out. "Yet you're still talking."

"I don't *want* to talk to ghosts. I don't want to be on a train with Ellis's crazy family. I didn't want to find a murdered ghost or a vandalized communications system. But here we are." I took a calming breath. Then another. We were in this for better or for worse. "Look," I said. "De Clercq is expecting you to investigate." This was bigger than Frankie. Bigger than my pride. "He admitted he's stuck. He won't let me help. He needs you. This dead girl needs you."

"Yeah? Well, there's a different dead girl who needs me more," he said, pointing a thumb toward the caboose, backing up, walking away from me and his responsibilities. He opened the back door of the car, then glided over the rickety walkway connecting us to the caboose. "You can't save everybody, Verity."

"I can try," I said, watching him disappear.

CHAPTER 12

I inserted my key and slid open the door to the compact luxury of my compartment—the velvet couch, the brocade curtains. The porter hadn't turned down our bed yet, which I could certainly forgive considering the circumstances tonight.

A single lamp burned on the table by the window.

If De Clercq was right, if the resurrection of the Sugarland Express meant this unfortunate woman was doomed to relive her murder each time the train set out, then I had to do my part to end the cycle.

I retrieved a wrap from the tiny, single shelf at the top of the closet and cast it over my shoulders. The silk chiffon was Melody's favorite, but she'd let me borrow it anyway.

My sister cared. She did what she could to help me and anyone else who needed it.

Frankie, on the other hand… He might have had the detective's ear, but he wouldn't be the partner the old investigator needed.

I would, provided the persnickety old ghost would allow it.

I watched the shadows of the mountains rush past.

No doubt the proud mobster was groveling to Molly, which

was absolutely the right move. After that, he could join us or not. But I couldn't let this go.

The room lay silent save for the rattling of wheels on the tracks as the Sugarland Express hurtled forward into the dark unknown. I should really get back to Ellis and the Abels.

But first, I tucked my wrap tight around my shoulders, planted a knee on the couch, and pressed an ear to the wall separating me from Beau and Stephanie.

Silence.

I waited, resting against the cool, polished wood. My eyes felt heavy and I let them drift closed for only a moment.

"I think they went to sleep," said a voice in my room, directly behind me.

I spun around. "Ellis!"

He stood in the doorway, rubbing a hand over the back of his neck. "You're starting to give me a complex about your ex."

"Ha," I said, hoping he was joking as I slid bonelessly down onto the couch. "Don't ever scare me like that again."

He stepped inside and secured our compartment. "If it makes you feel any better, I was out in the *hall*, listening at their door."

I stifled a laugh. "What are we doing?" I asked, feeling a touch —okay, a lot—foolish.

This was my ex-boyfriend and his new girlfriend, and the whole thing was starting to feel a bit Jerry Springer.

The couch sank as Ellis joined me and stretched an arm out over the back. "We're getting to the bottom of these odd happenings on the train. My brother included."

I leaned my head against his arm. "So much for fun and relaxation."

He looked at me for a long moment. "The night is still young."

He leaned down and kissed me, then deepened the contact into something sweet and full of promise. I was just getting into it when he pulled back slightly. "So what happened with Frankie?"

"You know how to kill the mood," I teased, wrapping my arms

around him, letting him fold me against his chest as I explained about Frankie's latest great idea and the vintage mystery unfolding next door.

"We can't let that girl keep on hurting," Ellis vowed.

"I know," I said, snuggling against his shirt. "We just need to solve a mystery where you can't see any of the suspects or the clues, and the lead investigator won't talk to me because I'm not a lying mobster pretending to be a cop." And most likely because I had girl parts.

"Makes sense to me." Ellis ran his fingertips through my hair, from temple to ear. "And, hey, I learned something interesting from the Abels."

"Oh, yeah?" I had to work to stay focused as he swept his fingers across that little soft spot behind my ear.

His chest rose and fell with his breath. "They were seated at dinner with the travel journalist, and when the lights came back on, they couldn't find her."

I lifted my head. "Beau didn't see her, either."

"She told Dave she works for *Southern Travel and Leisure Magazine*, but he's been a subscriber for years and couldn't recall reading any of her articles. She dodged the question when he asked her to name a few."

"That's strange." Maybe the journalist wasn't a journalist. I wasn't sure what to think about that.

Ellis gave a sharp nod. "I'm going to look her up once we have phone service again."

"I'll also put Melody on it." As soon as I could call.

I'd already asked her to check out the history behind the 1929 wreck. Knowing Melody, she'd have answers soon. I reached into my pocket for my phone and saw that I still had no signal. I sure hoped we'd move into a service area soon, and that my sister wouldn't worry if she kept getting my voicemail in the meantime.

This train was feeling more and more like a time warp from which there was no escape.

A faint tap echoed from the hall. "Turndown service?" a polite voice inquired.

We stood and Ellis opened the door for the young, wiry porter who had carried our bags onto the train.

"Thanks," my boyfriend said as he and I both shifted to admit the porter. In compartments this small, three was a crowd.

We watched as the young man lifted the top part of the couch, cushion and all, into an upper bunk. He pulled a mattress from the rectangular base of the couch and placed it on the upper bunk with quick efficiency. "My apologies. I was supposed to convert the cabins while you were at dinner tonight, but I didn't get to all of them."

"We understand," I assured him as he expertly unpacked sheets and pillows from the storage space and stowed them on the top bunk. "Were you helping wayward passengers?" Perhaps he'd seen something. "I know I wouldn't have wanted to get lost in the dark."

He emptied the space inside the base of the couch, then lifted a lower bunk out of the very bottom and straightened the mattress on top. "Luckily, all the passengers were safe in the dining car, ma'am."

I shared a glance with my boyfriend.

"I wasn't there," Ellis said, "not after the train stopped at least."

The porter didn't appear surprised or even fazed. "As you say, sir."

"I wonder if anyone else ventured out," I mused, keeping an eye on the porter.

"Not a one, I'm sure," he said, making up the beds.

It was difficult to tell if he truly hadn't seen anything, or if he simply wasn't one to gossip with the passengers.

"Anything else you might need?" the porter asked, turning to us when he'd finished.

"I can't think of anything," I said, not unless I could get him to talk. Or perhaps he truly hadn't seen anything.

"Thanks." Ellis pressed a tip into the man's hand as he left.

"We have to tip him?" I asked after the door closed.

"I have no idea," Ellis said, slightly embarrassed. "I figure better safe than sorry, and I'm sure he's earned it tonight."

Good point.

We stared at the pair of narrow bunks, one on top of the other.

"Our original compartment had a nice, snuggly bed, didn't it?" I asked.

Ellis gave a half-chuckle, half-snort. "I'd sleep in that spider-infested caboose if it meant being with you."

"I won't hold you to it," I said. Frankie already had dibs. Ellis grinned as I grabbed for my jammies. "I'll take the top bunk."

"So will I," he said. And I decided it would be a very good evening after all.

HOURS LATER, I woke with my head notched under Ellis's chin and his large warm body spooning me from behind. I felt snug, comfortable, yet…

My eyes fluttered against the faint glow of dawn. I couldn't escape the niggling sensation that something was wrong.

We'd neglected to close the curtains last night. I hadn't been thinking of anything besides racing Ellis to the top bunk and then enjoying the cozy space. In fact, I had no incentive to think about anything else at all—except…

My eyes opened wide.

The desolate landscape raced by outside the window. Bare dirt gave way to scrubby grass clustered against a sheer rock face. It was as if someone had cut a slice out of the mountains and then wedged us into it. It was downright claustrophobic. Even Ellis's arm, thrust casually over me with his heavy weight behind me, made me want to stand up and get some space.

I eased out from under him. He took a sharp breath, then

settled in and resumed his heavy breathing as I reached for my robe.

Ellis slept hard. So why was I so restless?

Maybe I just missed the familiar weight of Lucy the skunk curled up by my feet. She was always so warm. I hoped she wasn't also having trouble sleeping in an unfamiliar place.

A quick check of the hall and I'd be fine. I pulled the robe over my shoulders and tied it tight.

With a glance back at Ellis, I slipped from the compartment.

The view from the hallway window was the same as the one from my comfortable bed. Perhaps I was being silly to worry. I looked down at myself. It wasn't like I could go exploring a fancy train in my robe.

I turned toward my room and my bed when the front door of the car slammed open and Beau staggered through. He wore the same pale blue shirt and navy suit pants as he had last night, but he'd lost his jacket somewhere along the way. His collar lay open with his tie askew, and he looked like hell.

His gaze traveled over me with disturbing familiarity, and he managed a cocky smirk. "I remember that robe."

"Don't," I told him. Yes, I'd worn it around him, but I'd had it since college. He didn't own that experience. He drew closer and I wrinkled my nose. He smelled like the inside of a whiskey barrel. "Long night?" I asked, changing the subject.

He gave a small shrug. "I'm coming back from breakfast."

"Right," I said. I was usually good at sussing out the truth, but it didn't take a detective to figure out that Beau had most likely snuck off to the bar long after Ellis and I went to bed. I hoped he'd at least fallen asleep after his binge instead of drinking on into breakfast, but it wasn't my problem anymore.

"See you later," I said as he slid open his door.

There was no avoiding him on this train.

"Jesus!" he choked out, steadying himself on the doorjamb, slack jawed as he gaped at what he saw in his compartment.

I shouldn't look.

Yes, I should. It was the right thing to do, to offer my support, to steady Ellis's brother.

So I drew up next to him and saw his girlfriend, Stephanie, dead on the floor. She lay facedown on the floor in the exact same spot as the dead woman from 1929. Her arms lay askew, her legs tangled where she fell.

She'd been stabbed in the back in almost the same spot as the ghost, the bloody knife stark against her white silk nightie, the dark blood seeping out onto the rich gold carpet.

CHAPTER 13

J reached for my phone and realized I didn't have it. So I
turned to Beau.

"Call the police."

He brushed past me and banged on the door to my compartment. "Ellis!"

My boyfriend flung the door open, half-asleep. "Will you pipe
down?" he groused at his brother. Then he saw me. "What are you
two doing?"

"There's been a murder," I told him. "Stephanie," I added,
gesturing helplessly toward the open door of compartment 9.

"I don't believe it." Ellis swore under his breath. "Tell me you
didn't touch anything." He reached back to grab a T-shirt, grap-
pling it on even as he charged into the hallway.

"You know I wouldn't tamper with a scene," I said, indignant
and a little hurt. I never interfered with investigations.

"I was talking to my brother," he said, stopping at the
open door.

"I-I left the room at around midnight or one," Beau said,
retreating from the scene, scrubbing a hand down his face. "I
don't know. I couldn't sleep."

114

"And?" Ellis pressed.

"She was fine then!" Beau sputtered.

Ellis showed no reaction. "Have you been back since?"

"No," Beau promised. "I swear."

"Find a porter, a waiter, anyone who works on the train," Ellis instructed. "Tell them to try to alert the local authorities." He shook his head. "Let's hope somebody can get a cell signal."

"I'm on it," I said, leaving Beau slumped against a window and Ellis guarding the scene.

My legs shook at the knees and my breath hitched as I half-walked, half-ran up through the next passenger compartment, fighting the sway of the train. I made it through the lounge and dining room and up to the galley, where the skinny porter whispered frantically to the chef inside.

Wow. He was still on duty.

"I'm afraid breakfast doesn't begin until eight," the porter said, "and there is a dress code," he added, taking in my robe and lack of slippers.

"There's been a murder," I said, breathless, "a girl stabbed in compartment 9."

The chef's eyes grew wide. "Stabbed?"

The porter's jaw slackened. "Are you positive?"

"Pretty sure," I told him. This wasn't my first time reporting a murder, or even my second. "I need you to contact the local police, or find someone on the train who can."

The young porter nodded harshly. "Yes, yes." He appeared flustered, as if unable to muster his next move. I realized I'd given him a near-impossible task unless we'd somehow moved into a better service area in the last two minutes.

"Talk to the conductor," I suggested. He knew this train better than any of us. He might have a solution. "After you've done that, report back to Officer Ellis Wydell in compartment 9."

"Officer?" he asked, surprised.

"We got lucky," I said. "My boyfriend is a police officer in

Sugarland, Tennessee. He's secured the scene," I added, infinitely grateful that Ellis was doing what needed to be done.

When I made it back, I found Ellis pacing outside the door, about ready to toss his cell phone. "I can't get a line out. Did you have any luck?"

"They're working on it," I promised him.

"Good." His jaw was rigid, his body tense. "Beau is locating my mother and her high-end camera. I need to take some preliminary crime scene photos."

"I'm glad you can." There was no telling when or even where the local police would be boarding. "I have to tell you something," I said, drawing closer. "The scene looks almost exactly like the ghostly murder, down to the location of the stab wound."

"You've got to be kidding me," he muttered under his breath. But he knew better than anyone that I was telling the truth. "Why?" he asked me. "Do you have any idea what's going on here?"

"None," I confessed.

He ran a hand through his hair. "Okay, well, we're on it."

There was no one else I'd rather have on my side. "I'm going to go poke around," I told him, "unless you need me here."

"No," he said. "Go."

"Good." I leaned up to give him a quick kiss on the cheek. "I think I know just where to start."

I HEADED toward the back of the car and ended up on the wrong side of the rickety plank to the caboose. I'd been right. It looked worse with the train moving full-speed ahead.

Leave it to Virginia to get the history right, but then fail to fully restore the one car the passengers would never enter, the one she'd no doubt attached for historical accuracy only. Or maybe updating the caboose had been Beau's job.

I looked down at the ground racing past and at my lack of shoes. Well, that was one positive. As a Southern girl, I'd walked logs and climbed trees in my bare feet. Over time I'd developed quite a grip.

The train jerked and I resisted the temptation to panic. I had a three-foot run, maybe four. The low handrail—no higher than my thighs—wasn't exactly built to inspire confidence.

Heck with it. I wasn't going to solve this murder by standing on the back platform. I ignored the harsh wind and the nightgown tangling around my legs, and made a mad dash for the caboose.

The train shifted. I stumbled, but I kept going until I slapped up against the worn metal door and pushed my way inside.

Of course Frankie hadn't turned my power off last night. He'd been too busy arguing with me about it. So I barely saw the spiders, dust, and dirt Ellis had described as being a permanent part of the old caboose. Instead, I walked in on Molly resting on a plush red velvet couch twice the size of the one in my compartment, with Frankie painting her toenails.

To be honest, I might have preferred a hairy old spider.

The gangster stood and tossed the bottle over his shoulder. "Don't you knock?"

"Evidently not," I told him. Although I supposed I should. "Anyway, this is an emergency." I explained about Stephanie's murder, earning a gasp from Molly and a sigh from Frankie.

"This is a bad time," he said. "I got mimosas on ice and a wicked breakfast casserole on the potbelly stove."

I stepped around him to where Molly sat. She cared, and where Molly went, Frankie would follow. "Stephanie was killed the same way as that poor ghost we saw," I told her. "I'm not sure if Frankie mentioned it, but he was *mistaken* for a police detective when I located him last night. We met an officer who was on board the night of the murder and has taken it upon himself to investigate the girl's murder back in 1929. He's working on the case again and he asked for our help."

"My help," the gangster countered, unable to resist. And just like that, I'd trapped him.

"Oh, Frankie." Molly leapt up and hugged him, despite her wet toes. "I'm so proud of you."

He glared at me when he realized what he'd admitted.

Molly didn't notice. She was too busy fawning. "A detective..." She stroked a hand down his arm. "Wow."

"It is something," he said, still shooting me death eyes, the muscles in his neck so rigid they looked ready to pop.

She had to realize he wasn't an actual crime-fighting hottie. That honor went to Ellis. But I didn't bother telling her that as she gazed at Frankie like he was Captain America and Superman rolled into one.

At last he looked down at her and noticed. "Heh. Well, I do what I can," he said. Clearly, he wasn't used to being the object of girly fawn eyes, at least not for acts of valor. He straightened his shoulders and puffed out his chest. "That officer needs me on the case. I know how criminals think."

Did he ever.

"Still," he said, taking her hand, "I don't wanna steal that investigator's thunder by solving the case too quick. So I say we have that breakfast, hit the hot tub with our mimosas, and give the guy a chance to sort it out on his own."

"Frankie!" Molly appeared positively scandalized.

"Just kidding." He grinned, converting it to a sneer when he turned his attention back to me. "It looks like I'm the guy for the job."

"Hooray," I said. We had our very own reluctant crime fighter. Well, for as long as I could keep him on the case. "You should go with him and watch him work," I said to Molly, who nodded enthusiastically.

Frankie forced a smile for Molly. "You're killing me," he said through his teeth.

"Well, don't worry about that," I told him. He was already dead. Better still, I'd accomplished my first task. With the ghosts working on their side, that left me free to question some of the live people on our trip.

~

I MADE it back over the walkway to the main part of the train because I didn't have a choice. When I entered the rear passenger car, I found Manning standing outside compartment 9, looking a bit green in the gills.

"Morning," I said, leaving off the "good" part, fully expecting him to question my business at the back of the train.

He merely nodded as I passed. "We're lucky to have Mr. Wydell on board," he said, and I knew exactly which brother he meant.

"We are," I agreed, stopping at the door to compartment 8. "I'm just going to check on—" With the stress of the morning, I'd completely blanked on the reporter's name. "Her," I finished, with a genteel lift of my chin.

Much trust and goodwill could be gained by proper behavior, even if one still wore a robe minus slippers.

I knocked and the door cracked open. The redheaded woman from last night answered the door in a simple T-shirt and jeans, her short hair pulled back in a multicolor bandana. "Yes?"

"Hi." I gave her my biggest, brightest smile. "My name is Verity Long. From compartment 10. I wonder if I might come in and speak to you for a moment." I nodded toward the conductor, as if he approved of this meeting and so should she.

She followed my gaze and seemed relieved to see someone else in the hallway. "Is there something going on?" she asked, stepping back to let me enter.

"Yes," I said, not bothering to sugarcoat it, "I apologize for my dress." Or lack thereof. My grandmother would need a fan and a pinch of smelling salts if she saw me out like this. My mother would blame herself. "But after the tragic events of this morning, I'm not at my best."

She gave a quick nod. "Eileen Powers," she said, holding out a hand for me to shake. "I heard you in the hallway when they found her." She gestured toward a velvet couch just like the one in my room and moved a few file folders so I could sit. "How awful," she added, almost as an afterthought.

I forgave her casual concern. Perhaps she hadn't known Stephanie well, although she certainly had enjoyed some familiarity. I'd watched Beau's girlfriend visit this compartment last night.

"It is a tragedy," I said, watching for her reaction and getting none. We faced each other on the couch, with me nearer the window and the scattered stack of file folders on the table. I bumped my ankle on the lamp she'd relocated to the floor. "It appears she was killed overnight or in the early morning hours. My boyfriend and I are light sleepers, but we didn't hear a thing. Did you?"

She snorted out a laugh. "I heard plenty earlier."

"Ah. That." I wasn't sure how to respond.

"If they were dogs, I'd have gotten out the hose." She rubbed a hand along her jaw, amused at her own joke.

I felt the flush creep up my neck.

"My," I managed, embarrassed for them and for me. I had no reason to feel responsible, but there it was. Perhaps it was because I'd chosen him once upon a time. Or maybe because the reporter was so frank.

Her earrings, made from vintage, black-and-white typewriter SHIFT keys, swayed as she shook her head. "The kicker was, when I went over there to tell them to pipe down, she answered the door fully dressed. He was drinking scotch. I don't get it." She shrugged. "At least they kept it down after that."

"That is unexpected." And strange. Had they been putting on a show for Ellis and me? But that didn't make sense. Beau seemed to genuinely like Stephanie, and anyway, it wasn't like he'd invite a girl on a train just to make me jealous. Or would he? I wondered how much he knew about his perfect woman.

"How well did you know Stephanie?" I asked, realizing I hadn't even asked her last name.

"I didn't," she said plainly. "Never spoke to her before the incident last night."

She'd said it so easily, yet I knew she was lying.

"You're here by yourself and you didn't talk to anyone?" I clarified, giving her room to talk.

She folded her hands in front of her. "I'm here to write a travel piece for a magazine, not to make friends."

You'd think she'd at least want to conduct a few friendly interviews with the passengers.

I crossed my legs and kept my posture straight as if we were meeting at high tea rather than on a doomed train while I was still in my robe. "I heard you were a journalist," I said. It certainly explained the stack of notes. "I commend you for staying in your room and letting the police handle the situation next door."

She cocked her head to the side. "I'm a freelance travel journalist. I'm not after a crime story."

"Good," I said, watching her brows rise ever so slightly. "How long have you been working as a travel writer?"

She leaned back against the arm of the sofa. "Long enough," she said, not answering the question.

She was up to something. I just didn't know what. I folded my hands in my lap and leaned closer. "The police are going to ask me about last night, so I might as well warn you," I said, taking a risk. "I know you met with Stephanie last night." At her frown, I added, "I watched her enter your room as I was heading back for my wrap."

"Your wrap?" she asked dubiously.

"Yes." I notched my chin up. It was the wrap that kept on

giving. I'd have to thank Melody again for letting me borrow it, even if I hadn't actually gotten to wear it out.

She watched me closely. "You really saw her, didn't you?"

"Of course." I hoped I wasn't saying too much. The idea made me nervous.

She stood. "Son of a—" She tightened her hand and turned. "What time was it?"

In for a penny, in for a pound. "At around ten o'clock. Why?"

Her jaw worked and her cheeks flushed red. "I was out at the back of the car, on that tiny observation platform, trying to reach my editor."

"Without a cell signal?" I found that hard to believe.

"I didn't say I was successful," she snapped. "When I returned, my papers were scattered, which is pretty unlikely when the windows don't open to let the breeze in." She paced. "I complained," she said, as if she were working it out in her head, "and the porter blamed it on ghosts. I blamed it on bad door locks." She stopped. "But now I'm thinking I've been had by the owner's girlfriend."

"Over a travel piece?" There had to be more to it than that.

"It's not like I can promise a glowing report." She said. "I was going to say the same thing to my editor if I'd been able to reach her." She shook her head. "The Wydells are a scary bunch. My editor likes upbeat articles about new attractions like this, but frankly, I've seen a lot of problems, even before the disaster at dinner last night."

With Virginia Wydell in charge? "What kinds of problems are you talking about?" It must have been part of the project Beau handled.

She leveled her gaze with mine. "You'll have to read the article."

A knock sounded at the door.

She turned to answer, and I realized I was sitting near the

stack of files on the table. It wasn't like I could read any of them in front of her, but I did manage to lift the cover of the one on top.

It was an investigative piece titled "Addicts, Inc." about the heroin epidemic in Southern suburbia. And it was penned by investigative journalist Eileen Powers.

CHAPTER 14

*E*llis stood at the door to Eileen's room. "Can I speak with you?" he asked, all business.

He was going to question her.

"I was just leaving," I said, scooting past her out the door, as dignified as I could be for a woman in a bathrobe.

As I passed by compartment 9, I wondered if they'd removed the body.

Probably not. It took longer than an hour to process a scene, and Ellis had been handling it by himself. At least with this new turn of events, Virginia and her staff would be trying even harder to reach the outside world. Sabotage was one thing. Murder was another. We needed to stop this train and catch the killer, by any means necessary.

I gave a final glance down the empty hall before entering compartment 10.

Shivering, I ditched the robe and turned on a hot shower.

What if that had been me in compartment 9?

Would I have been a target by virtue of being there?

Or perhaps it was a coincidence that Stephanie happened to be in that particular place when her killer struck.

I stepped into the shower, grateful for the comfort of the warm spray. I tried to keep my mind clear and simply enjoy the moment. Yet no amount of hot water or soap could keep the gravity of the situation from settling over me.

If the tragedy next door did have something to do with the murder on the original train, then I might have been able to prevent it. If I hadn't been so determined to take a break from it all.

I wet my hair, letting the water wash over my head and back.

Melody had said I couldn't save everybody, and she had a point. But shouldn't I at least try?

When Frankie first exploded into my life, I'd thought of it as a curse. I still did, at least twice a week, and even more often when he was running his horse-racing operation out of the backyard, or when the Chicago mob had shown up at my door. Not to mention the time he'd gotten the idea to break into the bank downtown and hide the money under my porch.

But despite the drawbacks of my resident ghost, I'd been given an opportunity to make life better for a lot of people, both living and dead.

Who would I be if I didn't seize that?

I grabbed for the bottle of my favorite peaches and cream shampoo. Eileen was lying about her story. I wanted to know why. Maybe Ellis would be able to sniff it out. I wondered if she was here investigating her heroin epidemic story, or if that project was complete and she had another scoop in mind.

In any case, I should warn Virginia. No matter what the journalist was here to uncover, it couldn't be good.

I winced, and not because I got soap in my eye.

Virginia would likely shoot the messenger.

Ah, well, I couldn't let that stop me. It never had before.

Perhaps we could even work with her. Ellis would certainly want to try.

I stuck my head under the spray and let the water hit it hard.

Even after his mother's backhanded compliments and outright refusal to accept him for who he was, Ellis hadn't given up on her or his family. He still craved her affection. It would be wonderful if she could eventually open up and give him that. And while I didn't think she and I could ever be friends, I would like to be able to be in the same room with Virginia without being a target. I didn't think I could take too many dinners like the one last night.

Dating was supposed to be the easy part.

I dried my hair and dressed in my favorite white dress with blue hydrangeas. It had seen better days, but it had gotten me through some of my toughest mysteries as well. I'd need it today.

The hall lay empty when I stepped outside, and as tempting as it was to check the caboose to see if Frankie was indeed investigating, I didn't feel up to another run across the bridge of death. Not while wearing white kitten heels, at any rate.

Instead, I ventured up to the dining car. It was still early, and I found only two tables occupied. The large and imposing Ron had just finished a plate of eggs at a table on the right-hand side, closest to the window. Dave and Mary Jo Abel sipped coffee at the farthest table on the left side, in the same spots they'd taken at dinner last night.

I paused. While I'd like nothing more than to join the older couple—especially when I noticed Mary Jo was having cake again for breakfast—I focused instead on the broad-shouldered man I'd seen in the alley back in Kingstree. I didn't know much about him other than the fact that Stephanie had tried to deny any sort of association.

Before I could think on it too much, I slid into the seat opposite him. "Mind if I join you?" I asked, noticing a waiter approaching.

He glanced up and did a double take. "Hi," he said, a bit startled.

He was bigger up close, rougher looking, which made it all the more surprising when I noticed he had a manicure.

126

"Coffee for you, miss?" the waiter asked.

"Sure," I said. I preferred hot tea in the morning, but anything that planted me at this table was a bonus in my book. This man had seemed to know Stephanie well, at least well enough to threaten her. If I could get him on friendly terms, I might learn something. "We haven't been properly introduced," I said, unfolding my napkin and placing it in my lap. "My name is Verity Long. I'm from Sugarland."

"Ron," he said, offering a hand over the table.

His grip was firm and warm. So much so that I tried to ignore the way his close-cropped black hair and shadow of a beard lent an air of danger. He had the look of a predator. Under other circumstances, I'd have made my excuses and hightailed it the other way.

"I'm glad you sat down," he said, surprising me again.

Perhaps this would go better than I'd anticipated. Stephanie might well have provoked him in that alley. She'd certainly gotten on my nerves a time or two.

I gave him a bright smile. "Are you traveling with anyone?" I asked. I couldn't place him with a particular group. Eileen was traveling on her own. The Abels were a couple, as were the honeymooners and the couple celebrating their golden anniversary.

"I'm very single," he said, his eyes lingering on my chest.

Oh my. I'd wanted to start questioning him on a positive note, but never in a million years did I imagine he'd take it as a pickup.

"I'm traveling with my boyfriend, Ellis," I stated, wishing I could take my napkin and wear it as a lobster bib. That might keep his eyes where they belonged.

He leaned an elbow on the table, way too confident, and I watched as his muscled arms bulged against his suit coat. "If you're so into your boyfriend, then why are you sitting with me?"

"I know you were friends with Stephanie," I said, wishing again that I knew her last name. "I sat with her at dinner last night. She spoke of you quite fondly," I added, wishing it were true.

If I had to guess based on what I'd seen in that alley, I'd bet they had a romantic history. So he had to have been appealing to her at some point or other. She might even be the reason he was on this train.

"Stephanie is a two-timing slut," he said, as if it were fact.

"Oh." Well, there you had it.

"I don't want to talk about her anymore," he said, reaching across the table for my hands. "Serves her right if she saw us together right now."

I placed my hands in my lap. "I'm not quite sure how to tell you this, but Stephanie died last night."

Whatever derisive comment he'd been about to say froze on his lips. "What?" he asked simply.

I was surprised he hadn't heard already. Then again, this wasn't Sugarland.

"She was killed in her compartment overnight. They're not sure when," I explained gently, resisting the urge to offer him a simple, comforting touch. I couldn't possibly know how he'd take it. "I'm sorry to deliver such upsetting news."

He sat back, rubbing a hand over his face. He gazed into the distance for a moment, then back at me. "Are you messing with me?"

"No," I said, "she's really gone."

He blinked a couple of times. Hard. "How do *you* know?"

Because I was the one who'd found her. But this was tough enough without me telling him that.

I clasped my hands together in my lap. "My boyfriend is a police officer. He's with the body right now."

"Sucks to be him," he said, clearing his throat, avoiding my eyes so he could fiddle with his coffee cup. "Good thing I didn't know her that well."

Just looking at him, I could tell that wasn't true.

"How *did* you know her?" I asked, truly interested.

He glanced back toward the table where the Abels sat, as if he would catch them eavesdropping. "Stephanie did some business with me. It's over now. Obviously."

"The thing is, I was never quite sure what Stephanie did for a living," I began. She hadn't talked about it at dinner, and that was really all the time I'd had.

His lips twisted into a wry grin. "Market development," he said, with false sincerity. Lord, when he said it like that, he truly did look like one of Frankie's mobster friends.

"And you just happen to be on the maiden voyage of the Sugarland Express. With her," I added, saying it plain.

He held up a finger. "Not *with* her." The *not anymore* was implied. Before I could say anything more, he threw his napkin onto the table. "I gotta go."

"Wait," I said, standing with him.

"When you get tired of your cop, you know where to find me," he said, spearing me with a saucy, parting leer that glanced right off. He didn't have the energy for it, and I didn't have the time.

He walked past me, not looking back, heading to the passenger cars.

I watched him go. He'd seemed genuinely surprised when I'd told him about Stephanie's death. Before that, he'd spoken about her in the present tense, as if she were still alive.

He could be faking. A practiced killer would know to do these things, and I could say with a fair amount of confidence that Ron wasn't the nicest guy. He certainly didn't respect women.

But a jerk and a killer were two different animals entirely.

Unless he was a murdering jerk.

As I pondered my encounter with Ron, I began catching snippets of conversation from the Abels still ensconced at their table near the back of the car.

"Well, you shouldn't wander a dark train, even if you do have insomnia," Mary Jo scolded.

"I'll walk wherever I damned well please," Dave countered.

It was none of my business. And I wasn't the sort to pry, but this was literally a case of life and death.

Heavens. When had I gotten so dramatic?

I picked up my coffee cup—no sense letting it go to waste—and waved as I approached, giving them plenty of time to regain their composure. It would be rude to barge in on their conversation. Even if I was extremely interested in what Mary Jo had just revealed.

"Good morning," I said, glad when she motioned for me to sit.

"Is it good, dear?" she asked, clutching her cup. "Have you heard?"

I cringed as I scooted my chair in. "I was passing in the hall when her boyfriend opened the door and found her," I said. Mary Jo appeared as horrified as I'd felt. "It was awful."

"Poor thing," Mary Jo clucked. "Let's get you some breakfast," she said, waving over the waiter.

"I'm not hungry," I said.

She waved the waiter away. "I hope our son wasn't rude," Mary Jo clucked.

"Your son?" I asked, glancing back at the table I'd shared with Ron. "I hadn't realized you were traveling with anybody else."

"He's not talking to us," Dave said curtly. "A family issue."

"You're both so stubborn. Maybe I should go and try to talk to him again," she said, starting to rise.

"Mary Jo," Dave cautioned, touching her on the arm, "let him be."

"I hear he dated Stephanie," I said, fishing for information. And, truly, I think it had been said, if only by me.

"She had her hooks in him briefly," Mary Jo stated plainly. She waved a hand. "Oh, what am I saying? That poor dead girl." She closed her eyes and shook her head, her dangling sea-glass earrings swaying. "It isn't the same world I grew up in."

"It's not the world, it's this damned train." Dave clutched the handle of his cup. I could tell he hadn't slept well. He had dark circles under his eyes and appeared brittle in a way he hadn't before. "I said it last night. This trip is a disaster and it's only getting worse." He took a big gulp. "God, I hate decaf."

"You should at least try to get some rest," Mary Jo urged him.

"Maybe." He pushed his cup away.

"Go. I'll be fine," she said, patting him on the arm.

He closed a hand over hers for a moment, then rose from the table, a bit more at ease after her reassurance. "You two girls be careful," he warned, as if he were leaving us in a bad neighborhood after dark.

"He's really worried, isn't he?" I asked, a moment after he left.

Mary Jo watched him go, concern etched on her forehead. "He feels trapped, which has never happened on a rail trip before. And I tell you, we've taken plenty."

"We have gotten off to a rough start," I admitted.

"Dave likes being in touch, and when that Wi-Fi system went down—" she glanced around to make sure we were alone "—it was worse than you think."

"How so?" I asked, leaning my elbows on the table.

She did the same. "They touted this route as being historic, and it is. But it also means we're cut off from the main commercial routes. We're isolated. Dave liked the idea at first, and so did I. But it can't be a coincidence that the communications system was sabotaged shortly after we entered an area where that system was our only way to reach the outside world."

"We have to switch tracks right now," I said. Surely even Virginia would see the need to change course.

"Rail routes are carefully planned and assigned," Mary Jo said. "We can't just switch. Another train might be on that track and we'd have no way to even let them know we're coming."

"Shoot. I hadn't thought of that," I said, starting to get a bit claustrophobic myself.

"The route wasn't designed to stop at any towns along the way.

The ride is the entertainment. Or at least it was..." she trailed off, worried. "We have hundreds of miles to go, in isolated hills and forests, until we reach the next stop." She pressed her hands together in front of her. "It's spooky. We've been having trouble settling in, and Dave didn't sleep hardly at all last night."

"I heard you talking about his late-night walk," I confessed. "Did he see anyone else out?"

"I asked him the same thing," Mary Jo said, fiddling with her rings. "He says he didn't see anybody." She paused. "But I did."

"Last night?" I asked. They were in the first passenger compartment, just past the lounge car.

"Early this morning." She clutched her hands together. "It's going to sound strange."

"Try me," I urged.

"Well," she said, "I was worried about Dave. It was half-past two in the morning and he'd been walking for a while. I thought I'd go after him and see if I couldn't bring him back to bed." She fidgeted with her earring. "We're good together because when he gets worked up, I help him calm down. I teach him how to smell the roses, but he knows where the park is at," she joked, as if she'd said it a million times. "Anyway, I opened the door and I saw her."

"Stephanie?" I gasped.

"No." She appeared uncomfortable. "I saw a ghost in a kimono drifting down the hallway. I swear to St. Peter."

"I believe you," I told her.

"I slammed the door, turned on every light, and said about a hundred prayers to Jesus." She touched her fingers to her temples and let out a short laugh. "It feels good just saying it out loud."

"I understand completely." In ways she couldn't imagine. "My house back home is haunted. I have a gangster living with me."

Her jaw dropped open. "Then you're one of the few people who wouldn't think I'm half-baked," she said with obvious relief. "Anyway, I left poor Dave out there to fend for himself." She placed a hand on her chest, as if shocked by her own action.

"Course when he got back a half hour later, I said he couldn't go out again. Not with a ghost floating around." Her gloom returned. "Little did I know he'd be out there with a killer."

"We'll figure this out," I promised.

Mary Jo grew serious. "There's only one thing to do. We have to get off this train."

I was all for that. "You said it yourself. It's not safe out there."

She winced. "It's not safe in here, either. I'm not a fighter like Dave. I don't look for every problem ten steps ahead. But even I can see we're trapped here by design." She took my hands in her cold ones. "We're on this train with a killer, and whoever it is, he wants it that way."

$\mathcal{I}$t hadn't occurred to me that someone might have trapped us here on purpose. If that were truly the case, then the killings might not be over.

But why would anybody do that? This wasn't some Agatha Christie novel. This was real life. My life.

"Will you walk me back to my room?" Mary Jo asked, pushing up from the table. "I'd like to lie down for a little while." She paused and touched my arm. "Not that I think I'll be murdered en route, mind you. But at least this way, I won't hear about it from Dave."

"Sure." I stood and offered her an arm. "I'm glad you feel safe with me."

She smiled at the gesture and linked her arm with mine. "Now let's keep an eye out for killers behind the curtains," she said, eyeing the floor-length cream drapes.

"Not to mention criminals lurking behind potted palms."

That one was real.

The Abels occupied the very first compartment in the lead passenger car. I dropped Mary Jo off in a suite twice the size of our modest room, with a seating area and a real bed.

Dave stood by the window, watching the train rush through the mountain forest, while the skinny porter arranged a vase of roses on a nearby dining table for two.

"Good. You're back." Dave noticed me. "And you were smart," he said to his wife.

"I'm always careful, dear." Mary Jo dropped her sweater on the chair. "Now sit before you pace a groove in the carpet and eat all the chocolates."

"I wasn't pacing," he bristled.

Maybe not, but I did notice a half-eaten box of Irish cream truffles on the coffee table. Paper wrappers littered the polished surface like casualties of war.

"Will that be all?" the porter asked.

"Yes." Dave waved him away without a tip.

Okay, so you didn't have to tip porters.

"Would you like to stay for a while?" Mary Jo asked. "We can play some cards to take our minds off things."

That was the trick. I didn't want to forget our problems. I wanted to fix them.

"Normally, I'd love to," I said, "but considering the circumstances, I think I need to find Ellis."

"Be careful," Dave warned as I left the cabin alone.

I noticed he didn't offer to go with me. For once, I was glad to see a slip in traditional propriety. What I had in mind, I'd rather do alone.

While I was anxious to find Ellis and hear the latest on his investigation, I was more eager to locate Virginia and determine just how trapped we were on this train.

Ellis would certainly shoo her away from the murder scene, which meant—knowing Virginia—she'd be holed up at the front, trying to manage a trip that had clearly gone off the rails.

I passed through the lounge and dining cars, places meant for gathering and relaxing. The lack of patrons was eerie. Word had definitely spread.

I moved farther up the train and pushed open the door to the observation car. There, I found the newlyweds gathered in close conversation with the fiftieth-anniversary couple. From their dire expressions, I could tell they weren't trading happy marriage secrets.

Long benches lined the center of the car in rows, with an aisle up each side. The couples gathered on a bench at the front. Large windows ran up the sides and over the roof, offering a spectacular view of the stark wilderness. No one noticed.

"Hi," I said, drawing near.

The young woman on the end lifted her head, revealing a simple diamond stud in her nose. A tattoo of a dragonfly crested her shoulder. "Do you have any idea what's going on?"

"Other than the…incident this morning," I hedged. All eyes turned to me. "I'm sorry," I said. "We have a police officer on board who is working on it. I'm trying to learn more. Were any of you out and about last night?"

The petite girl blushed and shared a glance with her handsome new husband. "We were very much in."

"Us too," the older man said, without a hint of guile. "We go to bed early."

"Oh, I hear you," I said, to both points of view. "Verity Long, by the way," I added, offering the girl my hand.

She didn't seem like she knew what to do with it. "Madison Lemon," she said, giving a small wave.

"Xander," her husband said, taking my hand.

"Bruce and Barbara Danvers," the older man said, shaking my hand next.

I couldn't reach his wife. She was smaller than Madison and dwarfed behind her large husband. "So good to meet you," I said, giving my own little wave. "I'm hoping to learn more about what happened yesterday and this morning. My boyfriend is the police officer working on the case." That earned a few murmurs of appreciation, especially from the older couple. "I'm no detective," I admitted. I was just a girl who liked to help. "But I do have a question that I hope at least one of you can answer."

"Sit." Barbara motioned to me, her charm bracelet clinking.

I eased past the group and took the spot next to her. "Thanks," I said, enjoying her lilac perfume. "At dinner last night, when the train stopped, did you see anyone leave the dining car before or shortly after they passed out the drinks?"

I received four blank stares.

Madison raised her hand. "The Abels were looking for that reporter. She was sitting with them and then she was gone. She left her camera on the table."

"Did one of the Abels go after her?" I asked. That would have been the time Eileen was at the back of the train, calling her editor. If she was telling the truth.

"Not right away," Madison said, her husband nodding as she spoke. "People were scared and sticking together."

True.

"Mary Jo talked to us too," the older man said. "She said that if we saw that red-haired woman, to let her know that she was keeping her camera safe."

"They were so nice during the champagne toast," his wife cooed.

Yes, they were very nice. And they might have been sitting with a killer.

"Did you see anything else?" I asked.

"I don't recall." Bruce appeared tired as he took his wife's hand. "This was supposed to be a relaxing vacation."

Didn't I know it?

Barbara turned to me. "The Lemons sat with us afterward, and we learned Madison here works with our granddaughter."

"We're both maternity nurses up in Franklin," the newlywed added.

"That's great," I said, glad for them. These train trips should be all about meeting other interesting couples. I wished Ellis and I had more time to do it. "If you think of anything, let me know," I said, grabbing a pen from my purse. I wrote my name and compartment number on a napkin for each couple. I added my phone number along the bottom as well on the off chance we entered a service area. "Any time of the day or night."

I left them to their socializing and pressed forward. I'd have to ask Mary Jo exactly when she returned the camera to our intrepid reporter, and if she knew what Eileen might be investigating on the train.

In the meantime, I couldn't find Virginia in the library car or the small office beyond.

I slid open the door to the old radio room, and what I saw inside surprised me. It was the ghostly conductor I'd met at the hotel. He stood in front of a card table full of broken components and pieces of plastic that he couldn't touch or understand.

"No one is fixing this," he said, his hands moving helplessly through the mess. "We need this to work."

"I'm afraid it's a lost cause," I said, stepping inside, sliding the door closed behind me. "These are delicate instruments, and they've been smashed to bits. Even if we could put them together, they wouldn't work."

"We're running blind," he said, "same as we did when I was in charge."

That was right. The radio had been disabled on the original trip.

I faced him across the table full of broken parts. "There was also a murder last night," I said gently.

His face grew even paler. "The girl in compartment 9."

"From your side, and from mine."

He closed his eyes. "I tried to stop it. I did."

"I know. I wish I'd listened," I said, although I still couldn't imagine what I should have done. "I never dreamed it would turn out like this."

He nodded, his gaze hollow. "We'll run blind until we get to the bridge over the Holston River tomorrow. It's faulty. It'll give. We'll plunge to our deaths below."

Not this time, at least not in real life. I refused to believe that could happen to our train. At least I sincerely hoped it wouldn't.

The ghosts were another matter. But with any luck, we'd free them before their train crashed.

"We're working on solving both cases," I promised. We might even have a witness to the 1929 murder. "One of the passengers said she saw the ghost of a woman in a kimono. Do you know who she's talking about?"

He gave a small smile. "The Green Lady. She was a passenger on our last journey. She likes to wander and is fond of the library, but she only comes out late at night."

"I think I'll wait up for her, then," I said, formulating a plan.

Heels clicked down the hallway outside.

"Ellis," Virginia's voice rang out, clearly taken aback.

I opened the door and stepped directly into their chance encounter.

"I was just looking for you, Mother," he said. "And you as well," he added to me.

"I have a cause of death, but it's not what we thought," he added quietly. "Mind if we duck in here?" He nodded toward the radio room.

"Let's go somewhere else," I said quickly. The conductor didn't need to be listening to the gory details. He was upset enough.

"In my office," Virginia said crisply. She led us a short distance past the crew car to a hole-in-the-wall alcove with a desk at the very front of the library car. I was almost surprised we all fit. I leaned against the precisely organized desktop.

"Stephanie Marconi was stabbed in the back and bled out," Ellis stated. "The killer used a knife from the galley. The chef confirmed it this afternoon."

"Heavens," I whispered. Anyone could have taken that knife.

Ellis glanced from me to his mother. "The body is also showing clear signs of pre-mortem strangulation."

"I don't get it," Virginia said. "Why do both?" she added, as if it were a time-saving question.

Ellis crossed his arms over his chest. "Noise travels on this train. My guess is that the killer snuck up and had his hands around her windpipe before she could make a sound." He turned to me. "When she was sufficiently subdued, the killer ended it with the knife."

"So the killer got the jump on her, which means he had a key," I said.

"Not necessarily," Ellis cautioned.

Virginia stood rigid. "Compartment doors lock when a passenger leaves. Either the killer had a key, or Stephanie knew the person."

"Unless Beau didn't close the door all the way when he left for the bar," I suggested. I hated to bring it up, but my ex wasn't the most thorough person. "Ellis is right. All we know is that the killer closed the door tightly behind him."

Virginia shot me a look that could boil water. "It wasn't Beau."

"It wasn't," Ellis said, more relieved than put out. "He had the good sense to spend from eleven in the evening until six in the morning drinking in the lounge car. One of the waiters stayed up to serve him. He even talked one of the off-duty porters into drinking with him. Mom, you really need to establish bar hours on this train."

"I didn't think anyone would stay up all night," she snapped. "But I'm certainly glad it happened this time," she murmured to herself.

"The porter didn't happen to be the young, extremely skinny guy, did he?" I asked.

Ellis appeared startled. "Yes. Why?"

"I'm keeping my eye on him," I said.

Virginia drew back. "Is he offering subpar service?"

"It's not that," I said. "He's just always…there."

"He's a porter," Virginia said, as if I were daft. "That's his job."

"True," I admitted. Okay, so he was in the clear. "We also know the engineer didn't do it because he was driving the train."

"We need to get this train stopped soon," Ellis said. "I've processed the scene, but we need to contact the local authorities and get a team in there."

"All right." Virginia nodded. "We arrive in Gatlinburg tomorrow."

Ellis barked out a laugh. "That's not good enough."

"Well, it's the best I can do," she shot back. She paced the tiny room. "We're not cleared to leave our route. We can't call for help, and I can't make the Gatlinburg station any closer than it is, which is at least one day away!"

I braced my hands behind me on the desk. "Virginia, we have a killer on board, not to mention a body."

"And how does that fix my comms system?" she snapped.

"Calm down," Ellis said, stepping between us. "We at least need to put the body in cold storage and tell the passengers what's happening."

Virginia glared at him. "Absolutely not. You'd cause a panic."

"Most already know they're on board with a killer," I told her. I didn't mention that a few of them had heard it directly from me.

They had a right to know.

Ellis rubbed a hand over his face. "I just wish we had more facts. We have a sabotaged train, a murdered girl, and the killer potentially still on board. I'm not sure that calling the passengers together in a large group is a good idea, but you need to visit each of them individually and explain the situation."

Virginia pursed her lips. "I don't like that."

Of course not, it would mean admitting her latest project wasn't perfect. It would mean addressing their fears and concerns. A woman like her was more comfortable creating chaos than calming it.

"Let me explain," Ellis began.

"It's okay not to have all the answers," I assured her.

"Speak for yourself," she snapped.

Ellis cleared his throat. "Actually, I'm more worried about either one of you being alone with a killer," he said. "Both of you, please, be on your guard."

Shoot. I hadn't even thought of that. At least I'd only been alone with the Abels. Oh, and Eileen Powers. I'd be more careful in the future.

Ellis planted his hands in his pockets. "What I was going to say is that I need to question the passengers individually anyway. Mother, you can go with me. Your assurances will help put them at ease, and I'll be watching for their reactions when you talk to them about the killer on board."

Virginia ran her hand over her face. "This is a nightmare." She looked almost ready to cry. I'd never seen her this way.

"It is," Ellis agreed, "and we'll get through it."

"Fine." She held up a hand. "I'll talk to the passengers. But in the meantime, I need both of you on task. Figure out what's happening on my train."

"You want me as well?" I asked, genuinely surprised.

She raised her chin. "I don't always approve of your methods," she said to me, "or your job choices," she added to Ellis, "but, yes, I'm counting on both of you."

"All right," I said.

Ellis gave a sharp nod. "Let's do it."

CHAPTER 16

S o we had a plan. Ellis would continue to question the living, and I'd take care of the dead. I headed back to find Frankie and instead ran into Beau drinking a vodka and Red Bull at the bar and keeping company with the server behind the counter.

Goodness. "How are you doing?" I asked. He looked miserable, disheveled, and he still wore yesterday's clothes.

"Verity." He said it like an accusation. "Your *boyfriend* won't tell me what happened to Stephanie. Will you?"

Beau certainly wasn't in any condition to hear the details.

"I'm sure he'll let you know when there is something he can report," I said, forgiving his brusque manner. He was obviously hurting. I left out the part about Ellis wanting to call in the police in Gatlinburg, and about putting his girlfriend's body on ice. "These things take time. We're lucky to have him on board."

He rolled his eyes and went back to his drink.

"I'm sorry about Stephanie," I said gently.

He took a large swig. "Me too."

I paused, desperately wanting to say something to make it

better, knowing I couldn't. Any attempt by me would probably make it worse.

I just wished he would look at me or even turn toward me instead of tapping his red cocktail straw over and over against the bottom of his glass.

"Are you done?" he asked.

Yes. But I couldn't just leave him. "Ellis is doing his best and so am I," I promised. "I was up front, talking to your mother—"

"Now I really must be drunk," he snorted. At least he turned and looked at me. "What in hell did you have to say to her?"

"Beau..." I began. He never used to act this way or speak in such a vulgar manner. He'd been a fun party guy, but he'd never been such a drinker. I wasn't sure what had happened to him in the past year, and it worried me. I sighed. It wasn't my place to say anything. Not anymore. "Just...take care of yourself," I said, leaving him to his drink.

"Run away, Verity," he called after me. "Leave. You're good at that."

Shame on him for making it such an easy decision.

The kicker was, Beau could actually aid in this investigation—if he stayed sober and focused. We had a killer on the train and needed all the help we could get.

I passed through the hallway next to the galley and wondered about the knives I'd seen strewn on the floor after the near miss with the rocks on the track. I hadn't gotten a good look at the one that the killer had planted in Stephanie's back. But if they were the same, well, anyone could have gotten hold of it in the confusion.

But who would want Stephanie dead?

Despite Beau's callous attitude, I didn't believe for a minute that he'd killed her. His alibi held up, and besides, things had seemed to be going well between them. He'd invited a police officer to bunk next door. And even if she had somehow upset Beau enough to make him leave in the middle of the night, he'd barely started seeing her. He'd known me for two years, lost me the night before the wedding, and watched me date his brother. In all that time, I'd never once felt like Beau was out to physically harm me. He'd also appeared genuinely shocked this morning when we'd found the body.

So if not Beau, then who?

The train shuddered, and I paused between cars to gain my footing.

Ron was an obvious choice. Maybe he'd gotten tired of Stephanie pushing back on him. She'd denied any relationship to him, but he'd made it clear that they had some history. Mary Jo had confirmed it. And I knew what I'd seen in the alley. If I had to guess, I'd say he followed her on board. Let's face it, a vacation through the countryside on a train full of happy couples was not a mecca for randy, single guys. And it was clear he hadn't come to spend time with his parents.

Then there was the reporter, Eileen. There was no proof she'd gone to the back of the train when she'd left the dining room on that first night. She could just as easily have snuck to the front to sabotage the radio.

I suspected the murder and sabotage were connected. With communications out, our isolation made it too easy for the killer to remain at large and for potential evidence to be lost. No matter how well Ellis secured the scene, he didn't have the resources or the manpower.

He was supposed to be on vacation.

I'd almost made it through the lead passenger car when the last door on the right clicked open. I jumped, ready to flee the other way, when the skinny porter stepped out of the room.

"Good afternoon, miss," he said.

I looked behind him and caught eyes with Ron, who quickly looked away. Probably sheepish from his behavior this morning.

"Can I get you anything?" the porter asked.

"I'm fine," I said quickly. I flashed him a smile. "I do appreciate you taking care of Beau Wydell last night," I added, hoping he might say more.

He gave no reaction. "I take good care of all my passengers," he said, sliding the door closed behind him. When I didn't continue on, he hesitated. "Are you sure I can't get you anything?"

"Positive," I assured him, making haste for the last passenger car.

He nodded and strode up toward the dining room.

I watched him over my shoulder as I hurried the other way.

I let myself into my compartment and sighed in relief at the click of the lock behind me.

Of course, Stephanie had been in a locked room as well. It hadn't stopped her killer.

Our room had been cleaned and converted back into a formal day area. I grabbed a nutrition bar and a bottle of water and sat down on the plush velvet sofa.

Most likely Stephanie had known her killer and let the person inside.

It could have been Eileen, following up on their clandestine meeting, the one she'd lied to me about.

Would I open the door right now if the reporter knocked?

Not for all the tea in China.

I doubted Stephanie would have opened the door for Ron after the way he'd tried to manhandle her in that alley. She might have let me in, or for that matter, the newlyweds or the fiftieth-anniversary couple. If she hadn't felt under threat, she might have opened it for anyone. She could have answered a knock assuming Beau had forgotten his key.

I bit down on the chocolate-almond Kind bar. Perhaps Stephanie hadn't opened the door at all. That skinny porter had a key that unlocked both her room and mine.

I scooted to the far side of the couch, keeping an eye on the door. I wished I had a heavy piece of furniture to slide in front of it.

So I wasn't safe in my own compartment, or in anyone else's—lest they be a killer. And I could just as easily be attacked in an empty hallway.

My boyfriend and protector was busy safeguarding his barracuda of a mom and learning from the living, while my next move would be to risk life and limb to get back to the caboose, where I might or might not find a ghost.

"Oh, Frankie." I sighed.

How had this getaway gotten so complicated?

"What?" the gangster asked. His head popped out of the top drawer of the vanity, where I kept my unmentionables.

I leapt a foot in the air. "Frankie!" Of all the… "What are you doing in there?"

"Smoking," he said, his full body appearing in front of me, cigarette in hand. "Thinking. Small spaces are good for taking a load off." He took a drag. "Plus, I knew Molly wouldn't look for me in your personals." He flicked the ash off the end of his smoke. It disappeared on the way down to the floor. "Nice red teddy, by the way."

"Are you and Molly in some sort of fight?" I asked. He'd been trying to get closer to his girlfriend for days. What had changed?

"Nah," he said, making himself at home on the opposite side of the couch, elbow up to take another drag. "She's expecting some hero detective, and I don't know how to do that. So I'm lying low."

"You have to try," I insisted. "Your investigator buddy will get suspicious otherwise," I added, appealing to Frankie's sense of self-interest.

He raised his brows while taking another drag. "De Clercq will go off a bridge tomorrow. Besides, he can't figure it out. There was absolutely no motive. Everyone liked Emma, and the kid had no enemies, nobody who would want her dead."

"There's *always* a motive," I told him. "We just have to find it."

"You sound like De Clercq." Frankie shuddered. "All he's got is a scrap of paper he found under the body. It's got some kind of encrypted message. What am I supposed to do with that?"

I wasn't half-bad at puzzles. "Well," I said, "let me see."

He pulled a slip of paper from his pocket and placed it on the couch between us, then sat back and wedged a wing-tip shoe on the nice velvet.

"Foot off the couch," I said automatically, taking a good look at the ghostly paper. It wasn't a scrap. It was a very neat, although miniscule, note.

I knew better than to touch it. While I could handle objects from the ghostly plane, they felt uncomfortably cold and wet. Worse, my touch caused them to fade quickly. The detective had trusted Frankie to keep his clue in one piece.

The paper was no bigger than two postage stamps put together. It bore a scrawled message: *14/00 crow's nest.*

"It looks less like a code and more like a place," I told him. "I mean, the words are real words at least."

"So what does that tell us?" Frankie asked, unimpressed.

"The numbers could be room numbers, only the compartments only go up to 10 and there's no 00."

Frankie groaned and planted his foot back on the couch. "If you're going to point out the obvious, I'm going to hide somewhere else."

"Fine." We'd approach it from a different angle. "How many ghosts are on board right now other than you and the investigator?" I'd seen one in the dining room right after the train stopped. "Leave out the conductor for now." He wasn't involved as far as I could tell.

The mobster rubbed his chin. "Okay, then there's three ghosts who are back." He sat up, resting his elbows on his knees. "All from the original wreck. All of them knew the murdered girl, Emma Flores, who is gone now after reliving her death last night."

"Okay," I said, mimicking his pose. "Who do we have still on the train?"

"There's her sister, who shared her cabin. She's an heiress and quite the looker."

"And this impacts the case how?" I asked.

"I gotta pay attention to everything," he said. "There's some namby-pamby timber baron in compartment 8." He gave me a side look. "Oh, and I almost forgot the spinster from compartment 10."

"Are you joking?" I asked.

"No," he snapped. "Geez. I'm asking for help, here."

"Okay, so there are three suspects, plus the Green Lady."

"Oh, yeah," Frankie said. "I forgot about her."

Great. I could see exactly why De Clercq chose him over me.

I tried another tack. "I hear the Green Lady walks the halls after the passengers have turned in for the night. Have you met her?"

"Briefly. I tried to bum a smoke. She flicked my hat off my head and told me she didn't talk to fellas like me. She's a jerk."

It didn't matter. "We need to question the ghosts, see what they know. That will help us put together the events that took place on the night of the murder. We need to use all the evidence De Clercq has so far."

"This is the only clue we've got," he protested.

"All right." We'd make it work. "I need you to help me find the ghosts. Especially the Green Lady. She may know something about Stephanie's murder."

Frankie huffed. "Word has it she doesn't like the living."

"That's all right," I said, warming to my role. "Ghosts like me."

"You have a selective memory."

Okay, so some took a bit of work to get to know. "You'll help me talk to them. We'll get everybody chatting."

"It's like you enjoy this," he groused.

"Hey." I lifted a finger at him. "I'm trying to save these people."

"And I'm trying to impress my girl, but there's no time to interview all our suspects individually. And there are no other clues. Nothing else to do." His face fell. "Except hide out from De Clercq and let Molly watch me fail."

"I don't think sulking in my underwear drawer is the answer."

"It's a lost cause." He faced me, arms out to the sides. "I don't like it, either, but that's the reality. You and Molly think you can save the world. She expects me to be some hero cop, but I can't fix this. Nobody can."

I was getting fed up with his attitude. "We still have time," I insisted. Not much, but we could be efficient. "We'll just have to get them all together at once," I added, pacing the short area in front of the window. "We might even be able to read the situation better that way. Only my compartment is too small. The caboose is private—"

"See? Here's where you've got it all wrong. You're not thinking like a ghost," he said. "The Green Lady haunts the library. If we want a squirrely spirit like her talking, we gotta go where she's comfortable."

Good information. "See?" I asked. "This is why I need you."

He blew out a breath. "If we can pull this off, I'm aces," he said, shoving his hands into his pockets.

"We'll do it in the library," I said. It was secluded near the front of the train. I'd never seen anyone in there.

"Midnight," Frankie said, stamping out his cigarette onto my carpet.

"No. That's cutting it too close. We'll do it now."

He snorted like I'd asked him to the prom. "I gotta find every-body and let them know. Besides, it's quieter then, easier to haunt."

"Fine. Midnight," I said, facing him. "In the library."

He nodded, fading away. "I'll see you then."

CHAPTER 17

I spent the afternoon wondering about the clue Frankie had shown me. It was possible the killer had dropped the piece of paper next to the body by mistake. It could have belonged to the dead girl. Either way, I couldn't make sense of the message: *14/00 crow's nest.*

What crow's nest? We were on a train, not a ship.

I pondered the mystery while I also jumped at every noise I heard out in the hall. I didn't like being alone with a real live killer on the loose.

And when the sun had faded to streaks of orange and gold, and my compartment door rattled and edged open, I felt no shame in scrambling off the couch and greeting Ellis in a fighting position, with one kitten heel poised and ready to strike.

"It's you," I said, the fight draining out of me as I returned my weapon to my foot.

"Tough day?" he asked, sliding the door closed behind him.

How bad was it that he didn't even appear surprised?

"I'm so glad to see you," I said, attacking him with a hug. His chest felt rock solid under my cheek, and for the first time all day, I felt safe.

"I questioned everyone on board," he said, his voice vibrating against my ear. "Every last one of them claims to have an alibi."

"Dang," I said, lifting away from him. "How is that possible?"

He let out a frustrated sigh. "Half the alibis come from other passengers or crew members, who could be lying. Some people were just alone at the time. Sleeping, or so they said. Hard to argue when the killer struck overnight."

I moved to the couch and sat, smoothing my skirt under me. "What are we going to do?"

"We're going to keep at it," he said, taking a seat next to me, "and trust ourselves to catch a break." He rested an arm on the back of the couch. "Any luck with the spooks?"

Soon, I hoped. "We're gathering the ghosts tonight at the stroke of midnight. I'm helping Frankie solve the mystery of the murdered girl from the 1920s, and while I'm at it, I'm going to see if any of the ghosts can give us insight into Stephanie's death."

He tugged me close. "Want me to go?"

"Not for this." I didn't think the spirits would take kindly to us bringing more of the living. Some of them could be quite skittish. "You know what would help," I said, turning to face him, "if you could hang out in the hall and act as our lookout. That way, we won't be disturbed." I hesitated. "Of course, then you'd be alone in the hallway late at night with a murderer on the loose." I wouldn't forgive myself if something happened to him.

The corner of his mouth cocked up. "I can handle it," he said, gesturing to the spot at the small of his back.

He'd brought his police-issue gun on our vacation, which I'd deemed cute on the drive to Kingstree. Now, I was quite glad Ellis was always prepared.

"Frankie showed me a clue this afternoon," I said, "for the ghostly murder, not Stephanie. Neither one of us could figure it out." I told him about the slip of paper found with the body. "14/00 crow's nest. It's a strange message."

"It is." Ellis leaned back, running a hand over his mouth. "All it tells us is that a meeting likely took place at fourteen hundred hours in the cupola of the caboose," he said, "so we'd need to know why—"

"Wait. Hold it." I grabbed his arm. "How did you get that from what I said?"

"Well, I'm assuming somebody did a slash instead of a few dots in order to camouflage a time for a secret meeting," he said. "I could be wrong, but if they're giving a location, then it makes sense they'd give a time."

"The caboose does have a little top on it," I said, amazed at how quickly he'd made it make sense.

"Probably a small upper floor used as an observation area. Hence the term crow's nest," he reasoned.

"Of course." Dang. If he was right, this could be big. I gave him a big kiss on the cheek. "You should be a police officer."

He grinned. "It's like it was meant to be."

I settled back against the cushions next to him. "So either our killer or our victim—"

"Or both," Ellis interjected.

I nodded. "One or both had a secret meeting at 2:00 p.m. in the caboose. Most likely on the day of the murder, since the note was found with the body." I looked to him. "I don't know what to do with that."

"Find ghostly evidence," he supplied.

"I am good at that," I said wryly.

And as if I'd said "Beetlejuice" three times (which I would never, because who knows what would show up?) Frankie took form directly in front of us.

"That's brilliant!" he exclaimed. "I'm on it!"

The things that ghost would do to impress a girl. "I'll go with you," I said, standing.

Frankie held a hand up. "You're staying here. I'm getting Molly and De Clercq, and they're both gonna watch me crack this case wide open."

"Frankie," I admonished. I didn't trust him in that cupola. "Who's the real detective here?"

"He is," he said, pointing at Ellis.

Fair enough. But it would take De Clercq two minutes to discover Frankie didn't know clues from spiderwebs. "Listen to me—"

The gangster pointed a warning finger at me. "You steal my glory and I swear I'll be so depressed I'll camp in here all night."

Lord in heaven. Not that. The quicker he stopped popping up in our compartment, the better. Besides, if I wanted him to grow, I'd have to give him room to do it. "Fine," I said. He was a smart guy. Mostly. And he'd seen me look for clues plenty of times. "See what you can find and report back."

He gave me a salute, which was not what detectives did, but before I could even think to explain it, he'd disappeared.

~

NATURALLY, Frankie didn't report back.

"How long does it take to check a small room?" I asked, tempted to go find him.

"Let him go," Ellis instructed. "He may be doing better than you think."

"Have you met Frankie?" I asked.

"Actually, no." Ellis handed me a bottle of sweet tea from the mini bar. "He was before my time." And Ellis couldn't see ghosts.

But his meaning was clear. And Ellis had a point. We needed to hang tight and focus on what we could control. At the moment, it wasn't much.

So we ordered room service and had a picnic dinner on the floor of our compartment. He needed to unwind after the difficult day, and perhaps find a new perspective on his case. I needed to let go of the idea that Frankie had blown his cover and was soon to be under house arrest with me for all of eternity.

We talked, we told stories about Lucy—we both missed that furry little skunk—and then Ellis distracted me in the best way possible. For a few hours, I nearly forgot what we were about to face—until the alarm on Ellis's watch sounded.

He clicked it off, while I opted to bury my face against his shoulder. "Eleven thirty," he announced. "Time to go."

"I regret telling you to set it so early."

"Nah, you were smart," he said, running a hand through my hair. "It'll be good to scope out the library before the meeting."

It would. I forced myself to sit up and smooth my dress.

I was curious why the Green Lady haunted the library. Was it merely the place she'd been when she died, or had I missed something upon my initial inspection of the space?

Ellis pushed off the floor and reached down to give me a hand. "You're thinking pretty loud down there."

I let him pull me up. "If Frankie doesn't show up, I won't know if he's irresponsible or under arrest."

"If he's not there, we do it on our own," Ellis said, planting a kiss on my forehead.

We stepped out into the hall. I ran my fingers through my mussed hair and looked both ways.

"Nobody out and about," I murmured, "dead or alive."

"Speaking for the living," Ellis hedged, "I don't think anyone is in the mood after what happened today."

He hesitated as we passed compartment 9.

"Where's Beau staying tonight?" Ellis wouldn't have let him back in the room, not without calling in a local evidence team first.

"With our mother," Ellis said, continuing on.

Well, that would dampen any party boy's night.

We made our way up through the train. On what should be a night of intimate dinners and celebration, we found the social cars deserted and the bar closed down. An eerie silence had settled over the train, like the calm before the storm.

I didn't like it. It was more than just people turning in early.

The observation car lay dark, the moonlight glowing through the exposed glass, casting odd shadows as the train raced head-long through the wilderness toward its ghostly demise.

Security lights glowed dully against the walls. I hastened through the abandoned car, as if one of the shadows behind us would reach out and grab me at any moment.

"You okay?" Ellis called after me as I plunged into the darkness between cars.

"Fine," I breathed out, feeling his presence right behind me.

At least I hoped and prayed that was him.

Then I pushed out into the shadowy library car beyond and stopped short. A ghostly glow radiated from behind the half-closed door.

It seemed we hadn't arrived first, after all.

"This is it," I whispered.

Ellis placed a hand on my shoulder, letting me know he understood.

A woman in a kimono stood with her back to us, running her fingertips over a shelf of titles. Her image glowed a smoky green at the edges in a way I'd never seen on any other spirit. Most ghosts lost their color as they aged, and even though her image had faded to shades of gray and black, the dusky green tinge clung to her like an extension of her very nature.

Her dark hair was woven in a series of intricate knots. Polished, dark wood bookshelves surrounded her on three sides, and it appeared as if she was searching for a particular tome.

According to the ghost conductor, the Green Lady haunted the library. It could be that she'd died here when the train crashed into the river. Many ghosts felt a special connection to the place where they'd met their end. I could actually see traces of spectral energy, or soul traces, from spirits who had recently departed. But those spots faded over time and would be long gone in this case.

She paused, and I held my breath, trying to remain undetected.

The Green Lady glanced over her shoulder, and I pulled away from the door. But not before I saw her face.

I'd half-expected a Japanese woman, given the kimono. Or perhaps I just hadn't expected *her*.

Sharp cheekbones, piercing dark eyes, and an angular nose combined to form an arresting beauty reminiscent of old Hollywood. But she was no young ingénue. She'd lived, that much was written on her features. She couldn't have been older than thirty when she died, yet she wore her worldliness like armor.

She slowly turned back to the bookshelf, and I let out a silent sigh of relief.

The ghost pulled a book from the shelf and turned away, appearing to read with great interest for only a few short moments. She returned the book to its place and stood in front of it, hands clasped in front of her, as if on guard.

I tried to memorize the spot. Third shelf from the top, shoulder height, gray glowing book with scripted lettering down the side. Fifteenth...maybe sixteenth from the right. Either way, I'd find it.

Perhaps the Green Lady hadn't died in the library after all. Perhaps this was her hiding spot.

"Ellis?" Virginia's voice sounded from the hall behind me. "What are you doing?"

"Mom, you're up," Ellis said in a loud whisper, obviously trying to keep it down. "Let's go somewhere else."

Virginia's voice drew closer. "Of course I'm up. I'm working. Why are you outside my office?"

My heart sank as the Green Lady disappeared.

I turned. Virginia stood directly behind me, scowling.

"Well?" she prodded, as if I owed her the explanation.

"I was observing a ghost," I said, keeping my voice low in case the Green Lady was around to overhear.

"You—" Virginia began. Then understanding dawned. "*Ohh...*" She had the grace to appear slightly chagrined as she glanced from me to Ellis. "Well, keep at it," she ordered. "I'll be in my office." She turned toward her small office located next to the library.

"Mom, you really can't," Ellis said, as if he were expecting an argument.

Virginia hesitated. "Fine," she snapped. "I'll be in my compartment." She waved a hand. "With your snoring brother."

That was more like it.

"Just make it worth my while," she instructed.

"I'll try," I told her, biting my tongue. There was no use lecturing her on what she'd done. It wouldn't bring my ghost back.

I turned back toward the library and sighed. Her interruption had come at the worst possible time. It had appeared as if the Green Lady had been in the middle of something important.

Then again, while I had the place to myself, I was going to determine exactly what was so special about that book.

"Come on." I motioned to Ellis. "Before your mom popped up, the Green Lady was here. I'm going to see what she was doing." I hated to touch the ghost book. Ghostly objects that I handled tended to disappear shortly after. But I needed to know what was in there, and it wouldn't be gone forever. The ghosts could conjure it back at any time.

"You look," he said, backing out. "I'm guarding the hall."

Right. Anyone else wandering the darkened train might not be as friendly or as loud as Virginia.

I snorted at the idea of Virginia being the baseline for friendly.

"What?" Ellis asked from the hall.

"Nothing," I mused, counting down from the right side of the bookshelf.

And just when I'd located the volume in question—*Sir Charles Fouchet's Study of West Indian Botany*—I was interrupted by the sharp slap of a hand against wood.

Virginia... Dang it. Ellis said he'd keep her under control.

I turned and saw Inspector De Clercq standing in the doorway, glaring daggers at me.

Oh, well, no wonder Ellis hadn't seen him.

The detective's moustache twitched as he stared me down in some sort of old-fashioned power play, evidently waiting for me to make the first move.

"Hi," I said as cheerfully as I could. If I couldn't beat 'im at surprise hand-slapping, I'd kill him with kindness.

He wasn't amused.

Well, I wasn't, either. He was dead wrong if he thought I was going to let him dismiss me or intimidate me. I was on his side, and it would be nice if he started acting that way. We had less than twenty-four hours before the ghost train went off the bridge, and we didn't have time for him to sell me short because I was a live woman instead of a dead man.

De Clercq strolled into the library with precise, measured steps. "Miss Long," he said, clipping each syllable.

"Verity," I suggested.

"Officer Lawson told me about you."

"He'll always be Frankie to me."

De Clercq twirled the tip of his moustache. "He said you like to meddle."

More like solve everything, but who was keeping track?

He stopped in front of me. "I don't like meddlers. And I don't like the living."

I held my ground. "Frankie is expecting me to be here."

He glared at me, his eye sockets growing hollow, sinking down into his skin until I could see the bone of his skull. Holy cripes.

"Inspector!" a man called out a friendly greeting from the door.

A handsome ghost in a black suit stood in the doorway, looking stiff in a starched white collar and a tie. I guessed he was in his late thirties, with styled black hair and intelligent eyes. He escorted a gorgeous young blonde in a long silk dress that hugged every curve, yet still managed to appear classy and modest. This must be the older sister of the girl who had died in compartment 9. I saw some resemblance to the dead girl and to my own appearance. However, this woman's features were more defined, her look more polished. She wore a feather in her hair and clung to her man like he was the last cookie in the box.

"Monsieur Ward," the inspector said, with a slight tilt to the head. "Mademoiselle Flores." He lost the civility when Frankie drew up behind the couple. "Detective Lawson."

No telling what Frankie had done to get on De Clercq's bad side.

Leave it to Frankie not to notice.

"Hey, we're all here," the gangster said, clearly forgetting about both the Green Lady and the spinster.

"I'm very interested to learn what the inspectors have found," Mr. Ward said, eyeing our little party of detectives.

Mr. Ward escorted Miss Flores to a plush chair next to the table with a bust of Edgar Allen Poe. Meanwhile Frankie strolled up to De Clercq and me like he owned the place.

The inspector frowned. "Detective Lawson, I told you there would be no living souls at this gathering."

Frankie shrugged. "I'm training the next generation. You ever have a protégé?" He stood next to me. "Well, you're looking at mine."

Oh brother.

De Clercq didn't seem to believe it, either.

"You said it yourself." Frankie clapped the inspector on the shoulder. "Astute observation. A study of the clues. Our great methods are dying out. We need to pass them down. How else is this kid going to learn?"

"Her?" De Clercq said, as if it were impossible. "You picked one of the living," he clarified, as if I were a table or a piece of dead fish.

I swallowed my pride and went for it. I gestured to Frankie.

"This man is a truly great teacher and a great thinker," I said, trying to sound sincere.

He was certainly teaching me how to BS.

Frankie, at least, seemed pleased. He clasped his hands in front of him and addressed the inspector. "You called me in on this case because you've been unable to solve it. We agreed you would try my methods. Need I remind you that I've already offered stellar insight on a major clue?"

That was all Ellis, but I wasn't about to argue if it meant I'd be on the case.

The gangster glanced toward the ceiling, and I saw a glistening orb. It danced a greeting when it noticed my attention.

Molly.

He'd better not be showing off for his girl. Oh, who was I kidding? Frankie did everything for Molly these days.

I just had to hope he'd stay focused on the mystery as well.

"Let us begin," Frankie said. And just then, the Green Lady shimmered into being slightly behind me, in the same spot she'd been before.

I'd give anything to know why she was interested in that particular book.

Frankie opened his hands wide. "We are here to solve a murder most foul," he said, addressing the room. "We've returned to this train so that your souls may finally rest." He looked out over the gathered spirits. "Each of you is tied somehow to the death of young Emma Flores found murdered in compartment 9." Behind him, Emma's sister choked back a sob. "May we discover the truth tonight, and may the truth set us free."

"Lovely speech," I said, even if it was mostly borrowed. "May I suggest we conduct individual interviews—" I wasn't so sure how any person, living or dead, would react to being called out in front of a crowd.

"Silence, young one!" Frankie commanded. Clearly, he'd missed his calling in community theater.

And I'd made a mistake letting him watch *Clue* with me.

"We have Miss Flores"—he gestured to the plush chair where the blonde sat—"sister of the poor victim." She pulled out a handkerchief and dabbed her eyes. "We have her fiancé, president and founder of the Sugarland Lumber Company, Mr. Charles Ward." The man stood behind the distraught blonde and gave a sharp nod. "And finally..." Frankie swung around and pointed directly at me. "The spinster from compartment 10."

"Don't call me a spinster," I told him. I wasn't even a suspect. Really, this was too much.

"Not you, her," Frankie said, pointing to the Green Lady behind me.

"Oh," I said, glancing over my shoulder. It still wasn't very nice.

The Green Lady remained in her spot and shot a hostile look at Frankie.

"I've given that look to him plenty of times," I told her. "It doesn't work." The gangster hadn't even noticed.

"This murder has gone unsolved for more than eighty years," Frankie said, beginning a slow walk around the room. "I'm a special detective with the St. Louis office, and Inspector De Clercq asked me here to take another look at the only clue we have." He whipped out a piece of paper so fast I thought he was going to fling it over his shoulder. "A note! Found with the body!"

Mr. Ward's eyes widened, and his fiancée sniffled loudly behind her handkerchief.

That's it, I was never letting him watch old mystery movies with me again.

I studied the suspects and saw Mr. Ward's hostility, his fiancée's distress, and...I glanced behind me...the Green Lady was a blank.

Still, what Frankie was doing seemed to be working. He had the attention of the ghosts, at least.

Frankie waved the note at Mr. Ward. "This note spoke of a

crow's nest and gave us the location of a secret meeting place and time, a rendezvous with a killer," the mobster announced.

Ms. Flores reached up and took Mr. Ward's hand. The Green Lady pursed her lips.

I didn't know how he could possibly surmise that the killer hid out in the crow's nest.

"It led me to a small room above the caboose." He held a finger up. "And there I found a clue that gives us the undisputed identity of *the one,* the killer among us!"

The Green Lady gasped. Mr. Ward appeared distinctly uncomfortable, and Miss Flores crumpled into a flood of tears.

Frankie nodded to the stoic De Clercq and then whipped out a ghostly handkerchief. "This! With the initials CW." He pointed to the lumber baron. "Your initials, Mr. Ward!"

The industrialist inspected the handkerchief Frankie held with barely contained scorn. "That's a woman's handkerchief, Detective Lawson."

Frankie's eyes widened a bit. "Huh." He took a second look and ran his fingers over the lace edging. "It is kind of girly.

"Then it was you," he said, pointing at the Green Lady. "You've been looking guilty this whole time. And if I'm not mistaken, your given name is actually Clara! You go by the term 'Green Lady' to hide your true identity!"

She brought a hand to her chest. "My name," she said, in a clear, soft voice, "is Clara Elizabeth Bolton. And my initials are CEB." She notched her chin up. "You call me the 'Green Lady' and I like it about as much as I like the term 'spinster.'"

"I'm sorry," I told her. I'd been calling her the Green Lady this whole time without a second thought. "We should have known better," I said on behalf of all the living and the dead. It had to be hard to be renamed by people who didn't even know you, and don't even get me started on being called a spinster. She wasn't much older than I was.

"It's bad enough I boarded this train with no standing, no reliable funds or support," she fumed. "I don't need to be belittled in death."

"I agree," I told her, vowing to be more sensitive in the future.

Frankie appeared slightly confused at this turn of events. Then he gave a sharp nod. "So be it." He raised a brow. "That leaves us with..." He turned slowly. "Miss Flores, loving sister, and killer!"

"That's insane," Mr. Ward shouted.

"The inspector has no idea!" the Green Lady—I mean Miss Bolton—cried.

Miss Flores glared at the gangster, tears streaming down her cheeks. "Don't accuse me of hurting my sister. I loved her."

Frankie threw up his hands. "Well, one of you had to have done it." He turned to De Clercq. "Unless it was you."

The inspector stiffened. "It was not," he said hotly. "This is over."

"You're just going to give up?" Mr. Ward stormed toward Frankie and De Clercq. The three of them shouted while Miss Bolton maintained her vigil in front of the books and Miss Flores sobbed. "I loved my sister. I'd never hurt her."

I approached the young ghost as gently as I could. "What's your name, dear?" I asked, crouching down next to her.

She hiccupped and let out a loud sniff. "Bernadette Carter Flores."

"Those are not the initials from the hankie," Frankie declared. "Which is how I know *he* did it!" Frankie said, whirling and pointing to Mr. Ward. "I was right the first time. You, sir, own a girly handkerchief, and you are a killer!"

"This is ridiculous," I told him.

"I should never have allowed it," the inspector fumed. "The inspectors in the St. Louis office are hotheads, every last one of them."

"Everyone calm down," I ordered. We weren't going to solve anything this way.

"I never owned a handkerchief like that one," Mr. Ward

insisted, turning to me this time. "It's not mine."

"I'm sorry to put you through this," I told him and his fiancée as well. He'd obviously been a great support to her during this awful time. I couldn't imagine how horrible it would be to lose a sister like that. I didn't know if I could go on if I'd found Melody stabbed. "You have my deepest sympathies."

"Thank you," Miss Flores said, her eyes swimming with tears.

The men went back to blaming, and I stayed with the young socialite.

"It was her first train trip," she said. "Emma was so excited."

I rested a hand on the arm of her chair. "My sister and I took the train to Nashville together the week before she left for college. It was wonderful," I told her. "I'll never forget it."

"When they found her, she was wearing the fox stole I'd let her borrow," she said quietly. "She loved that stole." A tear rolled down her cheek. "It was my favorite, too."

"Oh, honey." I wished so badly that I could hug her.

She lowered her gaze and then raised it back to me. "Charlie's telling the truth, you know. That handkerchief with the initials, that's a sweetheart gift. You can tell by the lace edging and the way the initials are inscribed." She dabbed at her nose with her own lace-edged hankie. "I can tell you with one hundred percent certainty that I never made him a handkerchief like that, and he has no one else." She gave a weak smile. "We were engaged on this trip."

A tingle ran up my spine. "Congratulations," I said as warmly as I could with the ice-cold trepidation running through my veins. "Can you tell me when he proposed?"

She seemed pleased at the question. "At dinner." Her smile dried up. "Last night, before...before Emma died. She was so happy for me."

"I'm sure she was," I said.

And if I was right about what was in that book, I knew who did it.

CHAPTER 18

The gathering ended in chaos, but that was fine. I had a clear picture of what I needed to do.

I was almost glad when Mr. Ward stormed out, with Miss Flores on his heels. The Green Lady—Miss Bolton—took up vigil by the bookcase while Frankie huddled with the inspector by the door, speaking in urgent tones. I had no idea what the mobster-in-hiding was trying to pull now, but it ended up working out all right. De Clercq shot me one final dirty look before fading away. And once she saw she was alone with us, the Green Lady disappeared as well.

I'd have liked to have the inspector back, but you couldn't have everything.

Frankie cracked his shoulders, like he could dislodge De Clercq's watchful gaze, and strode over to me. "Can you believe it?" he asked, cocking a thumb over his shoulder. "That guy just hinted that I might not be a real detective."

"You're not a real detective," I reminded him.

"Hey, I'm doing the job. You see me." He shoved his hands into his pockets. "I just don't appreciate anybody thinking I might be anything but a hundred percent honest."

"You must get that a lot," I said.

He shot me a dirty look.

I let it go.

Worry tickled the back of my neck. I didn't mind so much about Frankie's view of himself as the good-to-his-word mobster, but we needed to keep him safely undercover until we could free De Clercq and the rest of the ghosts. Or until the ghost train plummeted into the river tomorrow. I really didn't want to see that happen.

"Just be careful around De Clercq," I warned. The inspector might be anti-woman and anti-living, but he was no fool. And if Frankie ended up under house arrest at my place for eternity...I shuddered to think about it.

Frankie turned his attention to the hovering orb in the corner. "Molly, sweetheart, can you give us a second?"

The orb dropped sharply then shot out of the room. I wondered how she didn't get dizzy doing that, but I'd say one thing for Molly—she didn't waste time.

The gangster turned back to me. "We really gotta solve this murder. I can't last another day with De Clercq."

Good thing he had me, and Ellis for leading us here in the first place.

"This way," I said, walking him over to the bookshelf.

"De Clercq needs to believe I'm the real deal," Frankie continued, "and besides, after seeing everybody tonight"—he gave a small wince—"I feel kind of sorry for that murdered girl and the spirits who are trapped on this train, reliving the same tragedy over and over." He shivered at the thought. "That's worse than living with you."

"Thanks," I said, stopping near the right-hand corner of the library. "Pull this book off the shelf," I said, pointing to *Sir Charles Fouchet's Study of West Indian Botany.* "Show me what's hidden inside."

He gave me an odd look, but he didn't hesitate. Frankie drew the ghostly book from the shelf and opened it. Tucked inside the cover page was an ethereal leaf of paper precisely folded in the middle.

"That's it," I said. She'd been hiding correspondence in the book.

The mobster opened the folded note and held it between us.

The flowing script read *01/00 Library.*

"I knew it," I whispered. Well, not the time and place, but I'd known what we'd find. I checked my watch. It read 12:48. "In twelve minutes, we'll have the proof we need."

The gangster cleared his throat, his discomfort audible even over the rumbling of the train. "What did we just find?" he asked, putting away his pride.

I glanced toward the open doorway. "Are we alone?"

Frankie paused, feeling for the energy of other ghosts. "Yeah."

"Clara Bolton killed Emma Flores," I told him.

"Yes! Of course!" Frankie exclaimed. He quickly ran out of steam. "Why?"

"If I'm right—and we'll find out soon—it was a case of mistaken identity." I walked toward the plush chair on the other side of the library, reasoning it out as I spoke. "Clara Bolton, otherwise known as the Green Lady, was Charlie Ward's lover. I'm assuming it had been going on for years. Why else would a woman in that day and age never marry?"

"Didn't meet the right guy?" Frankie shrugged.

I turned. "You and I both know it didn't work that way almost a hundred years ago." I placed a hand on the back of the chair, like Charlie Ward had done. "Clara Bolton is exotic, beautiful. But she admitted she had no social standing or money. Yet she could afford a private sleeper on this luxury train, very close to the lumber baron's room."

"Why not right next to it?" Frankie countered.

"Too obvious," I told him. "The two were better off meeting in secret—in the cupola of the caboose, in the library, where they hid notes for each other in Sir Charles's *Study of Botany*." I ran a hand over the back of the chair where his unwitting fiancée had sat. "I'm betting Miss Flores never suspected." She'd seemed comfortable. Trusting. Kept.

From all appearances, she appeared to truly care for her fiancé. She'd certainly defended him back there. Or at least, she'd tried. "I'm assuming she had position and money," I added. Frankie had called her an heiress.

"He wanted the girl with the money and the family, and the girl with the—"

"Watch it, Frankie." I suspected Clara Bolton had loved Charlie Ward, enough to put aside her life, take a position in the shadows, and sneak any bit of time she could with him. No wonder she'd haunted the library. It was her last, best tie to him. "He probably told Clara that the debutante meant nothing to him."

Frankie slapped a hand on his thigh. "But then he proposed to Miss Flores right in front of Clara and everyone."

"At dinner, and after a secret rendezvous in the caboose, no less." I hoped he'd at least broken the news to poor Clara before he asked another woman to marry him, but if she'd been mad enough to kill…

"Clara had given her life—or at least her future and her chance at marriage—to a man who would only want her as a mistress, at best. He made that clear in the dining car that day, in front of everyone, and didn't even give her a chance to respond."

"So Clara ambushed Miss Flores that night and killed her," Frankie concluded, as if the murder made perfect sense.

"But she killed the wrong Miss Flores," I said. De Clercq had been correct. "No one had a motive to kill Emma Flores. Only Emma looked a lot like her sister, Bernadette—especially from behind, wearing Bernadette's favorite fox fur."

"She could have stolen the key from her lover," Frankie said.

"She would have had to." I nodded. "Clara couldn't risk a direct confrontation, not in a small train compartment where sound carries. She had to take her victim by surprise." So she'd wrapped her hands around poor Emma's neck, subdued her, and then stabbed her in the back. "Poor Emma didn't have a chance. She was in the wrong place at the wrong time."

"Dang." Frankie blew out a breath. "I've been in that spot a time or two."

The grief Bernadette Flores displayed had been real. She'd lost her sister and she didn't know why. It had drawn her back as strongly as Ward's guilt had trapped him. He must have realized Clara had resorted to murder.

Emma had relived her murder back in compartment 9, unable to change the past or escape her fate. While Clara was trapped and turned smoky green at the edges, unable to escape her envy or helplessness.

It was so sad, so unnecessary.

Frankie shot me a cocky grin, and I was about to tell him to put a sock in it when a shot rang out from the doorway.

The mobster dropped like a rock.

I spun and saw Clara Bolton's snarl as she aimed her revolver at me next.

Cripes. I was tuned in to her world, which meant a bullet could kill me.

"Stop!" I cried, diving for the plush chair. Her shot hit the bookshelf that had been right behind me, spitting wood shards and debris. "Help, she's got a gun!"

"Verity?" Ellis charged into the room, but he couldn't do anything against a ghost. He couldn't even see her.

"Get the police!" I hollered.

"I am the police," Ellis countered, frantically searching for a way to help.

I stared from behind the chair as Clara walked straight through him, toward me. She took deadly aim and fired.

I ducked, and a bullet took off the top of the chair above my head. Goose-down stuffing rained down.

"Inspector!" I hollered. "De Clercq!" He'd get her. He'd arrest her.

Maybe too late for me.

"Stop!" I cried in final desperation as Clara rounded the plush chair and aimed just as the bust of Poe swung from out of nowhere and shattered against her head.

Clara went down like a load of bricks, and I dropped to the floor. I rolled to the other side of the chair, ready to scramble to my feet and make a break for the door, when I saw Molly's face hovering above me.

"I got her!" The petite ghost pumped a fist. She glared back at the fallen Clara. "How dare you shoot my man in the head, you tart."

I leaned back on my elbows, staring up at her. "You sure she's down?"

"Yes," Molly said, with relish. "Not bad for my first time."

Clara lay knocked out on the floor, glowing red, her hair falling from its elaborate coiffure.

"Not bad at all," I told her, trying to sit up and then giving up on it. "Heavens to Betsy. I almost died."

She nodded. "It's not so bad."

"Verity." Ellis rushed to my side and helped me sit straight. "Are you all right?"

"I am now," I said, letting him help me off the floor and onto the damaged chair. It looked all right in the mortal world.

"I didn't want to get too close and block you in," Ellis said, "but dang. You scared me."

"Me too," I told him.

"Poor dear," Molly said, rushing to Frankie, who lay several feet away on the floor.

He'd been shot in the forehead. Again.

"He's not dead," I rushed to tell her. "In fact, he and his old gang have shoot-outs for sport. He'll only be out for an hour or two."

"I know." She gently touched the gaping bullet hole in his forehead, very near to the one he wore all the time. She brushed a lock of hair off his forehead. "He tells me more than you think." She gave a small smile. "In his own way."

I was glad that it worked for them. "Thanks for sticking around," I said. If she hadn't been close, I'd have been a goner.

Molly nodded. She sat and rested Frankie's head in her lap, still playing with his hair and smoothing her fingers over his skin.

"You'd better grab the gun," Ellis said, "ghostly or not. Until De Clercq gets her into custody, Clara is dangerous."

He had a point. "How did you even follow what just happened?" I asked, standing on shaky legs.

Ellis reached out to support me. "I listened."

Her revolver had skittered away when she dropped it. I found it several feet from the chair, in front of the bookshelves. "Wait." I stopped just short of the gray, glowing revolver. "I can't touch it. Not the killer's fingerprinted gun. That'll make it fade away, and that's evidence."

By Ellis's pained expression, I could tell he agreed.

"I'll take it from here," De Clercq said from the doorway. Then he saw Frankie down. "Oh no."

"Frankie will be all right. He solved the mystery," I told him. And then I proceeded to tell him how.

"De Clercq wants to give Frankie a commendation and a medal," I said to Ellis an hour later as we made our way back toward our compartment.

"Aren't you worried that might expose him?" Ellis asked.

"Frankie will mess it up before that happens," I said, confident in the gangster's ability to tick off De Clercq, despite freeing the inspector from his last case in this life and the next.

Ellis closed the door to the car that held the library, and we passed through the rocking darkness of the space between cars.

Clara had woken up and confessed everything to the inspector. The fateful night had gone down exactly as I'd suspected, except for the fact that Clara was convinced her lover's fiancée was more practical than passionate when it came to Charles Ward. Either way, Bernadette had been innocent of it all, along with her sister, who had paid the ultimate price.

Ellis opened the door to the observation car, and I stopped short when I saw Bernadette Flores sitting in the front row, her hands clasped around the handkerchief in her lap, her gray evening gown flowing against her legs as if swept in an ethereal breeze.

I reached back and touched Ellis on the shoulder. "Can you give me a minute in here?" I asked, stepping into the car.

"Um, sure," he said, hesitating only slightly. "Call me if you need me," he added, staying in the space between and sliding the door closed behind me.

Ellis was the one who deserved a medal.

I approached the ghost cautiously. Even though she wasn't the killer, she was here for a reason. I had a feeling she'd been waiting for me.

"Do you know what just happened?" I asked gently.

She gave a small nod. "Thank you." Her eyes remained swollen from tears, but she kept her composure. "After all these years, it's good to finally *know.*"

I took a chance and sat next to her. "I'm sorry it had to happen that way."

She pressed her lips together tightly. "Emma was the light of my life. Our parents were never around. They were always too busy with one society gathering or another. She's my world."

"You'll see her again," I assured her.

"I can feel her growing strong again," she confessed, with barely restrained joy. "She's free now, you know. So am I." She smiled.

"I'm so glad." Moments like this made it all worth it.

Her eyes darted to her lap and she blinked hard. "Charlie saw her attack you." She twisted her rings on her fingers. "He didn't help. He came back to me and confessed it all. He begged for my forgiveness." She looked me in the eye. "I gave it because I want to move on."

"Good for you," I told her. "You don't need him anymore."

"I don't." She looked out at the stars blanketing the night. "He's already gone from the train, and I say good riddance." She turned back to me. "I'll be leaving soon and taking my sister with me. But first, I have to show you something."

"Whatever's holding you back, let it go." Or else she could be on this train when it went over. She didn't need to die again. "It's time to go to the light."

"This will only take a moment," she assured me. "You want to know what happened with the other murder in compartment 9. I was there right after it happened."

Oh, my word. "Did you see the killer?"

"No, but I saw the woman's spirit rise from the train. I was afraid it might be Emma again. When I went to investigate, I found a different girl's body and...I can't describe it exactly. Would you mind if I showed you?"

"Please," I urged.

This ghost, this insight, might give me the missing piece I needed to finally learn what had happened to Stephanie. Then we could arrest the killer and at last be safe in our own beds.

"It was like this." Bernadette stood, her attention focused on the floor at the front of the observation car.

I watched as she conjured up a vision of Stephanie's body. It appeared as I remembered it. She lay like a fallen rag doll, her cheek pressed to the carpet. She'd been stabbed in the back, the knife buried deep, the dark blood seeping out onto the floor.

It was exactly as I'd seen before. And then I noticed a single difference.

I stepped closer to get a better look at an impression in the blood. A single faint footprint made by a lady's high-heeled shoe.

"Are you sure this was there right after this woman was killed?" I asked the ghost. I had to know for certain.

Bernadette drew next to me, so close I could feel the chill of the ghost. "This is the scene exactly as it was when I saw it."

The killer must have returned to wipe it away. Or maybe the pool of blood had overrun the footprint. It still existed on the ghostly plane, however, just as Bernadette had witnessed it.

"Thank you," I said to her.

"Use it," she urged, her image glittering with a gorgeous silver light. She began to rise. "Find justice," she said, leaving me behind. "Make it right. Just like you did for me."

"I will," I promised.

I hoped.

"Wait." She hesitated. "I can't leave without my sister." As she spoke those words, a glittering golden light surrounded Bernadette and she began to cry. "Oh, my goodness. It's you, isn't it? Emma." Tears streamed down her face in relief and recognition as she reached out and touched the glowing mist. The light surged and grew stronger. "I've got you. I'll never let you go again," Bernadette promised. "Now let's go home."

I watched in wonder as, together, they rose up through the glass of the roof and up into the night sky until I couldn't see them any longer.

I turned back to the scene on the floor, memorizing it as it too faded into nothing.

The killer was a woman.

All right. There were only four other women on the train. One was Virginia, whom I dismissed immediately. If she were one for killing girlfriends, she'd have done me in long ago. The newlywed Madison was far too petite to have worn the shoe in question, and Barbara Danvers, the other half of the fiftieth-anniversary couple, was even smaller than Madison.

That left the journalist, Eileen Powers. And my friend, Mary Jo Abel.

CHAPTER 19

J had to figure out which woman made that footprint. The shoe might still have blood on it. Even if it was only a trace, Ellis could link it to the murder scene. Even if it didn't, if we could find the shoe, we'd know who killed Stephanie.

I was just about to return to Ellis and tell him the news when the ghostly conductor shimmered into view directly in my path.

"Excuse me," I said, barely dodging him.

"My apologies." He removed his black cap. "I'm not quite myself." He ran his fingers over the embroidered Sugarland Express script above the brim. "I didn't think you could save us. I didn't expect…" He broke off. "Thank you, Verity. You've done more than I could ever have imagined to protect my passengers. You freed us from this train."

"I'm so glad I could be here," I said, meaning every word. If I'd understood what I was getting into, if I'd let him warn me off, I might have had a vacation with Ellis in Kingstree, but I wouldn't have had the privilege of helping these ghosts find peace.

"Mr. Ward has moved on," he said earnestly. "The Flores sisters, as well." He looked past me to the place where Bernadette had been. "Those sweet girls will no longer suffer. Young Emma is free."

"What about Clara Bolton?" I asked. The Green Lady might not deserve a happy ending, but she shouldn't be trapped here, forced to relive her death. Nobody deserved that.

He grew somber. "Clara Bolton is gone," he said, "although not to a better place." He appeared uncomfortable, turning the hat over in his hands. "She's imprisoned herself in a place other ghosts have abandoned. I suppose I understand. She's going to be very lonely, though."

She'd sentenced herself in the afterlife. I wondered when it would end for the Green Lady. I could free her from suffering on the Sugarland Express, but not from the punishment she inflicted upon herself.

"What about you?" I asked the conductor, the man who'd started all of this.

He returned his hat to his head. "I'm leaving soon. I just saw the inspector off and told him I'd warn you."

That didn't sound good. "I've already stuck my nose into his investigation." And helped solve the case. "What does he have to warn me about now?"

"My dear, you've lost track of time." He drew his watch from his vest and clicked it open. "This train will plunge off the Holston River bridge in—" he studied the clock face "—seven minutes, and you're still very much attached to this world."

"No. Wait. That happens tomorrow." He'd said it himself.

"It is tomorrow. Very early, but still. The train goes over the bridge at precisely 1:17 a.m." He kept an eye on the watch. "You have six minutes now."

"*Six* minutes?" I stammered, my chest tightening. Why had he felt the need to warn me? "I'm on the mortal train." Only I'd crossed into the ghosts' world as well.

And then it occurred to me: When I was tuned in like this,

ghostly bullets could kill me. Therefore, so could the accident that doomed the original Sugarland Express.

I brought a hand to my mouth. "Sweet Jesus."

The conductor gave a solemn nod. "My train will split from the mortal train just before we reach the old rail bridge. You must not be attached to the ghostly realm when that happens. The steel walls of the original Sugarland Express will pass straight through your ghost friends. They don't have physical form. But those same walls will crush you."

"But those are ghost walls." Not real walls. Except, so long as I held Frankie's energy, they might as well be real to me. I'd thought our biggest problem was the phantom train nose-diving into the river with its original passengers on board—not flattening me on the way when its path diverged from the modern track. He had to be wrong. "I've never had anything on the spirit side try to crush me before."

Then again, I'd never been on a train racing through the countryside while tuned in to a ghost train, either.

Why couldn't I have just taken a vacation for once?

"I have to get Frankie to detach his power." But the mobster lay dead—again—in the library. The last time he was shot in the head, it put him out for hours.

This was impossible. "I need more time."

Glittery shards of light streamed from the conductor's image. "I'm sorry," he said. "You know I can't stop this train." His image began to break apart. "Release yourself now. Return to your world." I took a step back as he began to rise from the train. "Live your life. And know that I thank you," he said before he was gone.

Sweet heaven.

Sure. Live. Enjoy. He was going back to his afterlife while I had to try to save the one mortal life I had.

∼

I TURNED AND RAN. I had to wake Frankie.

Now.

The mobster lay unconscious on the library floor where I'd left him, his white Panama hat abandoned in the doorway.

Maybe the conductor was wrong. Maybe I'd be okay.

I didn't want to bet my life on it.

"Is he awake?" I asked, dropping to the floor next to Molly.

"These things take time," she said sweetly.

Yeah, well, I didn't have it.

Ellis hovered behind me. I'd caught up with him in the space between cars and filled him in on the mad dash back to the library.

"There has to be something we can do," Ellis insisted. "Shock him, douse him with cold water, anything."

"This train wrecks in six minutes, Molly." Probably five by now. "Before that, the new track will veer off its original course and the ghost train will continue toward the bridge. I can't be tuned in when that happens. I'll get crushed between the trains when they separate." I resisted the urge to shake her. "Come on. You're a ghost. You must know how to wake him."

"Oh my. Okay," she said, clearly nervous. She smoothed her hair over her shoulders. "I'll wake him with a kiss."

"That's your solution?" I pleaded. He wasn't Snow White. Not even close. I looked back to Ellis, glad he wasn't able to hear that.

"Trust me," she said, leaning to give him a sweet peck on the lips.

"Is he moving?" I asked.

"No," she said in dismay.

Frankie lay as dead as he ever was.

"Umm...!" She smothered him with a big wet one.

Heavens. She might be a ghost, but she had no idea how to rouse one.

The darkened landscape whizzed past the window. Mountains gave way to trees. We were nearing the river.

"Douse him with water," I urged.

"I don't have any," she pleaded.

"Well, I can't do it," I snapped, and she winced.

"I'm sorry," I said. But I couldn't manipulate things on her plane. I could barely pick them up. The shadows of the trees grew sparser, and we passed a ghostly bridge warning. "Molly!"

The conductor had been right about everything else. I really didn't want to test him on this.

She zipped out of the room and returned seconds later with a dozen gray, ethereal roses in a vase. "Here," she shouted, dousing Frankie from head to chest.

He didn't even flinch.

"Nothing," I gritted out.

Roses lay on his chest and under his chin.

"I don't know what else to do!" she implored.

"Molly, as soon as we hit that switch in the tracks, I'm out of time."

"Oh no! Oh no!" Her fear gave way to panic.

Then it hit me. I pushed aside a wave of fear and loathing.

I knew what to do.

I reached down, and before I could think twice or brace myself or even consider what I was doing, I enveloped the gangster in a big sloppy bear hug.

Wet, icy tendrils invaded my body, curling into my skin and bones, settling deep inside of me. The touch was too intimate, too damp and clammy and close. The chill turned to fire, hot and searing. I held on. I hugged tighter, embracing the pain.

"Aargh!" Frankie shot up into a sitting position, straight through me. I lost my balance and fell deeper into him, landing on my elbows, my chest and shoulders buried inside the ghost. "Get out! Get out of me!" He shot up off the floor, his energy curling into itself until he remained a shivering orb huddled in the corner by the door.

My teeth chattered; my brain scrambled.

Clang.

Clang.

Clang.

The ghost bell rang and, through the window, I saw the ghost engine split onto a secondary rail up ahead.

Just like the conductor had predicted. It was grossly unfair and terrifying, and I watched in horror as the coal car behind the locomotive peeled away, then the baggage car a mere two cars up from this one.

"Unhook me, Frankie," I ordered, watching the ghost train race for the ruins of a wooden rail bridge.

The ghost cowered in the corner. "Why would you touch me like that?" he demanded. "You're never allowed to touch me! You can't touch me!"

"Don't argue!" I yelled over the blistering noise of metal torn from metal. The ghostly walls shook. Dusty gray volumes fell from their shelves.

One struck me hard, the pain exploding through my shoulder. The conductor was right. He was right!

"For once in your life, do as I say." The floor trembled under me. "Frankie, unhook me. Now!"

CHAPTER 20

$\mathcal{F}$rankie ripped his power away so fast it made my knees weak and my head spin. I stumbled sideways into Ellis, who held me upright, his arms caging me and supporting me, and I needed it because what I saw next chilled me to the core.

The right side of the train bore down on me faster than Frankie's energy could loosen me from its grip.

I screamed and buried my head in Ellis's chest, waiting for the crushing impact of the steel outer wall of the car, feeling it whoosh through me like a blast of air.

I clutched his arms, stunned but alive. I was never asking Frankie to open me up to the other side again. It was too awful, too scary, too much of a risk.

"You've got to see this," the mobster hollered, hitting me with a fresh wave of ghostly power.

"Frankie," I protested as the shot slammed into my left shoulder, quickly spreading in a cascade of prickling energy, "stop." He couldn't just douse me like that. Seconds ago, I'd barely survived being pulverized by the steel carriage of a classic train car, and he wanted to power me up again.

"Too late now," the gangster said with glee.

"I don't want to see." I didn't want to know. Still, I watched in utter fascination as the faint gray outline of the ghost train rushed down the split track to my left, the rest of the train peeling away.

"What did he do to you?" Ellis demanded, shooting a dirty look in Frankie's general direction.

"The list is long," I said, stumbling toward the window, amazed I was in one piece. The ghost train curved along the sidetrack toward an old metal railway bridge.

The bridge appeared solid in the ghostly realm. Yet in the modern world, half the supports had rotted away. Moonlight reflected off the river below and shone up through the bottom.

The old Sugarland Express rushed headlong toward its destiny.

Clang.

Clang.

Clang.

I gasped as the bottom supports of the ghostly bridge gave way. They tumbled, gray and glowing, into the empty black void below. The train lurched and the engine tipped forward, plunging toward the churning river, taking the original Sugarland Express with it.

But this time, there were no souls on board.

No one to relive the tragedy. No voices crying out in terror over the grating of metal or the hiss of steam on the river. The old Sugarland Express fell in silence, dissipating as it dropped until there was nothing left to hit the water.

We'd averted tragedy tonight. And for that I was supremely grateful.

The new Sugarland Express thumped as its wheels charged over the modern steel bridge next to the old one. I remained at the window, watching the dark river churning below.

It was over. At least on the ghostly side.

I turned and hugged Ellis, who had remained at my back, always watching and protecting. "Thank you," I said into his shirt.

"I can still feel Verity touching me," Frankie groused from the other side of the room. "It's crawling all over me, like bugs in my brain."

"Let it go," Molly coaxed. "It's over now."

I lifted my head and saw she'd gotten Frankie down off the ceiling and stood embracing him.

His eye caught mine and he pointed a finger at me. "Don't you ever do that again."

"Believe me, I won't," I said, still nestled against Ellis. "As long as you stop getting shot in the head."

The modern train cleared the bridge and began a sharp ascent up the hill on the other side of the river. I turned back for one last look at the true, historic Sugarland Express before the curve in the tracks obliterated it for good.

"It's done," I said to Ellis.

He brushed a lock of hair behind my ear and I leaned up to kiss him. I was enjoying the warm touch of his lips when suddenly the train lurched and shuddered.

I stumbled backward, out of Ellis's embrace. The lights flickered. The plush chair slammed onto its side.

"Verity!" Ellis shouted.

I grabbed the bookshelves to the side of the window, realizing at once that it was a bad idea. Heavy volumes rained down, barely missing my head.

He reached for my arm and pulled me close, shielding me between the window and his body.

"Sweet heaven! What's going on?" I asked, my voice rattling with the heavy vibrations from the floor and the walls. It felt like we were going to crash.

"We're losing speed," Ellis's voice rasped against my ear as his body shook with the impact of falling hardbacks.

He was right.

Brakes squealed. The train rumbled and swayed, rapidly losing acceleration.

Darkened fields stretched from the tracks and ended in dense forest.

The train gave a hard lurch and ground to a screeching halt.

The lights flickered, but held.

Ellis and I shared a worried look. "Let's check it out," he said, releasing me, heading for the doorway. When I didn't move right away, he hesitated. "Are you all right?" He returned to me. "I can set up the chair again. You can sit."

"No," I said, shaking off the shock and fear of the night. "You need me. One of the ghosts gave me a clue to solving Stephanie's murder." I told Ellis about the shoeprint in the blood.

To his credit, the flash of surprise across his features was brief.

"Okay, let's figure this out," he said, taking my hand and escorting me out into the hall.

The door at the front of the car slammed open, and the conductor rushed toward us, his hat gone and his dark hair a mess. "Are you all right, folks?" he asked, his concern warring with his need to press on.

"We are," I assured him.

"What's happening?" Ellis demanded.

He paused, as if deciding what to tell us. "Rockfall on the tracks," he said quickly. Ellis was, after all, the law.

"Again?" Virginia asked from the back door of the car. She hurried forward, a white dressing gown wrapped tightly around her slim figure. I'd never seen her barefoot before. "It can't be an accident," she snapped, "not twice in a row."

"That's my fear," the conductor said, giving Ellis and me the side-eye, clearly not a fan of having this talk in front of us.

"They're fine," Virginia said, casting a crisp wave of her hand in our direction. "In fact, I want them to hear."

"All right," the conductor said. "If you want my opinion, this looks like a setup. I haven't been out on the tracks yet, but from what I can see up front, the rocks are too neatly stacked."

"Like last time," Ellis said flatly.

"Yes." The conductor nodded. "I know we didn't want to jump to conclusions then, not without proof, but this is more than a coincidence." He ran a hand through his hair. "We barely missed the boulders this time. They were set up on a blind curve, designed to take us out before we had a chance to stop."

Ellis cursed under his breath.

"What would have happened if we'd hit them?" I asked.

My question lingered in the darkness of the hallway.

The conductor stood rigid, and I saw a muscle jump in his jaw. "Best-case scenario, we would have derailed," he said. "Worst case, we could have lost the locomotive. The whole train could have detached and rolled back down the hill."

"Toward the river?" Ellis asked.

The conductor nodded.

Virginia shook. Whether it was from fear or anger, I couldn't tell.

Ellis's expression hardened. "I have a feeling whoever did this is also guilty of the murder in compartment 9."

It made sense. Earlier, when we'd nearly crashed, someone had used the confusion to sabotage the radio and kill Stephanie. If the rocks were stacked again in roughly the same manner, it had to be the same party at work. Still, I wondered how they'd managed it. It could have been a setup from the start, or perhaps the guilty party somehow had a way of communicating with the outside world. The killer could have ordered an associate to place a second blockade when the first wasn't enough to cause serious damage.

"Who in their right mind would strike at a train full of people like this?" Virginia demanded.

"I have the actual killer narrowed down to one of two passengers," I said, startling her. "In other circumstances, it would have been fun to see that wide-eyed, slack-jawed look on her face, but not tonight. "It's Mrs. Abel or Ms. Powers. I have no idea which." But we'd best get a move on.

We didn't know what plot our killer was hatching while we were standing here trying to figure out what to do.

"How do you know this?" Virginia demanded.

"Ghosts," Ellis said, with finality.

She shook her head, as if she couldn't quite believe what she was about to say. "All right. Let's keep an eye on both women."

"We need to do more than that," I told her. "We need to find the evidence to put one of them away."

"How?" Virginia asked.

"By securing physical proof." I explained about the unusual footprint in the blood. "Can you remember either Mary Jo or Eileen wearing a shoe with a large square heel and a pointed toe?" Virginia noticed what people wore. It was practically a sport to her.

Ellis's mother pressed a hand to her forehead and thought hard before she gave up, exasperated. "No. I can't recall." She dropped her hand. "I can't even imagine where you'd buy something that awful."

"We need to find it," I told her.

Ellis gave a sharp nod. "You work on that, and I'll take another look at the evidence in compartment 9," he said grimly.

That was right, he hadn't cleaned up the blood yet.

He'd gone into police mode, cool and collected. "In the meantime, we're trapped in the middle of nowhere with a killer on board," Ellis said, "so let's be careful."

Virginia crossed her arms over her chest. "Where are we exactly?"

"No more than fifteen miles from the Gatlinburg station," the conductor said. "Once we're there, we can call in the local police."

But until then, we'd better watch our backs.

Beau's voice sounded from the back of the car. "I'll go for help."

I hadn't even heard him arrive.

"You will not." Virginia kept her back turned to him. "I'd barely trust you on a five-mile hike."

Beau flinched, but he persisted, inserting himself next to Ellis in our merry little circle. "It's not your decision to make, Mother."

She had a point, though. He'd be out in the dark in rough country with a killer on the loose. And even if he wasn't stabbed from behind, he could get hurt any number of ways. He could run into wild animals, injure himself in a fall, or follow the wrong set of tracks and get lost.

"Mom's right," Ellis said. "It's not safe. I'll do it."

"Not this time," Beau vowed. "It's my train."

"We need Ellis to look at the bloodstains," I said. It seemed this was Beau's time to step up.

Virginia and Beau exchanged a look. "Go," she said, not happy about it.

Ellis gave a sharp nod to his brother.

"Come with me, then," the conductor said. "I'll show you the route. You can leave once the sun comes up."

Beau clapped a hand on Ellis's shoulder before following the conductor up front. He paused at the front of the car. "You won't regret it," he promised.

"I already do," Virginia said to herself as the door slid closed behind him.

"He can handle it," Ellis said when she stood for a long moment, looking at the closed door.

"I don't like it," she murmured. "He's not sturdy like you."

He might never be if she didn't let him strike out on his own. "You might be surprised," I told her. Beau never did what I expected.

She shot me a dirty look. "At least he's waiting until the sun is up. I'll tell the cook to prepare supplies." She turned to leave us, then stopped. "Verity, you said you needed to find a pair of bloody shoes."

"Yes," I said, not sure I'd put it quite that way.

"Then come with me." Virginia had donned the kind of crafty look that usually meant trouble. "If you're willing and able, I have an idea."

CHAPTER 21

"*D*on't do anything illegal," Ellis cautioned as the three of us made our way back through the train.

"Dear, I'm surprised your mind would even go there," Virginia said in a way that chastised while at the same time refused to tip her hand.

"He's right," I told her as we hurried past the club chairs in the abandoned bar. "Any evidence we find needs to be admissible in court."

While I'd be glad to accept Virginia's help—provided it was the kind I needed—she played by her own rules, and that made me nervous.

I was about to say as much when we entered the hallway of the kitchen car and encountered both the skinny porter and the cook.

"Most of the passengers are up," the porter said, looking frazzled. "We're assembling a continental breakfast."

"Is it that close to dawn?" Virginia asked, looking to the window. Faint light crested the horizon. Voices echoed from the dining room. "Give them mimosas as well," she ordered. "Wake the wait staff. And go comb your hair again," she said, continuing toward the back of the train.

We entered the dining car and found Mary Jo huddled with her husband, Dave, at their usual table. She didn't look like a killer. Then again, in my experience, killers rarely did.

Ellis leaned close to Virginia and me. "You two stick together," he said, low enough not to be overheard. "Our culprit might not be working alone."

The newlyweds clustered at the next table, in frantic conversation with the anniversary couple. It seemed that everyone was up except for Eileen Powers. The reporter was nowhere to be seen.

"Go," Virginia said, ushering her son along. "We've got this."

"I'm counting on it." He grabbed me sideways, kissed me hard, and walked on toward the bloody mess in compartment 9.

"I'm going to pretend I didn't see that," Virginia muttered under her breath. She held up her hands, showing her palms to the room. "May I have everyone's attention for a moment." She spoke with the ease and authority of someone used to addressing groups. "I'm so sorry for the inconvenience this morning. Rest assured, there's nothing to worry about," she lied through her teeth. I frowned, along with half of the other passengers. "That jolt you felt was the train stopping suddenly."

"What did we hit?" asked Xander. The young newlywed appeared shaken as he clutched his wife's henna-tattooed hand.

I wanted to know what made him assume there had been anything on the tracks to hit. Virginia hadn't said anything of the sort.

His young wife crossed her legs nervously, and I saw that she wore a pair of wedge heels with a pink flamingo print. Her feet were too small to fit the killer's shoes. But what about her husband?

"We didn't hit anything," Virginia assured Xander. I was pleased for once at her slick nature when she left out the part about the rocks on the track. It wouldn't make anyone safer to know, and keeping our cards close to our chest on this one might just help us suss out the killer. "The driver thought he saw a bear. After such a sudden stop, he needs to check the engine." She added quickly, "We should be on our way shortly."

"A bear?" Dave Abel asked, as if he couldn't quite believe what he was hearing.

At the next table, Barbara scooted her chair closer to her husband, Bruce. "I didn't even know there were bears in these mountains."

I doubted my almost mother-in-law knew, either.

"I need to complete a quick safety check," Virginia said, as if they'd never questioned her. "Breakfast will be served shortly. Please enjoy. I'll report back here when I'm finished. In the meantime, the waiters and porters will bring you anything you need." Her bony fingers found my elbow. "Thank you." She smiled sweetly before giving me a firm nudge toward the rear of the car.

Because she had this under control.

"A bear?" I hissed once the door closed behind us.

Dawn peeked through the distant mountains.

"What other wandering animal can stop a train?" she snapped, hurrying down the hallway of the first passenger car, and into the second. "Or do you think there's a dairy farm in these hills?" She drove her key card down into the door to compartment 7. "Now wait here," she said, leaving me outside. Alone.

Lovely. I wondered if they'd hear me scream in the dining room should the killer attack.

I leaned back against a window and kept my eyes peeled for knife-wielding maniacs, or even pleasant historic train enthusiasts turned murderers.

There were too many suspects and not enough evidence.

I mean, how bad had it gotten that I was partnering up with Virginia Wydell? Most days, she'd just as soon throw me under a train than help me solve a mystery on one. I looked over my shoulder at the rapidly approaching dawn. At least she cared about the Sugarland Express and her two sons. Beau was going to be out there soon. I hoped he knew what he was doing.

Scant minutes after she'd disappeared into her room, Virginia emerged wearing fresh lipstick, a pair of fitted trousers, and a sleeveless cashmere sweater. She'd twisted her blond hair into a sleek knot at the back of her neck and completed the ensemble with a string of pearls. She could have been on her way to a Rotary meeting.

"You look good," I said reflexively, suddenly conscious of my wrinkled sundress and day-old hairdo.

"It's not hard," she said pointedly. She closed the door behind her, eyeing me from head to toe. "You just need to take a little time."

And now I wanted to throw her under the train.

"Speaking of time," I said, unable to keep the ice out of my voice, "it seems to me we have a killer to catch right now."

"We do," she said, drawing a plastic key card out of her pocket and giving it a dainty wave. "I have my master key, so let's get started. After all, Mary Jo is in the dining car."

"That would be breaking and entering," I said, feeling for a moment like I was talking to Frankie. "You heard what Ellis said. This has to be legal."

"Oh, it's quite legal when you own the train," she assured me, moving swiftly up to the first passenger car and to the door to the Abels' compartment. "There's fine print on the ticket that specifically allows me to enter." She slipped the key into the lock. "Besides, I'm in charge of housekeeping. We'll straighten up a bit while we're in there."

"Don't even think about it," I said, looking quickly to make sure we were still the only ones in the hallway. "The Abels will know if we start moving things around."

"Leave it to me," she said, entering like she owned the place, which I supposed she did.

Darn it.

I followed her into the plush suite.

Virginia busied herself adjusting a ceramic lamp on the carved wood table next to the couch. "See? I just straightened," she said, her tone innocent, fire in her eyes. "Perfectly in line. Now let's go see if any of Mary Jo's shoes are crooked."

"This is so wrong," I said, making a quick dash to the closet attached to the vanity while Virginia threw open the curtains to the small bedroom at the back.

Mary Jo had placed her shoes at the bottom of the closet—three pairs of flats and a pair of slippers. "Well, she wouldn't have put those shoes with the other ones," I reasoned. Even if she'd cleaned them, she might not want to look at them. I checked the top shelf of her closet before going for her stored luggage on the racks next to the vanity.

"We're lucky the windows don't open," Virginia said, ducking beneath a reading lamp attached to the wall, inspecting the compact wooden dresser beneath. It was the only freestanding piece of furniture in the luxurious, yet efficient space.

"The killer would be foolish to toss incriminating evidence from the train," I said. "Besides, right now, the killer doesn't realize anyone is looking." The killer either wiped the print away or didn't realize she'd left the evidence before blood seeped over it." We only know about the print because of the ghost."

"Well, there's nothing in here," Virginia said after a few tense moments of hurried searching.

"I'm coming up empty, too," I said, completing one final check to ensure I'd left the Abels' possessions the same way I'd found them. "I'm glad it's not them," I admitted, while Virginia turned off the light above the bed and closed the curtains to the room, fluffing and adjusting them just so.

"Really?" she asked, stepping back from her work. "You do realize that means we're probably sending my son into the room with a killer."

She was right. Ellis would be the one to confront Eileen Powers.

"At least he knows who he might be up against," I said. I also trusted him to do the right thing. "Now let's get out of here."

~

WE STOOD IN THE HALL, as innocent as could be. Virginia even treated me to a small smile. I had to admit I was a little surprised when we slipped out into the hallway without getting caught. It didn't seem right, what we'd just done. There should be consequences for lying, for keeping the Abels in the dining car while we inspected their belongings. And yet…

My almost mother-in-law had just stowed the key card in her pocket when the door slid open at the back of the car and Eileen Powers stepped inside.

"Hello, dear," Virginia greeted her as if they were old friends. It would have been stunning to watch if I hadn't been so horrified. She strolled toward our suspect with artfully placed concern. "I'm sure you felt the train stop."

Eileen met her halfway. "What's wrong this time?" she asked, cutting to the chase.

Virginia smiled, as if that kind of questioning didn't make her seethe inside. "You know, I'm just about to address the passengers and give all the details."

I had to give her credit. She said it in a way that would tempt the reporter, and it worked. Eileen's expression went from sour to curious.

"Care to give me a preview?" the redhead asked.

"Go have a seat, and I'll be right in," Virginia assured her.

The reporter shot me a curious glance, and I gave her a bright smile. "I'm just going to help Virginia carry something," I said.

It wasn't necessarily a lie. Maybe she'd let me hold the key card before we broke into compartment 8.

"All right," Eileen said noncommittally. She headed for the dining car.

As soon as the door closed behind her, I turned to Virginia. "This is such a bad idea."

"Someday, you'll learn to be practical," she said, tucking the tag into the back of my sundress. "Now let's get down to business."

The back of the train was on a definite downward slant. It seemed the final cars hadn't fully cleared the hill before the conductor hit the brakes. I tried to ignore it and focus on our mission.

We entered Eileen Powers's room the same way we had the Abels'. I took the closet again. Virginia took the reporter's single suitcase down off the rack. As if we had a system.

"At least this room is tiny," she mused.

It was a little bigger than the one I shared with Ellis.

Eileen didn't keep her shoes on the floor of the closet, though. She'd spread them out to the side of the vanity area. I checked the top shelf anyway.

"What I don't get is why she'd wear heels to commit a murder," I said, finding only folded clothes on the shelf.

"Maybe she wasn't planning to kill," Virginia said, dropping to her hands and knees to check under the stacks of paper beneath the window table. "This woman needs a couple of file boxes."

"Nothing in this part of the room," I said, trying to think of where else she could have stashed them. I looked in the shower.

"I'm coming up blank, too," Virginia said, sitting back on her heels.

"I don't get it." It would be crazy for a killer to hide such a personal piece of evidence outside an area they could control. It had to be hidden in the culprit's room. Virginia said herself the windows on the train didn't open.

Unless the killer had indeed tossed the shoe off the end of the caboose. Still, even then they risked exposure. As soon as we contacted the authorities in Gatlinburg, they would be scouring the tracks for it.

"If I were the killer, what would I do?" Virginia mused.

"I'd lie better," Eileen said, sliding open the door to her compartment, trapping us inside.

Virginia stood quickly. I remained in front of the vanity. "This isn't what it looks like."

"Two people trying to pin a crime on me?" Eileen asked, in no hurry to get out of our way. She reached into her bag. I braced myself, expecting her to pull out a weapon, my eyes settling on a can of aerosol hairspray as she pulled a stick of gum from her purse.

I relaxed—barely—as she opened it and began to chew.

"Tell me why you suspect the Abels," she said, giving no hint of what she was thinking.

I exchanged a glance with Virginia.

"I don't recall saying that," I told her.

For all I knew, Eileen could be the killer. She looked as if she could fit the shoeprint found in the blood, and she'd been absent from the dining room during the time of the murder.

Then again, I hadn't ruled out anyone on the train. And Eileen hadn't attacked us yet. That was certainly a point in her favor.

And there was the fact that she was a reporter. I had a feeling she was here to dig up the truth rather than put someone in the ground.

"Fine. I'll level with you," I said, going with my gut.

Virginia pursed her lips, but didn't argue. "Join us on the couch," she offered, her tone cool.

"I'd rather stand where I can see you both," Eileen countered. "You can't be too careful on this train."

"Good point," I said.

Then I told her everything—about the body, about the ghosts, about the bloody footprint we'd found. She stared at me like I'd lost my marbles when we got to the part with the spooks, but she listened, and she didn't interrupt once.

When I finished my story, I heard a click echo from her pocket.

"What's that?" I stiffened.

She removed her hand and displayed a mini voice recorder.

"Verity never said this was on the record," Virginia snapped, taking a step forward.

Eileen held up her hands. "Stay where you are. I'm within my rights."

She'd tricked me. And now she was going to make me look like a fool. "Did you ever intend to share information with us?" I demanded. "I want the truth about what you're here to investigate and what you learned from Stephanie the night she died."

"Oh, we'll have that discussion," the reporter said, lowering her hands. "This," she said, slipping the recorder into her pocket, "I'd intended to use as insurance, but frankly, you sound like a loon."

"Get to the point," I told her.

"You want the truth?" she asked. "Here it is. I'm working on a story that's very big and that will be going down very soon. Stephanie was my informant. She's dead now, and I think the people I'm investigating were behind it."

"The Abels," Virginia said flatly.

She didn't deny it. "I think I know what happened, and your bloody footprint seals the deal. Let me check out my last good lead," she urged. "If it works out, I can point you to your evidence."

Or she could just as easily destroy it if she were so inclined.

She pressed her lips together. "Trust me on this one," she urged.

"I don't see where we have a choice," I told her. We were at a dead end with the bloody shoe, at least for now.

"If I'm right, we'll have our answer in an hour or less," Eileen promised.

"Come find me as soon as you do," Virginia ordered, taking a risk and approaching Eileen at the door, displaying her empty hands as she did.

"Where are you going?" I asked.

She glanced back at me. "I have to see to a room full of passengers."

Right.

Eileen backed out of the room ahead of us. "I'll find you," she said to me. "In the meantime—" the reporter fished in her pocket and withdrew a tube of lipstick "—here." She handed it to me. "You need this."

"O-kay…" I said, not sure why she'd given it to me. I opened it and saw a used tube in a terrible orange-pink color. "Thanks."

The reporter gave a slight nod and headed in the direction of the dining room.

"I'll see you in there," I said to Virginia once we were both out in the hall. I hated to separate, but Ellis's mom would be safe with the crowd in the dining room. And I had to find Frankie. I needed him to act like a ghostly investigator one more time and tail Eileen to wherever she was headed.

While he was at it, I'd have Molly search the rest of the train for those missing shoes. She could do it faster and better than any mortal, and while managing those two might drive me a bit crazy, I was pretty sure it wouldn't violate any law.

A smart killer would have indeed tossed the bloody shoes from the train, but it would have been hard without windows that opened. It would also be risky to lose possession of evidence like that. It would be safer to keep the shoes hidden until they could be disposed of properly.

Besides, the killer didn't know anyone had even seen the print. I was willing to bet she'd wiped it away.

I made my way to the very back of the train and found my crack team of ghost investigators canoodling in the caboose. This time, the room looked like a small-time 1930s jailhouse. Newspapers plastered the walls, with brash headlines praising Lead Investigator Frankie Lawson, the country's hottest new crime fighter.

Molly perched on the desk, with Frankie nuzzling her hair.

"Oh brother," I said, stopping short in the doorway.

Frankie's back stiffened. "Don't you knock?" he spat.

Why start now? "I have a job for you," I told him.

CHAPTER 22

The ghosts took the job without complaint. I didn't know if it was because Frankie now saw himself as the next Columbo, or if he only wanted to impress Molly, but either way, I'd take it.

And as I stood alone in Frankie's ghostly jail, I noticed the caboose had stopped on even more of a downward slope than the passenger car before it. I made my way toward a plain metal door at the back, careful not to touch the many awards cluttering his detective's desk.

Did they even give awards for solving crimes? I certainly hadn't received any.

I pushed the door open and stepped onto a small squared-off platform that thankfully had a rail, because I could feel myself being drawn downward.

We were definitely clinging to the hillside on an angle. Bare tracks dropped sharply toward the wide river below.

Gray clouds hung low overhead. I could see the modern steel bridge we'd crossed, and at the switchback, a second set of tracks branching off toward the ruins of the trestle and the wreck that lay buried under the churning water.

Enough of that. I climbed down the steps on the side of the platform and jumped the final two feet to the gray rocky rail bed.

A raindrop touched my forehead, and before I could wipe it away, another pelted my arm.

I walked sideways from the train, toward a towering hillside. Hardy trees clung to the crumbling shale. From this angle, I could see that most of the train had cleared the curve around the hill and had stopped on more level ground. Only the last few cars hadn't made it.

Yikes. Surely, the brakes could take the weight.

I mean, it couldn't be dangerous or the conductor would never have allowed it. Although he hadn't exactly been given a choice. Either way, I'd be glad when help arrived.

I walked farther up the tracks, toward a figure I saw sitting on a fallen rock near a scraggly bush. When I drew closer, I almost stopped and retreated.

It was Beau.

His shoulders slumped. His head hung low. His hair stood out at all angles in a way that would give Virginia heart palpitations. And at that moment, no matter what he'd done to me, I couldn't find it in me to abandon him.

I made my way over the rocks in kitten heels. I didn't bother trying to spare them. They were ruined by that time anyway.

"Town is that way," I joked, pointing toward the front of the train.

He stood quickly, as if I'd surprised him. "Yeah," he said, embarrassed. He looked to the path ahead rather than back at me. "I told them I needed a minute."

Another raindrop touched down on my arm.

"You don't have to go," I told him. Yes, Ellis had a lot on his plate, but he was probably the better choice.

"I do," Beau said, decisive as he turned to me. He let out a huff. "I should have stepped up a long time ago."

I wasn't sure what to say to that. To agree would be rude, but I wasn't going to lie to Beau and tell him it wasn't time for him to stand on his own two feet.

My hesitation turned into uncomfortable silence. "Is there a way back onto the train over here?" I asked, eager to make a quick escape, already retreating toward a break between the passenger cars.

"Verity, wait," he called after me.

I'd really rather not. And in my first cowardly act of the day, I pretended not to hear.

"Please," he called, "stop." I could hear him crunching over the rocks after me. "I need to talk to you."

I turned. He'd followed me several steps, and we stood awkwardly between the hill and the lead passenger car.

"I'm sorry," he said earnestly, "for everything." He made a weak gesture with his hand. "In case I don't make it."

I took a few steps toward him before I realized what I was doing and halted. "You're going to be fine," I assured him. "You can do this."

He shook his head sharply. "I don't need reassurance. I need—" He paused, frustrated, muttering a curse. "I used to be able to talk to you."

Those days were over. A lot of things were over.

"I don't know what to say to you, Beau," I admitted.

He pressed his lips together. "I know," he said, resigned. "That's my fault."

"I really should go," I told him, backing up.

"Listen." He closed the distance between us. "I was a dick. It was wrong to try to ruin your trip with Ellis."

I froze. "You were," I agreed.

I wasn't sure what it cost him to admit that to me, but he certainly had my attention.

"I was an ass to you after you called off the wedding," he said quickly. "Hell, I was an ass to you as soon as you told me we were over." He pinched the bridge of his nose between his fingers. "I just didn't know how to deal with it. I didn't know how to face you and make it up to you and make it so you wouldn't hate me every time you looked at me."

He faced me then, and the raw pain I saw took my breath away.

"I don't hate you, Beau."

I'd never let him have that kind of power over me.

"But you don't want me back." He said it like an accusation.

"No," I said simply.

He blinked hard a couple of times. "I don't know how to do this. I don't know how to stand here and watch you date my brother." He cursed again. "My own brother, Verity!" he pleaded. "If it wasn't you, I'd think you were doing it on purpose—driving the knife deep. But you're not like that. You honest to God like the guy. Hell, knowing you, you might even love him." His breath caught on a huff. "I have to stand here and watch him have what I lost, and it's killing me. Do you get that? I get physically sick every time I see you with him."

"I don't know how to fix that," I said, holding my ground. "None of what happened with us was my fault, but you made me pay the price."

The fight drained out of him. "I know I did," he said gently. He pulled away, running a hand through his messy hair. "I think I just wanted you to suffer like I am. I screwed up, Verity. I know I did. It's my problem, not yours."

That was where he was wrong. "It is mine too, because we have to learn to be around each other."

I couldn't dismiss Beau or his mother or anything about my past if I wanted to have a real future with Ellis.

Beau stood quietly for a moment. "What you have with my brother is getting serious, isn't it?"

"It is," I said, ignoring his flinch. "I really care about Ellis."

His head hung low. "I didn't even know Stephanie that well. I just wanted you to see me with a hot blonde on my arm."

I'd suspected as much. "It's okay."

A muscle in his jaw jumped. "Now she's dead."

"It's not your fault."

His eyes met mine. "It is. I brought her on this train. I left her alone to go drink and wallow because I couldn't have you."

"Beau—" I began.

"Don't try to make it better," he warned.

"I'm not going to let you feel guilty about something you couldn't control," I told him. "Stephanie made her own decisions. Based on what we've learned, I think she might have been involved with some pretty bad people."

He stood shocked for a moment and then barked out a laugh. "Of course. My life has been one big screwup since I lost you."

Actually, what he'd done right before he'd lost me had been pretty messed up as well. "You'll find someone else," I told him. "You will." After that, with any luck, he'd forget all about me. "Just...learn your lesson and try not to screw up next time."

"I'm trying to be a better person." He rubbed the back of his neck. "I should apologize to your sister."

"You should," I agreed.

He looked up the tracks, toward town, then back to me. "I'm going to do better, I promise. Starting now."

I reached out and took his hand. "We're counting on it."

He slipped away, and I watched him go up the side of the tracks toward the bend around the hill. He'd get his supplies up front and then he'd be gone.

Beau needed a purpose, a direction bigger than vintage train tracks through the wilderness. But I supposed it was a start.

A voice sounded near my ear. "You gonna stand there all day staring at the horizon?" Frankie asked.

"You have something better for me to do?" I countered.

"Yes, as a matter of fact," he said, every bit the cocky gangster. "Molly found those bloody high heels."

Frankie grinned and zipped straight into the passenger car to my left. I, however, had to do a bit more work to get back onto the train. It turned out you needed a stepstool to reach the side doors on the train when there was no platform involved.

I ran back to the caboose and trekked it from there, out of breath by the time I slid open the door to the last passenger car.

Frankie stood in the hall with a smug grin. Molly hovered at his side, clasping her hands in front of her.

"Where are the shoes?" I hissed as soon as I reached the two ghosts. The bloody evidence sure wasn't out here in the hall.

"You have to understand, I searched everywhere," Molly said earnestly, leading me up through the train car.

"Let's go in here," Frankie said, stopping in front of my compartment of all places.

"Why?" I asked, drawing my key from my dress, wasting no time unlocking it. I glanced up and down the hall. We were alone, but I supposed we could be overheard in the hall.

Molly had already passed through the wall next to me and stood in front of my vanity.

Frankie glided up next to her. "I got to say, kid, we don't think it's you."

"Think what's me?" He wasn't making sense. "Don't start your crazy detective mumbo jumbo," I told him. "I don't have time for that."

"Open your luggage," the gangster instructed. My suitcase sat on a small rack next to him. "Go on."

"All right." At this point, I was a little afraid of what I'd find. I clicked the double clasps on the tan leather case and lifted the lid. And there, on top of my extra nightgowns and unmentionables, lay the pair of bloody heels.

CHAPTER 23

I stared down at the silk heels in my suitcase. Size ten. White, except for the rusty bloodstains on the bottom.

This could mean only one thing: the killer was onto me.

Worse, she could get into my sleeping compartment. There was nowhere safe on this train for me to go, and suddenly, I felt very much alone.

"I've got to get out of here," I said, slamming the suitcase lid down over the heels. "I need to be with people."

"Excuse me," Molly chafed. "I believe we count."

"Get used to it," Frankie told her. "She treats me like that all the time."

I shoved my hands into my pockets, encountering Eileen's nasty tube of lipstick. I tossed it onto my vanity and held up a hand, trying to control my racing thoughts. "You are people," I assured them. How had this become my life? "But I need living, breathing souls around if this killer comes after me." It wasn't like Frankie or Molly would be able to help fight off a knife-wielding psychopath, or tell any flesh and blood person what had happened.

But I couldn't just leave the bloody evidence behind. And I

didn't dare touch it.

"You should hide in the crow's nest," Molly suggested. "It has a nice, big window and plenty of elbow room."

I wasn't going to hide. I needed to track down our killer and end this once and for all.

"You two"—I pointed at the ghosts—"stay here and guard those shoes. Molly, I need you to find me and let me know if anyone comes in here after them. Frankie, stick with any intruder and don't let them out of your sight."

"You see how she barks orders?" Frankie groused to his girl.

"I think it's a good idea," Molly countered. She smiled at me. "I like to see the ladies in charge."

"Great," I said automatically, kicking off my kitten heels and reaching for a pair of running shoes. "I'm counting on you two."

I laced my Nikes in record time and headed out.

Hopefully Ellis was still in compartment 9, locating that bloody print. I knocked on the door hard. "Ellis," I said.

Nobody answered.

"It's me." I knocked harder, my knuckles taking the brunt of my discomfort. I felt conspicuous out here by myself, like I was asking for trouble.

No response. He wasn't in there.

Darn it.

I glanced up and down the hall. Rain pelted the windows.

The door to compartment 8 stood open a crack. Was Eileen trying to listen in on me?

Lovely.

I wondered if she'd been spying from the start.

She was certainly positioned well enough. When I'd first told her about Stephanie's murder, Eileen admitted she'd heard the commotion in the hall. Yet she hadn't come out to join us. She'd merely listened through the door.

It made me wonder whose side she was on.

Eileen also hadn't reported back about the evidence I'd shared with her, not that I'd been around to hear it.

Well, she couldn't hide from me now.

"Eileen," I called, as if she hadn't already heard me out here, "I'm back." She'd claimed her fact-finding mission wouldn't take much time at all. I sincerely hoped she'd found something. I wanted her to prove me wrong.

I slid open the door to compartment 8. "Eileen," I called from the doorway.

The room appeared as it had before. Files cluttered the table by the window. More lay strewn underneath. Her bed hadn't been made, and clothes littered the room. It didn't seem as if there was anyone inside. Yet the door had been open.

I itched to make a more thorough investigation, but didn't like going in alone. I'd be a sitting duck if a killer lurked inside.

I should get Ellis. I would if I knew where he was. I had no cell signal, no way to reach him. I couldn't waste time knocking on all of the doors from here to the locomotive. Meanwhile, I'd tipped my hand to Eileen. I'd set the wheels in motion and needed to see it through.

Perhaps it wouldn't hurt to take one quick look around. An umbrella leaned against the front wall. I took it, wielding it like a weapon as I took another step into the room and then one more.

The room appeared empty. That was the good thing about compact train compartments. There were very few places to hide.

And then I saw the figure in the shower stall. No water ran. No towel was laid out.

I screwed up my courage and kept my voice even. "Come on in here, Ellis," I said to my imaginary partner, hoping whoever was in there would at least think I wasn't alone. "Or you can wait right by the door with your gun."

The figure didn't move.

"Eileen?" I asked, approaching slowly. "Are you okay?" I spared a quick glance to the empty hallway behind me. "Ellis and I are worried about you."

Then I struck. In one fluid motion, I raised the umbrella, ripped open the door, and found Eileen Powers fully clothed and very dead in the shower, her throat slit.

Blood drenched her white blouse and khaki pants. Her knees were bent, her body wedged into the tiny space with no room to even crumple to the floor. She began to pitch forward, and I slammed the door.

Sweet Jesus.

With Eileen dead, that left Mary Jo as my last suspect.

But the only proof was in my own luggage.

My mind swam. Eileen had been investigating the Abel family business. She must have known something about Mary Jo, something incriminating. The reporter's files lay in a heap by the table, and once this room became the site of a murder investigation, I had no hope of seeing any of it.

"I'm sorry, Eileen," I whispered, easing away from the shower door, hoping it remained closed.

It did. For now, at least.

"I'm sorry I had you asking questions for me." If I'd known what to ask, whom to confront, that might have been me dead in the shower.

"I'm sorry I got you involved." I retrieved her notes from the table and from the floor. Then again, it was possible she'd been involved from the start.

Rain pelted against the windows as I rifled through the dead woman's notes on the Abels and their business. I found an employee listing, background checks, a folder with truck schedules and shipping routes. It didn't make sense, not without any idea of what lead Eileen had been chasing.

I lifted my head, desperate for inspiration, and saw a figure reflected in the window glass. I turned—too late—as someone grabbed me.

A hand covered my mouth and my scream.

CHAPTER 24

I woke up on my knees, fuzzy headed, with a spider crawling over my cheek.

"Mother Mary!" I reached to wipe it off and realized my hands had been zip tied to the rail of a rusty ladder that led up to the crow's nest in the caboose.

Rain fell heavily outside the tiny windows, the dampness seeping into the metal car.

I dislodged the spider with a swipe of my shoulder and turned to see the skinny porter standing behind me.

"You—" I gasped.

The corner of his mouth twitched. "Nobody ever suspects the help."

I didn't understand how he could be working for Mary Jo. Had she bribed him?

Somehow, I didn't think he'd answer that question, so I went for an easier one. "How did I get here?"

It couldn't have been easy. Someone had to have seen.

His cold grin shook me to the core. "I packed you in my big roller bag," he said, confident. Proud. "Nobody suspected a thing."

I tried to stand, but with my legs shaky and my hands bound

low, I slumped back to my knees. "Ellis will find me," I warned. "Whatever you have planned for me, it won't work. Ellis is looking for me right now."

"Your *Ellis* is busy investigating Eileen's cause of death," he said simply. "I made sure of it."

The door at the back of the train flung open. Dave Abel stood on the threshold. "Stop." He ordered. He slammed the door behind him. "You can't do this."

The skinny porter turned to him. "She knows about the blood on Mom's shoe," he said. "I don't know how. I wiped the print. The police didn't find it, but she saw it. Eileen Powers knew, too."

Dave went pale. "What did you do to the reporter, Jordan?"

"I shut her up," he snapped.

Sweet Jesus. "Let me go," I ordered, doing my best to remain calm. "You said it yourself. I can't prove a thing about your mom's shoe." Which meant this Jordan guy was Dave's son, which meant he'd listen to his dad. I hoped. I focused my attention on Dave. "You know I was only on this train for a nice vacation. I don't want to get mixed up in any of this."

Dave adjusted his glasses. "I realize that, dear," he said, sounding like the guy I'd seen in countless Abel Windows and Doors commercials. A fire burned in the potbelly stove next to him. The door hung open, the firelight playing against his features. "I don't think you mean this family any harm."

But he didn't move to let me go. He knew as well as I did that I'd go to the police.

"She's the last one, I promise," Jordan vowed, slipping a knife from under a large rolling duffel bag next to the wall. That must have been the luggage he'd used to transport me. It would have been heck to get me over the rickety walkway.

Yet he'd been determined enough to manage.

"I burned the reporter's notes," he said, cocking a head toward the old stove by the back door. "With this blonde taken care of, the police are out of leads."

"Then you don't know Ellis," I countered. He'd fight for me. He'd avenge me. Although I really, really didn't want to be stabbed to death in a caboose.

Jordan strolled toward me, the blade of the knife long and deadly in his hand. I clenched my fists, unable to move, scarcely able to breathe.

"Christ almighty." Dave cringed. He turned toward the stove. "I'm not going to watch."

But he was going to let him do it.

I struggled against my zip ties. They sliced into my wrists.

"This had better be the end, Jordan," Dave said, like a stern father.

My assailant adjusted his grip on the knife, agitated. "It never would have started if you hadn't cut me out of the business."

"I had no choice. You were putting us all at risk," Dave insisted. "You don't know when to quit. Like now. Where do you get off showing up on my vacation to threaten me?"

Jordan spun to face his father. "If you would have said yes, I'd have been out of there by dinnertime on the first night. I'd have warned the conductor about the rocks, not made such a show out of it. I do have some decency."

"You killed Stephanie," Dave said flatly.

"How was I supposed to know Ron's ex would be on board? She recognized me and started asking questions. She'd have blown my cover for sure." He glared at his dad. "You're the one who made me stay here to convince you. It's your fault she's dead."

With Jordan's attention diverted, I doubled my efforts, ignoring the way the plastic bit into my skin, and the blood that began trickling down my arm.

"I was as surprised as you were to see Stephanie," Dave scolded. "Poor Ron was blindsided."

"The golden child," Jordan sneered.

"Cut it out." Dave snapped. "Ron tries hard. I never condoned what he spent to keep that girl happy, and I wasn't surprised she left when we tightened our belts. But Ron's problems are nothing compared to yours. You can't threaten me, and you can't go around killing people. What happens when Ron finds out?"

He pointed the knife at his dad. "You'd better not tell him."

Dave held his hands up. "You got what you wanted. I signed over your inheritance, your portion of the business." His forehead shone with sweat. "It's over now. I don't want to see you ever again."

Jordan showed him the knife, approaching him slowly. "I wouldn't have had to stop the train the second time if you'd signed it over when I asked the first time. Hell, we were less than a day out of the station. You could have avoided this whole mess."

"You don't deserve that money and you know it," Dave said softly.

If he wasn't careful, he was going to end up next to me.

I looked down at my bloodied wrists. The ties remained intact. I wasn't getting anywhere, and I was almost out of time.

"I made the company millions," Jordan seethed.

"By using my trucks to transport heroin over state lines," Dave hissed.

"Our trucks," his son corrected. "And I didn't hear you arguing when the money started rolling in."

"I didn't know," Dave shot back. "I trusted you."

Think. I frantically tried to recall the details of the Personal Safety and Self-Defense workshop Melody had set up at the library. She'd been so excited, so worried nobody would show up. I did, with Lauralee. The woman giving the class had talked about how to get out of zip ties. At the time it had seemed like a rather extreme bit of information, but now I wished I'd paid closer attention.

Jordan leveled the knife at his father's throat. "You kicked me out of the house with nothing. No job, no savings, a shitty apartment where I was supposed to hide out and do what?"

Dave kept his distance. "Let your mother and me fix it."

His son barked out a laugh. "I fixed it."

I couldn't look anymore. I focused on untying the laces on my sneaker, praying I was remembering the library seminar right.

"You're breaking your mom's heart," Dave pleaded.

"I'm covering her butt. She's the one who brought the bloody heels back to your room. She was the one who followed me that night. I didn't ask her to go tromping around in the blood. Did I tell you she closed the stupid compartment and let it lock behind her? I'm one of the only ones with a skeleton key!"

"She can't sleep. She can't eat."

I threaded my shoelace through the zip ties, fumbling. I realized I had to untie my other shoe as well.

What was I even going to do if I could get free? Attack the guy holding the knife? I still wasn't sure whose side Dave would be on.

"We'll be okay as long as Mom keeps her mouth shut," Jordan spat. "I think she will. Mom likes nice things. So do you. And there aren't many nice things in prison."

"We didn't do anything," Dave pleaded.

I tied the free ends of my laces together and started sawing. He was going to stab me for sure once he saw what I was up to.

"She covered up a murder," Jordan said, waggling the knife at his father. "So will you. You're going to forget all about this."

Dave seized the handle of the knife. He wrenched it out of his son's grip and shoved him backward.

"How dare you threaten me after everything we've done to cover for you?" He tossed the knife into the fire burning in the potbellied stove.

"What the hell?" Jordan raged. He shoved his dad against the wall while Dave gripped his son's arms to maintain some distance between them. "Now how are we going to kill her?" He gave one last, hard push. "I dragged her all the way down here so I wouldn't leave evidence anywhere else."

Dave stood with his back to the door. "This is how you think," he said, as if he still couldn't quite believe it.

"The police can still find out about you. It won't take too much digging in your business records to find the truth. You want to go to prison, old man? Lose the house? The business? Tell Mom you gave it all up to teach me some lesson?"

I sawed harder.

"Or do you just want to let it go?" Jordan taunted.

Dave rested his hands on his hips, thinking.

"We do this and it's over," Dave commanded. "You don't come crawling back to your mother or me. You don't expect us to cover for you anymore. It's over."

"You'll never see me again," Jordan promised.

Dave looked past his son, to me. I blocked my hands with my back and crouched perfectly still.

"Then what do we do about her?" Dave asked.

The corner of Jordan's mouth turned up. "Same plan, we get rid of the evidence."

CHAPTER 25

"We'll send her into the river," Jordan told his father.

It was a death sentence. I couldn't swim with my hands tied. Even if I could, the fall would probably kill me, just like the passengers on the old Sugarland Express.

Jordan brushed past his father and opened the door. Rain poured down hard, but he barely seemed to notice.

He drew down the brim of his porter's hat and jumped out sideways, to the left of the rickety crossing to the main train. "There's a switchback halfway down the hill. I'll pull it. You unhitch the caboose."

Dave looked back at me. I locked eyes with him, daring him to see me as a person, not just a complication. But I saw no trace of guilt, no humanity. Nothing.

"The tracks are slick," he said to his son. "It won't take anything for it to head down that hill."

"Dave, please," I called. "You're better than this."

He'd taken the knife. He had some sway over his son. He could stop this. There was a good person in there.

Somewhere.

This was the man I'd had meals with, I'd shared drinks with. Now he ignored me.

Dave jumped down next to his son. "Show me how to unhitch the caboose."

They stood right outside the open door, with a clear view of me.

Luckily I had my back to them. I was nearly through the zip tie. Only a thin strip of plastic remained.

I was so close. I twisted my wrists. If I had my hands, if I could only break free...then what? I'd attack two grown men who wanted to kill me? That was insane on about ten different levels, but so was staying on a train car that they were about to send into the river.

Footsteps echoed on the metal floor behind me. I peered over my shoulder.

Jordan.

He held something low next to his leg. A weapon?

I hunched over my hands, praying he didn't see the laces wound through my ties.

He tossed a pair of bloody heels onto the floor next to me. "You wanted these so bad. You can go down with them."

The rusty bloodstains nestled against the cheerful blue hydrangeas on my dress.

"You sure that's a good idea?" Dave called from the door.

"Her idiot ex went for help. We can't risk having the shoes on the train when the police get here, or Mamma is going to jail for sure."

Sweet heaven. I tried to keep my breathing steady, to remain calm.

The metal door slammed closed behind them.

I went back to sawing for all I was worth.

My arms sweated, my wrists bled, my breath came in pants. I worked the bands until they snapped hard. My hands were free.

Thank God and hallelujah.

I grabbed the metal ladder and hauled myself to my shaking feet, knees weak and mind racing. I had to go. I had to get out of here. I made a dash for the window, forgetting my shoelaces were still tied together, and went down hard on my knees.

It was okay. It was fine. I kicked my shoes off rather than try to untie them.

I stood again, gripping the rain-splattered window for support. I saw Jordan sprinting down the hill, toward the junction in the tracks.

Okay, so I just had to take Dave, a large man who would be fighting for his life and his family. Good thing I could scream really loud.

I grabbed for the metal door on the side closest to the hill, hoping to avoid him for as long as I could.

It was locked.

I ran for the door on the train side. I'd swing it outward—hard —and hope to hit him with it.

It didn't budge, either.

Through the foggy window, I saw Dave, his focus trained on a spot down the hill, waiting for his signal to cut me loose. I had to get off before then.

Think.

I could break a window, but they were too small for me to fit even my head through.

I could use the wood-burning stove to set a signal fire, but the caboose was metal. I didn't have anything to burn. Besides, it was raining hard outside, and anyone who might see my fire would be snuggled indoors.

Then it hit me: the crow's nest.

Molly had talked about the view.

That meant windows, hopefully big enough for me to at least poke my head out and scream bloody murder.

The car shuddered as Dave dislodged something in the front.

Oh, no, no, no.

I scrambled up the ladder, the rounded rungs hard against my bare feet. I crawled up into the crow's nest, past the old observation chair, to the long, wide window at the back. Jackpot!

Only I didn't have anything to break it.

My mind swam.

It's fine. I'm fine.

I forced myself out of panic mode—barely—in time to see a latch on the bottom. Of course! It would be stuffy up here. In olden days, the watchman working the caboose would need fresh air.

I flipped the latch and shoved at the old window. It protested. I forced it open anyway just as the caboose began rolling down the tracks toward the river.

Rain pelted my face and wind blew my hair into my eyes as I shoved my head and shoulders out the window. I squeezed the rest of my body out until I was sitting facing the rapidly disappearing train as the caboose picked up speed down the hill.

Cripes! The car jerked and rattled hard on the tracks, a light, loose, barreling disaster.

I slipped and nearly fell.

For a second, I considered jumping. Only the caboose was moving too fast. I'd break my neck.

The caboose hit the switchback and I struggled to hang on. The car shuddered hard, jerking onto the old tracks, clattering straight for the ruined bridge.

It felt like I was on an old wooden roller coaster from hell. Only this roller coaster had no seatbelt, no safety system, and a dead drop at the end.

I gritted my teeth and climbed on top of the slick roof of the crow's nest, grasping the wet, metal handles above the window and hoisting myself over, the metal rumbling under my stomach as the car screamed toward the ruined bridge.

It was at least a four-story drop into the river.

I had no shot if I was inside the caboose. None.

A water landing was my only chance.

We hit the bridge, almost hopping the old rails, which hadn't been part of the renovation project and now were barely held together by rotting planks. My hands went numb as the caboose rattled hard, losing some speed but not enough to save me. Up ahead I saw jagged wood, broken rails, and the churning river below.

I tucked my legs under me, dug the balls of my feet against the cold metal roof, and braced myself as the caboose tipped and plunged through the gaping hole in the bridge.

My stomach lurched at the sharp drop.

And then I jumped.

I shoved up off the roof, launching myself away as far as I could. It wasn't pretty or athletic or even smart. I squeezed my arms and legs tight and kept my body as streamlined as I could.

The plunge into the water felt like getting knocked in the head by a two-by-four. I dropped down deep and fast, the sudden punch of impact knocking the breath out of me. For a second, I let the water cocoon me. I was shocked to be out of that train car. Amazed to be alive.

Gray light shone from above the waterline. It was quiet down here. Peaceful.

I pushed up, and with several hard strokes, I broke the surface.

Water streamed down my face, momentarily blinding me. I wiped my eyes, but the rain hit them and blurred my vision again. Thunder rolled overhead. I spotted the shore and swam for it, fighting the current that pulled me sideways.

If I could just get to the river's edge. If I could just get up the hill and to the train and find Ellis before the Abels found me. Choking and gasping, I made my way toward shore. I was ten feet from safety when I saw Jordan on the bank.

He glared at me, as if incensed to see me in the water, to see that I'd lived. I stifled a scream as he waded into the water after me.

I turned and swam the other way, to the far bank. I was already exhausted and out of breath. My muscles felt weak and rubbery, like I was kicking against nothing. I hit a spot where the current swirled in a whirlpool and prayed I wouldn't get sucked into an undertow. But I didn't have time to go around it. I didn't have the energy. I was working hard and not going anywhere. It took everything I had to keep pushing forward.

I'd almost reached the middle of the river when a hand grabbed my back leg. Jordan. He'd caught me. I kicked and tipped forward, earning a mouth full of water.

I spit it out and took a deep breath.

Rough hands found my neck and shoved me under.

I couldn't swim forward, I couldn't go back. He held me down hard.

I kicked off him and inhaled a huge, fast breath before going the only way I could. I swam deep down, as deep as I could go.

His hand caught my ankle. He was right behind me.

I swam hard, down, down, down until I glimpsed a twist of metal through the gloom. My lungs burned and my brain screamed *wrong direction*! A window gaped at me, crusted with barnacles.

I'd found the wreck of the Sugarland Express.

CHAPTER 26

The maze of ruined metal was a dead end, a death trap. I turned and saw the looming figure of Jordan right behind me.

I blew out a little breath to ease the pressure in my lungs, which were already screaming for oxygen. I was desperately trapped. It couldn't get worse—until I felt the sickening, invasive touch of a ghost on my wrist.

Ick! I grabbed my arm back.

The Green Lady reached up through the dark water. She was supposed to be imprisoned somewhere. The ghost conductor had said she'd exiled herself to a place even ghosts had left behind, and I hadn't asked him to explain.

She'd chosen the wreck of the Sugarland Express.

She floated inside the remains of the old dining room. Ghostly plates drifted in the water behind her. Her hair streamed with the current.

Her mouth formed a single word: *Come.*

Sure. To her creepy water prison. I could get lost in there. Drown. Encounter sharp metal, shifting debris. Ghosts didn't always understand the limitations of the living.

Jordan burst out of the murky darkness and grabbed for my other wrist.

I yanked it back and dove straight into the wreck of the Sugarland Express.

The ghost of Clara Bolton zipped ahead of me, glowing gray against the murk of the river. I avoided the hulking ruins of toppled tables and chairs. A gray, glowing chandelier brushed my elbow and I shivered.

I dodged a piece of fallen roof as Clara twisted around a bent door and down farther, through the remains of a kitchen car.

I looked back. Jordan was right behind me.

My lungs seized. I needed to get to the surface. I needed to breathe.

Ghostly knives were scattered over the floor or the roof or whatever I was looking at. I couldn't see windows anymore or a way out.

I followed Clara anyway. I was in too deep already. She was helping me.

She *had* to be helping me. I was betting my life on it.

My brain fuzzed and my vision went blurry. I let out little bits of air, craving the relief. Blackness began to overtake me. Either we were too far down in the wreck or my body was shutting down.

I gave in to panic and grabbed for something to hold onto. It sliced my hand.

The pain shocked me back to my senses.

Clara turned back to me. Her lips moved: *"Swim!"*

With the last of my energy reserves, I swam as hard as I could. I'd die swimming as I focused on the glowing dot of the ghost. I pushed and I struggled until there was no more wreck above me and I was floating up, up. I kicked hard, but I was hardly moving. It felt like I was pulling against my own weight. I stroked with everything I had, gasping as I broke the surface of the water.

Air!

I let the river carry me, floating on my back, sucking in oxygen.

A hand grabbed my arm and I let it. I couldn't fight anymore.

CHAPTER 27

"*V*erity!" Ellis's arm snaked in behind me, lifting my head and upper chest out of the water. "I've got you."

I couldn't believe I'd actually made it.

I blinked. Then I turned my head and coughed on him.

"Don't try to say anything," he ordered.

He swam to the bank with me, and I gave in to him. I let him take charge—until I saw Dave standing at the water's edge.

"Ellis!" I kicked and struggled to get the words out of my raw, swollen throat. I had to warn Ellis.

"Calm down," he urged, keeping a vise grip on me. "Mom's got it."

Virginia scrambled down the hill in the rain behind Dave. She called out to my would-be killer.

Dave turned, and Virginia pointed a pistol at his chest, the deadly intent on her face almost daring him to give her an excuse to shoot.

"SAVED BY THE WYDELLS," I said, tucking Melody's wrap closer around my shoulders, watching Ellis hand Dave and Mary Jo Abel over to the Gatlinburg police. I'd been asked to stay on the train with the other passengers, which was fine by me. I couldn't shake the chill of the river.

Outside the window, Ellis handled the official business while Virginia embraced her youngest son.

In this case, he deserved it. Beau had not only made it to the next station, he'd run half the way there.

Help had arrived in the form of police, as well as a transport van Beau had rented for the passengers.

"I'll bet we'll still be on the train for half the night." Bruce took his wife's hand. The anniversary couple sat at the table next to me, across from the honeymooners.

The police needed to question the passengers and staff before releasing us to the hotel Beau had booked in Gatlinburg.

Still, I'd take an evening on the train over a swim in the river.

I stepped back from the window.

Jordan Abel's plan had almost worked.

Almost.

I wore a clean yellow sundress and flats this time as I walked alone toward the back of the train, past the gleaming gold compartment numbers set in lacquered wood.

A remorseful Dave and Mary Jo had confessed everything to Ellis. I'd also gone back and taken a second look at the lipstick Eileen had given me. It wasn't just an awful shade of pink-orange. It was a thumb drive case. She'd uploaded the evidence she'd found against the powerful family.

The story it told had killed her and almost ended my life as well.

The Abels' youngest son had learned the business early. He'd managed shipping routes while still in college. And when his parents placed him in charge of them, he took a new approach.

The youngest Abel son began selling the route space to a drug runner with ties to his hometown.

When a set of custom doors shipped to Memphis or St. Louis or even Chicago, they came with a little extra hidden inside the custom containers. It was easy enough to do, since Abel Windows and Doors hired its own distribution staff and manned its own trucks.

I stopped and ran a finger over the scripted gold number on compartment 2.

The Abels made money. Lots of money. Dave's orders increased. Many doors, windows, and parts were bought and shipped precisely as a means of safe, easy delivery for illicit cargo.

It was all about delivery these days.

They had money for a vacation home, Dave's vintage train passion, even trips like this one.

Until Mary Jo found out.

A misdirected shipment, her worry about a scratch. It all came out.

Or so she'd claimed after Ellis arrested her this morning.

To have their livelihood, their business, tied to drug dealing—well, she was afraid they'd lose it all. The government confiscates the assets of those involved in drug running. Their house, the cars, their retirement—it was all at risk.

Unless they covered for their son.

I passed compartments 3 and 4, another luxury suite, this one occupied by the Danvers to celebrate their fiftieth, secure in the knowledge that their legacy was safe.

Not so for the Abels.

The last passenger car stood silent as the grave.

The Abels had removed their son Jordan from the company, but didn't turn him in. They seized his bank account, which they held jointly with him. They put him up in an apartment in the next town while they cleaned up the mess.

Dave Abel cut ties with the criminals Jordan had courted. Business went back to normal.

Life didn't.

According to Dave, his son threatened him. He wanted his job and his life back. Dave refused.

Dave and Mary Jo needed to get away, so they booked a luxury double compartment on the Sugarland Express. It would be an epic journey.

Jordan wasn't content to watch them go, to spend lavishly after he'd been sidelined into a tiny apartment, to have a life when he had none. Dave talked about going to the police despite the consequences.

So Jordan boarded the train as well. Not as a ticket holder. He couldn't afford it. Instead, he got a job as a porter. He'd trap his parents and force them to give him a share of the business before he departed for good.

Jordan lied about his qualifications and his past. He presented himself as the perfect applicant.

I stopped in front of compartment 9.

Beau had been delighted to give him responsibility for all of us. Of course he hadn't checked references.

In handcuffs, Mary Jo confessed how Jordan had hired two of his crooked delivery drivers to leave the rocks on the tracks on the first night. He'd sold her diamond tennis bracelet to pay them, or so he'd claimed. It had been a fiftieth-birthday gift from her husband, and her favorite. Selling it was another way to punish her.

That night, Jordan was waiting for his parents when they returned to their room. He'd stopped the train and disabled the radio. He asked them to sign a contract giving back his share of the business as well as the entirety of the money he'd earned illegally. Then he'd disappear from their lives for good.

Dave refused. He didn't have that kind of liquid cash. Plus,

Jordan didn't deserve it, especially after he'd tried to blackmail his own father and break his mother's heart.

Jordan was angry and frustrated, and then he ran into Stephanie.

She recognized him. In fact, she'd broken up with his brother only after Jordan's crimes nearly spelled disaster for the business. The Abels had tightened their belts when it came to their sons, which meant no more trips to the islands paid for by the company. No more fancy dinners. Stephanie had dumped Ron and gone in search of bigger fish.

But she claimed she still loved him. She believed he was holding out on her, refusing to treat her well because he'd been taking her for granted. She used Beau to taunt him.

When Stephanie saw Jordan working as a porter, she had too many questions. And she'd never been the subtle type.

The reporter, Eileen, had noticed immediately and invited Stephanie to talk.

Stephanie had swiped Jordan's skeleton key in order to check Eileen out.

That was the end of Stephanie.

Mary Jo saw Jordan leave Stephanie's compartment. She'd been up, looking for Dave, who hadn't been able to sleep. She saw the body. She stepped in the blood.

After that, Dave and Mary Jo must have truly feared for their lives. Jordan had become unhinged. It was getting harder to cover up. But if they turned him in for murder, he'd also go down for the drugs, and so would they.

I reached the last compartment, number 10, the one I'd shared with Ellis.

The Abels had to have been doubly nervous with a police officer on board. Jordan, too. He hadn't planned on that.

But he did have a backup plan after the first one failed. He'd already arranged for a second blockage on the tracks, this one above the river. He cornered his parents one last time and threatened to send the entire train backwards, careening toward the river, if he didn't get his way.

A crying Mary Jo described how Dave had signed the contract.

It would have been done and over if Eileen Powers hadn't found Mary Jo and asked her about her bloody heel.

Eileen had been taking pictures at the bon voyage party in the lounge car. She had a picture of Mary Jo wearing white silk shoes with a pointed toe and a square heel.

Jordan told his father he killed the reporter because he loved his mother and couldn't bear to see her hurt.

I might have gotten off with a bloody-heels-in-the-suitcase warning if I hadn't walked in on the murder scene and begun rifling through those files.

I looked out the back of the train, bare now without the caboose.

I would have been dead if it hadn't been for Virginia Wydell, who could not have been more thrilled when she saw the porter taking what she'd presumed to be Ellis's large black bag out of our room.

Assuming Ellis had decided to spend the rest of the trip sleeping in the caboose without me, Virginia located him in Eileen Power's room, processing the scene. She offered her love and support. That alone was enough to tell Ellis that something was horribly wrong.

He ran to the caboose. He watched from the window as Dave shoved it down the hill, with me on top.

Ellis ran down the long, steep hill, with Dave close behind. Unbeknownst to either of them, Virginia grabbed her gun and followed.

Ellis saw Jordan take me under and jumped in after us.

Dave grabbed a large tree branch, ready to take Ellis out, but Ellis was already in the river, swimming toward the place where I went down. When I popped back up again, he grabbed me and took me to the shore while Virginia secured Dave.

Ron, meanwhile, had fled the scene. Police apprehended him several hours later in the woods.

Dave and Mary Jo had believed that only their youngest son had gone bad. Ron had boarded the train with his parents, who wanted a family trip with their "golden child." But Ron had come on board to aid his brother's cause.

Jordan had never reported Ron's involvement in the smuggling operation, and he wouldn't if Ron helped him get what he deserved.

It was Ron who sabotaged the radio. On the way back, he hid behind the counter in the bar car when he heard me coming. While he crouched in the shadows, his large frame dislodged the bottle that had come rolling toward me.

Then Ron had returned to the dining car in time to be counted among the stunned passengers.

After that, Ron spent most of his time holed up in his room, reading an Agatha Christie novel.

Amazing how one could be so close to the truth, yet have no idea.

I shuddered. It was over. Perhaps now the Sugarland Express could finally find peace.

THE NEXT MORNING, I carried a plate of sausage and eggs to a table Ellis had secured on the patio of the hotel in Gatlinburg.

He smiled and stole a link before I'd even put my plate down.

"I see you worked up an appetite," I teased.

The poor guy had been up half the night assisting the local police. We hadn't gotten to bed until almost two in the morning.

"Happy to oblige." He winked, and it took a minute for me to realize he was talking about what had happened after he made it back to the room. I'd been so happy that we were safe, whole, and occupying a normal-sized bed that I hadn't let him sleep too much.

He downed the sausage in two bites. "Your cooking is better," he said, meaning every word.

He was lying, but I loved him for it. "I am looking forward to getting home," I admitted.

I missed it.

Despite the hour, I'd called Melody last night, figuring she'd want to hear the latest and know why I'd never called her back after that first day. She'd been shocked and confessed that she'd hoped it meant I was enjoying my vacation too much to worry about solving a mystery.

Maybe next time.

I'd cut halfway into my first sausage link when I heard my name called out over the parking lot beyond the dining patio.

"Verity!" Lauralee waved from behind a gaggle of kids.

Oh, my goodness. I dropped my fork and knife on the plate. "What's she doing here?"

Ellis grinned. "I figured you could use a little love from Sugarland."

I dashed out to the parking lot, where I found Lauralee, Hiram, Ambrose, and George. Plus Tommy Junior walking my little skunk, Lucy, on a leash homemade from six colors of potholder bands.

"Y'all!" I exclaimed, rushing for them. Lucy wriggled with joy as I picked her up. Ambrose clasped my leg. Hiram and Ambrose stroked Lucy. Lauralee gave me a monstrous hug in greeting. Tommy Junior, at age seven, was too cool for it all, but that was all right. "I don't think I can take it," I said, raising my head as Lucy burrowed hard against my neck and shoulder. My little skunk had a red ribbon hanging from her collar. "What's this?"

"She won!" George shouted with glee.

Tommy Junior reached up to pet her. "We entered her in the Kennel Time Best Dog Contest up at the park."

"And she won?" I asked, bending down with her so the kids could pet her, too. "Those judges may need glasses," I said, with a wink to Lauralee.

Lucy smelled like peach shampoo, and she wore a pink bow behind one ear.

"There was no rule against entering skunks," Lauralee pointed out. "In fact, there was a banner that said *welcome one and all*."

Leave it to my friend to take that to mean skunks, too.

"Third place is quite impressive," I told the boys. Even if only two dogs entered.

"Third in the Smallest Pet category," Tommy Junior announced proudly. "I walked her to the measuring stand myself. She stood very tall. Just like I told her."

Lucy looked at me with her round little skunk eyes, as if daring me to debate it.

"That's wonderful," I said to the boys. "It's obvious she had a great time."

Tommy the showman grinned back at me. "She did."

I handed her to him and he snuggled her tight.

It was obvious the boys had done wonderfully with her. And this had been their test to see if a pet was right for the family. I nudged my friend on the arm. "So does this mean you're getting a dog?" I asked under my breath.

She laughed. "Tell her, Tommy."

"No dogs for us, Miss Verity," he said, with the seriousness of a judge handing down a verdict. "We want a skunk."

I BROUGHT Lauralee and the boys (and yes, Lucy) back to the table to celebrate.

We ordered the boys all-you-can-eat servings at the buffet. Lauralee showed Ellis my award-winning skunk's new leash. I spread homemade strawberry jam on my toast and shared a smile with Ellis, all the while thanking heaven for the little things.

This was all I needed. Good company, good food, laughter. Love. I was just about to slice into a sausage link when Frankie shimmered into view next to an ornamental evergreen in the parking lot.

I'd really been looking forward to that sausage link.

"Excuse me, it appears I've got a meeting with a wiseguy," I said to the adults at the table, reaching over to give Lucy a scratch as I stood.

The wiseguy in question shot me a slight grin, and that was all the warning I got before he hit me with his power. The prickling energy washed over me, making me catch my breath and almost miss the step down off the curb into the parking lot.

After this, I was going to insist he unplug me for a month. Maybe three.

He glided ahead, leading me to a secluded alley just off the lot.

"How very mobster of you," I said, ducking into the cool shade between the buildings.

He lit up a cigarette, inhaled, and blew it out. "I'm glad you're not dead."

Please. "Who else do you think took your urn to the hotel?" It wasn't like he could go far without me.

Molly shimmered into view at my side. "We didn't know what was going on after that porter stole the bloody heels out of your compartment," she said, immediately making me feel bad for my attitude. I swore sometimes Frankie wore off on me.

"You weren't anywhere," Frankie said, smoke curling out his nose. "And I'm telling you, we looked."

"They had me in the caboose," I told them both.

"Oh!" Molly drew a hand to her mouth, then leaned in closer. "We were wondering where that went."

Frankie shook his head. "I liked that caboose," he mused. "You're not so bad, either."

"Thanks," I told him. "I'm glad you're not in jail."

He grinned. "Yet." Molly punched him on the arm as he took a drag. "I gotta tell you, it ain't bad being the law."

"You sure fooled that investigator." Molly giggled.

De Clercq took form behind the mobster. "You might think so, but you'd be wrong."

Frankie spun around and pulled his gun on the officer.

De Clercq merely held up a hand to ward off the attack. "If I were going to arrest you, I'd have done it when we first met, Mr. Franklin Rudolph Winkelmann."

Heavens. "You knew all along?" I asked him. He hadn't said a word.

He looked me up and down as if I were a simpleton for asking. "I recognized him the moment I saw him on the platform." He made a slow walking study of my reluctant housemate. "Frankie the German is a legend. A master criminal. He also takes a very clear mug shot photo." De Clercq stopped at his side. "He's slick. He's crafty. He was just the kind of man I needed to help me solve the case."

Molly made doe eyes at her favorite mobster.

Frankie fought back a grin. "I get that a lot," he said, keeping an eye on the officer. If De Clercq made any sudden moves, I had a feeling he was going to get shot in the kneecap for sport.

"I would not fail again," De Clercq said. "The stakes were too high." He clapped Frankie on the shoulder. "I meant it when I said you deserve a commendation. It will go to the newest special officer in the Chicago bureau, undercover agent Frankie Smokes."

"It's a good name." Frankie nodded, taking a drag.

"You're so brave," Molly cooed.

Wait. So he lived a life of crime, avoided arrest by impersonating an officer, and basically tripped his way through an investigation, and we were celebrating that?

"He's not in trouble?" I asked. Not that I wanted him arrested or anything, but, "You're not going to do anything about the smuggling, the shooting, his entire previous life of crime?"

"That is the problem with the living," De Clercq said, "they are always so shortsighted."

"I tell her that all the time," Frankie said, offering his lit smoke to the investigator.

De Clercq took it. "What good would jail do?" he asked, taking a long drag. "As it stands, Frankie the German is trapped in a house with you." He raised his brows. "That is punishment enough."

"It sure is," Frankie agreed.

"I can agree with that," I told them both.

De Clercq stubbed out the cigarette on the ground. "I may need you again," he said to Frankie, his gaze finding me as well. He knew. He had to know. "I've been tasked with yet another impossible case, this time in your own hometown of Sugarland."

"Oh my." Molly fanned herself. "My man is both the bad boy and the cop."

"What does this have to do with Sugarland?" I asked. I'd discovered a lot about my town in the short time I'd been a ghost hunter, but there was no doubt plenty more to uncover if I was brave enough.

"It might be grisly," Frankie warned, holding out his arm for Molly to take.

"Most likely scandalous as well," she agreed.

"Don't forget historical," I told them. "And probably terrifying."

"It is all that and more," De Clercq promised.

And I had a feeling my life was about to get complicated again.

NOTE FROM ANGIE FOX

Thanks so much for hopping on the crazy train with Verity and her friends. I grew up reading Agatha Christie and have always wanted to write a "trapped on a train" mystery. If you like these mysteries, and want to know when the next one comes out, sign up for my newsletter at www.angiefox.com.

You'll receive an email on release day, and in the meantime, your information will be kept safe by Lucy and a pack of highly-trained guard skunks.

Thanks for reading!

Angie

ABOUT THE AUTHOR

New York Times and *USA Today* bestselling author Angie Fox writes sweet, fun, action-packed mysteries. Her characters are clever and fearless, but in real life, Angie is afraid of basements, bees, and going up stairs when it's dark behind her. Let's face it: Angie wouldn't last five minutes in one of her books.

Angie earned a journalism degree from the University of Missouri. During that time, she also skipped class for an entire week so she could read Anne Rice's vampire series straight through. Angie has always loved books and is shocked, honored and tickled pink that she now gets to write books for a living. Although, she did skip writing for a week this past fall so she could read Victoria Laurie's Abby Cooper psychic eye mysteries straight through.

Angie makes her home in St. Louis, Missouri with a football-addicted husband, two kids, and Moxie the dog.

If you are interested in receiving an email each time Angie releases a new book, please sign up at www.angiefox.com.

Be sure to join Angie's online Facebook community where you will find contests, quizzes and special sneak peeks of new books.

Connect with Angie Fox online:

www.angiefox.com
angie@angiefox.com

Printed in Great Britain
by Amazon